Margaret Elizabeth Sandford

Thomas Poole and his Friends

Vol. 1

Margaret Elizabeth Sandford

Thomas Poole and his Friends
Vol. 1

ISBN/EAN: 9783337396299

Printed in Europe, USA, Canada, Australia, Japan

Cover: Foto ©Andreas Hilbeck / pixelio.de

More available books at **www.hansebooks.com**

THOMAS POOLE

AND HIS FRIENDS

yours most truly

Thos Poole

THOMAS POOLE

AND HIS FRIENDS

BY

MRS. HENRY SANDFORD

IN TWO VOLUMES

VOL. I

London

MACMILLAN AND CO.

AND NEW YORK

1888

THIS BOOK IS INSCRIBED

TO THE LOVED AND HONOURED MEMORY OF

MY FATHER

GABRIEL STONE POOLE

PREFACE

THE memoirs which are here offered to the public have absorbed most of the leisure of a somewhat busy life for between three and four years. When I began I hardly contemplated anything more than a magazine article, but the unsuspected richness of the stores of material entrusted to me, and the ever-increasing interest that these gave to my subject, soon showed me that the task which I had undertaken was altogether too large to be dealt with on that scale, and that I stood committed to an amount of labour and research which I had little dreamt of at the outset.

Once, as I sat surrounded by old letters and notebooks, wearisome to copy, and not always easy to decipher, I was rather amused at finding myself interrupted by a faithful old servant, who gravely remonstrated with me for allowing myself to become entangled in what to her appeared to be a very unnecessary expenditure of time and pains.

'*And what for?*' she demanded, very emphatically ; '*there's many a hundred dozen books already as nobody ever reads.*'

'And What For?' This is, after all, a question which may be fairly enough addressed to any one who is proposing to add to that 'surfeit of too much,' through which the readers of the present day have to find their way ; but surely if it can be replied that the new book will bring fresh contributions to a department of literature that is at once interesting and incomplete, the answer is one that cannot but be accepted as sufficient. It is from this point of view that I venture to hope that this record of Thomas Poole and his Friends may meet with a welcome in more than one quarter, as throwing not a

little additional light on an important epoch
in the moral and intellectual life of England,
and on a group of men who, in no small
degree, helped to make it so.

By the kindness of Mr. Ernest H. Coleridge, an entire series of letters addressed by
Thomas Poole to S. T. Coleridge has been
placed in my hands, and as regards the other
side of the correspondence, I have been permitted to make use, not only of the letters
that have already appeared in the *Biographical
Supplement*, but also of many hitherto un-
printed letters of S. T. C.'s. I should add
that the letters I have published are merely
those which illustrate the friendship that
existed between Coleridge and Poole ; they
are but an instalment of that astonishing
wealth of biographical material which we
hope will be, at no very distant day, given to
the world in Mr. E. H. Coleridge's Life of
his Grandfather.

My best thanks are also due to Miss
Edith Coleridge for permission to use letters

from her parents, Mr. and Mrs. H. N. Coleridge; to Mr. Gordon Wordsworth for permission to use Wordsworth's letters; to Mr. Godfrey Wedgwood for permission to use the letters of Josiah and Thomas Wedgwood; and to Mrs. Lefroy for obtaining for me a similar permission to use the letters of her father, Mr. John Rickman.

I gladly also take this opportunity of offering my grateful acknowledgments to all those who have aided me in my work by entrusting me with letters and papers, or by bringing to my notice books and circumstances illustrative of my subject. And, amongst these, I must make special mention of those few who could actually remember Mr. Tom Poole, and whose reminiscences have been of the utmost value in enabling me to form something like a living idea of the man as he actually was. And here I cannot forbear to mention my own father, Mr. Gabriel Stone Poole, who died in 1875, but to whom, more than to any one else, the writing of this book is due. He had a sincere and affectionate admiration for his cousin, and very often, in days long gone by, I remember that he would frequently speak to me of Mr. Tom Poole and his friendships, and would urge upon me, if ever I should have the opportunity, to make inquiries after the mass of correspondence and of other materials which he was confident must still exist, in order that I might make some attempt, should it lie in my power to do so, to rescue that remarkable personality from oblivion.

Next to these, nothing has been of more service to me than the counsels and criticisms of my kind friend Mr. J. Dykes Campbell, whose acquaintance I was so fortunate as to make just as my work had nearly reached completion, and whose aid has been simply invaluable to me.

CHAPTER I

'Long years have flown since last I lay
On seaward Quantock's heathy hills,
Where quiet sounds from hidden rills
Float here and there like things astray,
And high o'erhead the sky-lark shrills.'

Adapted from S. T. COLERIDGE.

THE paper that I hold in my hand is yellow with age; the ink has faded, and, at the place where the sheet was originally folded, it has worn into tatters. No wonder! for the date of the letter is December the 31st, 1799, and it was written, on the last New Year's Eve in the century, from S. T. Coleridge in London, to his friend, Thomas Poole, at Nether Stowey. Coleridge was, at that time, writing regularly for the *Morning Post*, and describes himself as extremely busy :—

'I work,' he says, 'from I-rise to I-set (that is, from 9 A.M. to 12 at night), almost without intermission. . . . I hope you receive the papers regularly. They are regularly sent, as I commonly put them in myself. . . .

'*Being so hurried for time I should have delayed writing till to-morrow ; but to-day is the last day of the year, and a sort of superstitious feeling oppressed me that the year should not end without my writing, if it were only to sub-scribe myself with the old words of an old affection. . . .*

'*God bless you, and him who is ever, ever yours—who, among all his friends, has ever called and ever felt you the Friend.*   S. T. COLERIDGE.'

These words have been chosen by me as a kind of introductory motto, because they present to us, in a vivid, yet perfectly natural manner, the principal claim which the memory of Thomas Poole has upon all who care for literature—I mean his intimate friendship with some of the most distinguished of those men of note and genius who illuminated the close of the eighteenth and the beginning of the nineteenth century, and more particularly with Coleridge ; and they also suggest the thought, which I think a closer study of his character will but develop and confirm, that there must have been found in him an unusually high degree of the gift or faculty of friendship,—a much rarer endowment than those persons suppose who are apt to use the word in a loose, miscellaneous way, making it cover all the various grades of social acquaintance, and extending it to the most transient intimacies, in which not the slightest particle of real affection is either felt or

pretended.   Yet it is hardly possible to imagine
any set of circumstances, not wholly outside the
bounds of probability, less apparently favourable
to the cultivation of friendships of the closest and
most intimate description, with some of the foremost men of his day, than those which seem to
have surrounded the early life, and determined
the prospects, of the subject of this memoir.

He was born on November 14, 1765, at the
little country town of Nether Stowey, a town so
tiny it might easily have been mistaken for a
village, even in those days, but for the market
cross in the centre of the principal open space.
It nestles at the foot of the little-known, but very
beautiful Quantock Hills, whose near neighbourhood to the grander scenery of Porlock and Linton,
which will always be preferred by the ordinary
tourist, together with their comparative inaccess-
ibility by rail from any of the great manufacturing
centres of population,[1] have so far preserved them,
even till now, from the foot of the explorer, that,
if not quite so wild, they are, in many places,
almost as solitary as when, a hundred years ago,

---

[1] Far be it from the present writer not to rejoice, as in a great
and signal benefit, that railways *have* thrown open so much of
the beauty of hill and moor and sea to the foot of the cheap
excursionist, thus enriching the lives of thousands with new possibilities of enjoyment.   Nevertheless there is, and ever must be,
a special charm in untroddenness, which we cannot but lose with
some regret.

Tom Poole and his brother Richard used to scramble up and down their steep *coombs* in the days of their boyhood. A coomb (*cwm*), in Somersetshire parlance, means a deep little valley with wooded sides, and a stream at the bottom; and, if it be true that the very name of Quantock [1] signifies in Celtic '*many openings*,' this is a very good instance of the happy gift in the naming of natural features, which seems to have distinguished the ancient inhabitants of these islands, for it is a chief characteristic of these delightful hills that they are thus broken up into the loveliest glens and dells, each the special home of some brook or brooklet, green nests where nothing is to be heard but woodland murmurs, and nothing to be seen but branches against the sky. Coleridge's *Fears in Solitude* was evidently written in the bottom of a coomb—Cockercoomb, perhaps, or Seven Wells— whence ascending, '*by the green sheep-track, up the heathy hill*' (for '*the hills are heathy*', except that here and there the eye is caught by the sunny splendour of some

'. . . *swelling slope,*
Which hath a gay and gorgeous covering on,
All golden with the never-bloomless furze,')

any one may see, as Coleridge saw long since, the wonderful '*burst of prospect*'—

[1] Paper on Topographical Etymology by Rev. W. A. Jones, M.A. Proceedings of the Somersetshire Archæological Society, 1854.

> *'. . . here the shadowy main*
> *Dim-tinted,[1] there the mighty majesty*
> *Of that huge amphitheatre of rich*
> *And elmy fields. . . .'*

and, beyond them, the far expanse of marsh country, stretching away on the right to the furthest horizon, above which Glastonbury Tor is just visible, rising like a bluish-gray island against the sky ; whilst on the left, and opposite, the view is limited by the pale outline of the Welsh mountains, or by the nearer purples of the Mendip Hills, between which and the Quantocks, the level land spreads inward many a mile from the mouths of the Parrett and the Brue,[2] sometimes in rich dairy farms, sometimes in long tracks of moorland, brown and spongy, to the very foot of the famous Tor, guiding both the eye and the imagination to that ancient isle of Avalon where King Arthur lies buried, and where the ruins of the sanctuary which Briton and Saxon alike held sacred are still to be seen.   The marsh is simply the well-drained bed

---

[1] 'The shadowy main, dim-tinted,' is an entirely perfect word-picture of the effect of the dun waters of the Severn Sea beheld from that distance.

[2] It was down the River Brue, of course, that the mystic barge came from Glastonbury to receive the dying king.   Tennyson's picture of the 'coast of ever-shifting sand,' and 'far away the phantom circle of a moaning sea,' with the 'death-like mist,' in the midst of which the 'last dim weird battle of the west' was fought, exactly recalls the scenery.   But there were certainly no 'zig-zag paths and juts of pointed rock.'   How could there be, on such a coast ?

of what was once the estuary of the river Parrett, that river which long formed the boundary between the two races,[1] and, on the north-eastern side, the very names of the villages—Chedzoy, Middlezoy, Westonzoyland—reveal the homes of these early *settlers by the sea-meres* with whom the name of Somerset originated, and who were the pioneers of the West Saxon folk in this direction. So that 'seaward Quantock' looks, as it were, along the actual line of contact, an interesting landmark always, but especially so to the lover of English literature ; for, as if to remind us of our national descent from both, and of the share that Celt as well as Teuton has had in the moulding of the English mind and character, it is here, along this line of contact, just where the latest struggles for the mastery were fought out, and conquerors and conquered at last settled down peaceably side by side and began to mingle and to become one people, that English poetry has ever had her surest abiding-place,[2] and discovered her freshest springs.

[1] *i.e.* between Dyvnaint and Wessex *zoy* is pronounced *zee*, and z stands for s in the West Saxon dialect.

[2] Do not forget that Stratford-on-Avon lies along this line ; and Langland was born in Shropshire ; and Spenser came originally from that North Countree where Northumbria ran parallel to Strathclyde ; so did Burns ; and if we are to speak of those poets who, each in his degree, were the instruments of that reawakening of the national imagination, that extraordinary revival of English poetry, which has in this nineteenth century given another great age to our national literature, Wordsworth was a Cumbrian ; and Devonshire gave us

I know of no other point of view from which this line is so distinctly traceable, and so enriched and illuminated with historical and legendary associations.

Twelve hundred feet is the highest elevation to which 'smooth Quantock's airy ridge' ever attains; but although the scenery never rises into grandeur, these hills have a character and a beauty of their own, and once thoroughly known and loved in youth, they will always retain their hold on the affections. One special charm consists in the loveliness of the foliage. The sloping sides of the coombs are clothed, not, as a general rule, with fir, but sometimes with forest trees, or more commonly with oak underwood; and perhaps it may have been to the near neighbourhood of these oak woods, once more abundant than now, that the large and thriving tanning business owed its origin in which our Tom Poole's father, who was also named Thomas Poole, and his uncle John Poole[1] were both engaged. At any rate, this

Coleridge; and Southey, a sharer, though with inferior powers, in the same impulse, was born at Bristol.

[1] There were two other brothers also, I believe, engaged in the tanning trade, but not in the same business. I have been told that old Mr. Kinglake of Taunton, the father of the author of *Eöthen*, used to say that these four brothers were all amongst the cleverest men he had ever known. They were the sons of a Mr. William Poole of Marshmill, who died in 1750. There was one sister, an Alice Poole (died 1773), who was not clever, but like other maiden aunts, a great cherisher of old family traditions. She it was who

constituted an important part of the family property, and it was natural enough that Thomas
Poole, the elder, should decide that his first-born
son must, as a matter of course, take to the tanyard, nor is there anything to show that the
younger Thomas disliked the prospect, or in any
way revolted against it.   But there was another
part of his father's arrangements against which he
did revolt, and that in the most determined
manner.   Whether it be that his father thought
that bare reading, writing, and arithmetic, represented all the book learning that a man of business
required, or whether it be that he detected in his
son a love of literature that he feared might lead
to a distaste for trade, must remain a matter of
conjecture ; what seems certain is, that Tom was
never sent to a good school, his bookish tastes

remembered how, when a child, she saw *her* aunt 'weep' at the
death of Queen Anne. Another of her favourite sayings, ' My uncle,
Sir Richard, was knighted for valour,' carries us much farther back,
for it refers to a Sir Richard Elsworth, who raised a troop of horse
for the king, and was knighted during the Civil Wars. His grandson, another Richard Elsworth, besides founding various schools,
founded two small exhibitions at Balliol College, Oxford, for the
benefit of natives of the county of Somerset, with a preference to
certain parishes, and to founder's kin, one of which was actually
held by the eldest son of the John Poole mentioned above—another
John Poole, of whom much will be said in these memoirs. This
Richard Elsworth died in 1714. The present generation of founder's
kin has been pretty numerously represented at the University, but,
of course, all special claims upon such endowments have, with
Spartan impartiality, been long ago disallowed.

were discouraged and sneered at, and he was apprenticed to the tanning trade at as early an age as possible. This may have seemed all the harder to him because his uncle's sons were educated at Tiverton Grammar School, then considered the best public school in the West of England, and the eldest, who showed talent, went thence to Oxford, where he did not fail to distinguish himself, and to become, in due time, a fellow of Oriel. Even Tom's own younger brother, being intended for the medical profession, was fitted for his future work by a suitable education. Happily, Tom was of too sweet and wholesome a nature for envy and jealousy; he loved his cousin John, and took affectionate pride in his successes, whilst between him and his brother Richard there was always the strongest possible bond of fraternal love and sympathy; but he got on very badly with his father, and showed his resentment of the whim that condemned him to ignorance by ostentatious inattention to his work in the tanyard, whilst, in such fragments of spare time as he could command, and always oppressed with a disheartening sense of the difficulty of making progress without better advantages, he seems to have continued his studies with steady persistency, year after year, getting on very slowly, no doubt, but never losing sight of the determination to become a well-educated man. Family traditions represent the elder Thomas as venting his disappointment in taunts and sarcasms. He chose to consider Tom simply in the light of an idle apprentice, and as long as he lived he never ceased to 'twit' his son with ignorance of his business, though, as time went on, inefficiency was the last thing of which he could justly be accused, whatever may have been his inattention to detail at the outset.

His mother was a woman of great sensibility, and of so much sweetness of nature that her tender tolerance, and 'overflowing good-will' to any one whom Tom wanted her to like, made her, in after years, very dear to his friends, and especially to Coleridge, who sends her his love, sometimes his 'filial love,' in almost every letter. Thus in 1799, at a time when Mrs. Poole was recovering from an illness, he wrote :—

'In this hurly burly of unlucky things, I cannot describe to you how pure and deep joy I have experienced from thinking of your dear mother! O may God Almighty give her after all her agonies, now at last a long, rich, yellow sunset, in this her evening of Life!—So good, and so virtuous, and with such an untameable sensibility *to enjoy* the blessings of the Almighty— surely God in heaven never made a Being more capable of enjoying with a deeper Thankfulness of Earth, Life, and its Relations !'

Of his one sister, Sarah, Tom Poole was both

fond and proud, but the chief happiness and compensation, both of his boyhood and early manhood,
must have been the perfect affection, and thorough-
ness of understanding, that existed between himself
and his brother; whilst, outside their own household,
the main resource of both, and probably of their
sister also, was found in the society of their cousins,
the John Pooles, whose home was at Marshmill, a
plain but pleasant country-house in the neighbouring village of Over Stowey, and in the sympathy
and counsel of their Uncle John, a man described
by Tom Poole as one whose

'natural sense was incomparable, his information extensive, and his desire to use those blessings for the good
of his family, his friends, and the neighbourhood, greater
than that of any man he ever knew.'

He was younger than Tom's father, and yet
'generally considered and treated as the head of
the family ;' and, whilst the desire and the determination to achieve usefulness, that noblest of all
the various forms of young ambition, was working
in Tom's mind from boyhood, in his uncle he saw
a living example of the very kind of life upon
which his imagination was dwelling, the life that
he one day hoped and intended to lead himself.
Besides this, at Marshmill was to be found the
soothing atmosphere of a home, in which the jarring
notes of discord were never heard. 'The tender

affection which the seven children bore their father,
and the mother her husband,' was 'beyond anything
Tom ever saw elsewhere, and realised as much
happiness in that united family as can ever be
enjoyed here below.'   There were four sisters and
three brothers, of whom the eldest, John Poole the
young Oxonian, was the special pride of the entire
clan.   The sisters were brought up to be perfect
housewives, complete mistresses of the art of
domestic comfort as it was understood by our
great-grandmothers ; but they were also, what in
those days was much less a matter of course, very
cultivated women.   The third sister, Charlotte,
kept a journal, from which we gather that Tom
must have been almost as much at Marshmill as
at his own home, and that nothing of importance
ever happened to him that he did not at once proceed to share with his cousins.

Of course he had his special favourite amongst
them.   The youngest sister, Penelope, was a
beautiful, dark-eyed girl, with a voice of unusual
power and sweetness, and a fine taste for the best
music which made Handel her favourite composer.
But Tom's attachment to this attractive cousin
was never returned.   The family tradition goes
that she told him she had been too long accustomed
to think of him as almost a brother, to be ever
able to regard him in the light of a lover.   In due

time she married some one else ; and, if he had
been like the majority of human beings he would,
after a while, have taught himself to like some
other woman.   But natures gifted with very strong
affections are apt to be also very slow to change,
and it seems probable that the family impression
that it was this unrequited feeling for his cousin
which kept Tom Poole single to the end of his life,
was a correct one.   Much as he loved poetry, it
may be *because* he loved poetry so much, he was
little given to verse-making on his own account,
but a few stanzas still remain in which he expresses
his delight in her singing, or, perhaps, merely seeks
to lay the homage of an extravagant compliment
at Penelope's feet, by the image of 'sweet Philomel,
at Marshmill gate,' listening in a passion of jealousy
to strains that outdid her own—

> ' Come unto me all ye who toil,'
> Was echoing to the zephyr's round—
> She heard, she owned herself surpast,
> And vanquished, sunk upon the ground !

It is not poetry ; it is merely the restless feeling after some vehicle of expression for that which
is not to be said in direct words, that is common to
all young lovers.   Often such verses are the merest
effervescence of youth, the outcome of passions as
short-lived as the froth upon the wave.   With Tom
the case was different ; and therefore it seemed

rather sad to be told, when collecting reminiscences
of these early days from the daughter of this very
Penelope, that though, in later life, there was no one
that her mother 'respected' more than her cousin
Tom, yet there actually had been a time, when she
was a dainty, gentle little girl, and he a 'great,
strong boy,' when she did not even *like* him, and
rather dreaded the frequent occasions when he and
Dick came over to spend the day at Marshmill.
Tom, indeed, was always kind ; it was Dick who
teased, and who even once hung her doll in the
cellar ; but they were both so rough and eager, and
so vehement in all their ways, that it was quite
enough to make a small and rather timid cousin
shrink into herself, and incline to the opinion that
all boys were rather objectionable, except her own
brothers.

Then, as time went on, Dick was more and
more habitually absent from home, until he finally
settled at Sherborne, and his sister Sarah went to
keep house for him, and Tom was more and more
thrown upon his Over Stowey cousins for companionship. He seems to have been an affectionate light-hearted young fellow in those days, taking
his full share in the jolly, sociable life continually
going forward among the lesser gentry of the Stowey
and Bridgwater neighbourhood, which his cousin
Charlotte's journal records. Beyond their own

immediate surroundings the cousins' chief intimacy was with an American family of the name of Coulson, who, having taken the Imperial side in the Struggle for Independence, had been prudent enough to leave their home in Massachusetts at the opening of the American War, and had settled in Bristol. It is not improbable that their first introduction to the Pooles may have been through the medium of a business connection, and, afterwards, assistance may have been given in the transfer of themselves and their property, of which they seem to have been able to save some considerable portion, to the mother country. What is certain is that the friendship between the two families was very close and intimate, and that the younger Pooles were constant visitors at the Coulsons' hospitable house. It was there that Sarah—more commonly known as Sally Poole— met her husband,[1] and the first mention of Tom Poole in his cousin Charlotte's journal, dated December 15, 1789, records his return, with her sisters, from a visit to these very friends. They found their little parlour at Marshmill as comfortable as ever, sat down to sup on a turkey, and talked of all that had happened during their absence, 'particularly of the dangers Tom Poole had encountered on his voyage to Ireland.' He

[1] She married Mr. King, a Bristol merchant.

had apparently merely rested in Bristol, on his way home from a longer journey.

The Coulsons seem to have delighted in society, and to have entertained a great deal. Tom Poole always spoke of their daughter, Mrs. Marchant, and of her niece, Mrs. Darby, as the two most lovely women he ever saw in his life—whence it would appear that beautiful Americans are not a speciality of the nineteenth century. The former lady was the chosen friend of the Marshmill sisters. She was extremely young when the family first came to Bristol, and already the wife of a husband who was understood to have an appointment in India, and who never appeared upon the scene. After his death, many years later, she became Mrs. Harford, and a small portrait of her, painted at the time of her second marriage, is still in the possession of the Poole family—a dark-eyed woman with an olive complexion, and short, dark, curly hair, clustering round a small and shapely head. It was probably Mrs. Darby who gave Tom Poole the lock of Washington's hair, which he regarded as a sacred treasure, and kept in a special casket, placed within the precious copy of the Barberini Vase,[1] presented to him by the Wedgwoods. He used to say that it was given to him by the most beautiful woman ever created, and if we knew for certain

[1] Now in the possession of the King family.

whether he received it from the aunt or the niece,
we should know to which of the fair kinswomen he
gave the palm ; but, whichever it may have been,
the incident shows both that Tom Poole was a
favourite in the Coulson family, and also that,
whatever sacrifices Mr. Coulson may himself have
made out of loyalty to the British government,
the politics of his home circle were by no means
uniformly of the same complexion.

One other American friend must be mentioned
—a Mr. Garnett, who, in the last years of the
eighteenth century, seems to have been very frequently in Bristol.   Charlotte Poole in after years
described him as a 'prince among men,' highly
gifted both in mind and body, and a thorough
gentleman, and used to declare that 'all the girls
would have been in love with him,' but that it was
well known that he was wasting his life in a 'useless' attachment to the beautiful Mrs. Marchant,
who, on her side, seemed to be wasting hers in
solitary lingering under her father's roof, apart
from a husband who had almost become a stranger
to her.   When at last set free by his death it was
too late—Mr. Garnett had returned to America, and
was on the eve of marriage to another woman.
His name finds a place here because he was one
of the very first people who took kindly notice of
young Tom Poole, and encouraged him in his

endeavours after self-improvement. Whether he
was quite the paragon that he seemed in the eyes
of the young ladies may be questioned, for John
Poole, who kept a diary as well as his sister, notes
that he 'was not at all the kind of man he had been
led to expect;' but perhaps this only means that
he expected a man of sentiment, and a *cavalier des
dames*, and was surprised to find instead a person
of considerable practical shrewdness and ability.
His name occurs again and again in Tom Poole's
letters, as the inventor of improvements in the
machinery used in the tanning trade. But although
the main subject of the correspondence may be the
'new bark mill,' or 'patent anti-friction roller,'
which Tom Poole wishes to introduce at Stowey,
there is always an undercurrent of mutual understanding upon topics of a very different order;
and there is one letter [1] in particular in which,
many years afterwards, Tom Poole recalls, 'with
sincere affection,' Mr. Garnett's 'kind and friendly
attention' to him 'when he was an ignorant boy.'
'Often have I thought of you with affection and
regret,' he writes, 'and, I may truly say, with
gratitude. . . .' And he adds, 'Whether I have
made a good use of my time or not, I often doubt;
but I have endeavoured to be as useful as I can.'

[1] Letter to Mr. Garnett written in 1808, of which a copy has been
preserved in Mr. Poole's Copying-book, No. 2.

'*To be as useful as I can.*'   This was, as almost
every page of this book must show, the keynote of
Tom Poole's life ; but, indeed, the passion for usefulness was a kind of characteristic of the Poole
family, and provided a path in which, as we shall
see, not even the very deepest division of opposite
political opinions could prevent their working hand
in hand through life, with a still deeper sense of
united sympathies.

CHAPTER II

'You welcomed this stupendous event, Sir, with the spirit of an
    Englishman ; with a spirit which, even in its excess, was truly
    English.   If you shall ultimately appear to have erred, posterity
    will add more to your heart on this account, than it will detract
    from your sagacity.   To have hoped too boldly of our common
    nature is a fault which all good men have an interest in forgiving.'
    —S. T. COLERIDGE's Letter to Fox, *Morning Post*, Nov. 4, 1802.

As Tom Poole entered manhood it soon became
apparent that, in spite of his father's sarcasms,
books had by no means spoilt him for business.
He may, indeed, have been unversed in the
practical details of the art of tanning, but with the
trade in its wider commercial relations he was so
well acquainted that, some time in 1790, he was
elected at a great meeting of the tanners of the
West of England, held at Bristol, as their delegate
to a still more important meeting in London, where
he was again chosen for an interview, on behalf of
the meeting, with Mr. Pitt, in February 1791, of
which the object seems to have been to lay before
the Prime Minister the distressed state of the

tanning trade, caused partly by the alarming scarcity of oak bark, and partly by the restrictive effect of the different legislative enactments which insisted upon particular methods of manufacture, and almost made it penal to introduce any improvements. A further effort seems to have been made in the winter of 1792, but without much result; for in 1793 we find Tom Poole drawing up a memorial for the tanners of Bristol, 'to the Right Honourable the Lords of the Committee of Council for trade and foreign plantations,' to point out that the scarcity of oak bark 'continues and encreases,' and to entreat that the exportation of that article may be forbidden, or else bounties granted for the importation of foreign bark. They are aware that 'bounties have not always produced the desired effect,' but believe that 'in the present case it is easy to prove that a moderate bounty would encrease the trade and revenue of the kingdom,' whilst it is hinted, 'with the greatest diffidence,' that the heavy excise duty paid on every ton of bark does furnish some claim to special consideration.

The tanning manufacture was indeed so heavily handicapped in those days, that one would almost think nothing, short of the absolute necessity of leather as an article of daily use, could have prevented the complete decay of the trade as a branch of national industry. Yet it was not till 1808 that even *some* of the vexatious enactments, which hampered manufacturers and discouraged inventors, were, after long parliamentary investigation, at last removed by the repeal of the statute 1 James I. c. 22 ; whilst the heavy excise duty of first 1d. and then $1\frac{1}{2}$d. a lb., imposed on all tanned hides in the reign of Anne,[1] was not only not abolished, but was actually doubled in 1812 ; such being only a mild example of the burdens to which nations find themselves compelled to submit in time of war.

Except then that, even in minor matters, such as the prospects of a single trade, years of per- sistent refusal to let the question rest are usually needed before the public mind can be awakened to consider the importance, or desirability, of any proposed revision of methods, or change of ancient routine, we might say that Tom Poole's mission on behalf of the tanning trade was not crowned with success, and that the months that he spent in London were, therefore, of little interest and importance.   But in the history of his own life and character this first visit to London does form a noticeable epoch.   Hitherto, family traditions, a few brief entries in the diaries kept at Marshmill,

---

[1] The imposition of a duty *by weight* was, in itself, peculiarly harassing and inconvenient, and placed obstructions in the way of trying improved methods.   In 1815 this tax seems to have pro- duced £500,000.

and such scanty references to his early life as I
have been able to discover in letters written long
afterwards, have been my only materials ; but from
this period a regular series of written records begin,
and, in particular, several long and intimate letters
have been preserved by a Mr. Purkis,[1] known in
the family as 'the great London tanner,' who, although a much older man than Tom Poole, seems
to have been strongly attracted by the clever young
delegate from Somersetshire, whose literary tastes
he shared, and whose political opinions he probably
helped to form.   When Tom returned home in
March 1791 he was soon at his uncle's house at
Marshmill 'in high spirits,' and no doubt full of
the adventures and experiences of his London
visit.   Great, however, was the reproachful astonishment, not only of his cousins, but of the
entire neighbourhood, when it came to be perceived
that he had brought back with him to Stowey an
ardent sympathy with that, which, even in 1791,
was felt to be a doubtful and incomprehensible
portent, to be regarded by all right-minded persons with the most suspicious caution—I mean
the French Revolution.

[1] For a long time I believed that Tom Poole had been *sent* to
Mr. Purkis to improve his knowledge of business ; but when the
entries in Miss C. Poole's journal were carefully compared with the
memoranda in Mr. Tom Poole's Copying-book, new light was thrown
on the subject.

Of old Thomas Poole's thoughts about the matter no record remains. It seems impossible but that he must have been rather proud of a son who, at twenty-five, stood so high in the confidence of all the leading men in his own trade; but the making of disparaging remarks had become a habit, and, if old stories are to be believed, he never left it off as long as he lived. Now, however, Tom occasionally attempted to turn the tables, as when, upon one occasion, he advanced the opinion that his father's practice of keeping no accounts, was a manner of conducting business which was actually barbarous in its simplicity. But the elder Thomas's confidence in himself remained unshaken. 'Tut, tut, boy; why, what would you have?' he made answer. 'I owe no man anything; the pits are full, and there's money in the stocking—what better do you want?'

Neither of the Thomas Pooles possessed a very yielding disposition; they disagreed upon many points, and the contentions between them were frequent; but the chief fault seems to have been with the father, who could not let his son alone. The irritable, arbitrary old man, who might have been better tempered if it had not been for the gout, was not a favourite in the family. 'Uncle Thomas is often very disagreeable,' recorded Cousin Charlotte. Nevertheless it appears that Tom was always able to invite his friends to his father's house whenever he would, and the summer of 1792 brought him the delight of a visit from Mr. Purkis, which was evidently a great success, though Tom is half apologetic to his London friend for the primitive plainness of life at Stowey. They rode and walked over the Quantock Hills, and spent evenings at Marshmill listening to Penelope's singing, and, in short, entirely enjoyed themselves.

And, if that old life were primitive, it had, at least, the advantage of being a good deal less expensive than our present modes of existence are found to be. Remember what it costs *now* to send a son to a private tutor's and read this reply of Tom Poole to a letter of Mr. Purkis's about a boy in whom he was interested [1] :—

'You ask me if we have a cheap boarding-school in this neighbourhood. A Mr. Roskilly, the clergyman of this place, a most amiable, liberal-minded man, and a very good tutor, takes a few pupils ; if your friend wishes to give his boy a classical education there is no situation that I could with so much confidence recommend. The treatment of the children is affectionate and kind to a degree, and, as he takes no day scholars, and not above a dozen boarders, the utmost attention is paid to their studies. Indeed he dedicates his whole time to his boys. His terms are £20 a year; no presents of any kind are

---

[1] Copy of this letter preserved in Mr. Poole's Copying-book, No. 1. The date is June 10, 1792.

expected, unless you chuse to give the servants anything at the vacations.   For the twenty pounds they
are boarded, their linen washed, they are taught Latin,
Greek, English Grammar, to which particular attention
is paid, and Geography ; but what is more valuable than
all is the exceeding healthiness of the situation, and the
particular attention he pays to their morals.   Indeed his
boys are as healthy, innocent, and happy, and in as good
a train of instruction, as any I ever met with. . . .
There is a very decent man who attends the school
three times a week to teach such boys as wish it
Writing and Arithmetick, for which they pay him five
shillings a quarter.   There is also a Dancing-master—
but these things are optional.   I have a charge of mine
with him, the son of an eminent merchant at Bristol,
and he learns neither of them.' [1]

The letter was written just before Mr. Purkis's
visit to Stowey, and continues as follows :—

'I am happy Government pays some attention to the
bark business—their ordering bark to be procured from
Canada, etc., seems at least to show some goodwill towards
us.   Pray, are you to send a ship on purpose, or do you
take advantage of a back freight?   Let me know the
steps the committee designs taking. . . . A bounty on
the importation of bark would certainly be desirable, and
in all probability a prelude to some restriction on the
exportation of our own bark, inasmuch as a very strong
argument would arise against allowing the free exportation of that which we were granting a bounty to import.

---

[1] It is puzzling to find writing and arithmetic classed with danc-
ing as non-essential extras !

I wish the circumstance may not stare Government in the face and prevent their giving us the bounty. . . . When you come into Somersetshire I shall reckon upon your taking a particular account of every object worthy of your attention. I would recommend you to begin with Wells, where the Mail stops a quarter of an hour, and where the cathedral is one of the finest pieces of Gothic architecture in the kingdom. The celebrated and splendid ruins of Glastonbury Abbey would next demand your admiration, but as the coach does not stop at Glastonbury you must defer your view of that interesting scene till your return, when perhaps we may together tread the holy ground. I am already in my mind disposing of the time when we shall be together. . . .'

The Mr. Roskilly mentioned in this letter was the curate of Stowey. The vicar was always rather a personage, and, for the most part of the year, non-resident, as the living was in the gift of the canons of Windsor, and they usually appointed one of themselves. In Tom Poole's early manhood the vicar was a Dr. Majendie, who must have been both a good man and a man of very enlightened views, for we find him, in those remote days, when the very idea of such a school was a recent, and in the eyes of many, a questionable novelty, deeply interested in the establishment of a Sunday School in Nether Stowey, which was the earliest effort made in that place for the education of the children of the poor. It is also the first direct

work in the service of the labouring classes in
which we know Tom Poole to have taken an
active part, and it is certain that the question of
education, as one of the crying needs of the poor,
had already begun to take possession of his mind,
though, in 1789, the year in which the first report
of the Stowey Sunday School was published, he
was only twenty-four.   The Marshmill journals
abound in notices of a similar school at Over
Stowey, of which his cousins, the John Pooles,
were the chief promoters.   For Dr. Majendie
himself Tom Poole entertained a strong feeling of
affectionate admiration, which finds expression in
many letters, whose rough copies, blotted and
interlined, are still to be seen in the pages of
his Copying-books.   Tom used to take a great
deal of pains with his English in those days, and
must have spent much time in the translation of
his thoughts into elaborately rounded periods,
formed upon the model of Dr. Johnson ; but some
of these ceremonious epistles are so characteristic
of the manners and feelings of a bygone age that
they have seemed to me well worth preserving.

The year 1792 ended, for the whole Poole
family, in the deepest gloom.   As summer passed
into autumn a malignant fever broke out in the
Stowey neighbourhood, and Tom's enjoyment of
the visit of his London friend was barely over

when his Uncle John, after a short period during
which his unsatisfactory state of health had caused
his family vague uneasiness, sickened unmistak-
ably on August 13th of 'the same fever of which
so many had died,' and growing rapidly worse
and worse, breathed his last on the 30th day of
the same month. Tom Poole was present. At
the very first alarm he and his sister Sarah had
hastened to Marshmill to stay with the sorrow-
stricken household ; and perhaps this may be a
good place to note that, in spite of the rough
abruptness of manner which all his cousins
thought so much to be regretted in poor Tom,
his wonderful tenderness in times of trouble, and
especially of sickness, was so well known as to
make his presence continually sought for and
desired at such seasons. To his Uncle John he
was 'as a nurse,' and I think scarcely one of that
uncle's own children can have felt a deeper sense
of bereavement at his loss.

'The death of my dear uncle,' he writes to Purkis,[1] ' is
the severest stroke I ever felt. . . . He was taken off in
the prime of health and strength by the dreadful fever
which has carried so many to the unknown country.
His death has caused a shock in the neighbourhood you
can scarcely conceive, and has thrown a gloom over
every countenance. . . .

'When I last wrote I was in such distress of mind I

[1] September 19, 1792.

scarcely recollect what I said, but if I did not then remember to do so, my dear friend, let me sincerely thank you for your kindness in paying that short visit to me at Stowey, and to beg you to excuse anything which you must have remarked deficient in the reception I gave you. A time will come, I hope, when I shall welcome you to my home, be it where it will, in a manner more to my mind . . . but of one thing be certain, that whatever was amiss sprang rather from our inability than from any want of goodwill.

'This letter, my dear friend, must be gloomy, for such is the present state of my mind that I wonder at the cheerfulness I have heretofore experienced, and almost despair of its ever returning again. I reflect, with melancholy pleasure, on the delightful scenes and days through which I have passed, and they appear almost as a dream to me. Do you remember that evening, Purkis, the last I spent with you? I think I never remember a more delightful one. The heavens smiled upon us, and the pale moon shed her mild lustre on that pleasing, rational conversation, which so swiftly beguiled the way. You then promised to send me some charming lines which you repeated, and which I beg you will transmit to me in your next letter. You also promised to throw into a regular form your account of our little excursions. I do enjoin you to send it to me as well, on the earliest opportunity. . . .'

To another London friend he writes :—

'My uncle was a man who is regretted by all who knew him. He had a good head, and an honest, feeling heart, which prompted him to exert the means Providence

had placed at his disposal to the advantage of all around
him.   His death has overwhelmed his wife and children,
who tenderly loved him, with affliction you can better
imagine than I describe.   But why do I thus write to
you of a person you did not know?   Because it is a
subject that so eternally fills my mind that I cannot help
it. . . .'

Indeed the shadow of death still rested darkly
on the once happy home at Marshmill.   In the
course of September, John, the beloved elder
brother, who had just gained his Oriel Fellowship,
was taken ill, and brought to the very brink of
the grave, by the same terrible disease to which
his father had fallen a victim.

'For a fortnight he was in a state of raving madness,' wrote Tom Poole, 'and it was the opinion of his
physicians that, even if life survived, his senses must be
lost, and that a wretched maniac was all that could be
preserved of what John Poole once was,—the most
accomplished and best of men.'

The only remedy used seems to have been
large doses of opium, and these John Poole, a tall,
powerful young man of two-and-twenty, and
'suffering from severe delirium, attended by such
spasms in the throat it was feared locked-jaw would
ensue,' resisted so violently that even his mother
was for giving up in despair.   Those were not the
days of trained nurses, and no one knew how to

act. But, 'What!' said Tom Poole, 'let a fine young man *die*, for want of a little resolution?' Whereupon, 'calling in the strongest men from the farm,' he administered the required medicine by main force. 'I believe I may say with truth,' wrote Cousin Charlotte, 'that our dear John owes his life to him.' His recovery was so unexpected that he seemed 'almost as one risen from the dead, and given anew to those who loved him from the hands of the Creator.'[1]

[1] Letter to Purkis.

CHAPTER III

'. . . Lo ! the giant Frenzy,
Uprooting empires with his whirlwind arm,
Mocketh high Heaven ; burst hideous from the cell
Where the old hag, unconquerable huge,
Creation's eyeless drudge, black Ruin, sits
Nursing the impatient earthquake.'

COLERIDGE, *Religious Musings.*

THE death of his uncle would, under any circumstances, have been a great blow to Thomas Poole ; but the particular time at which it occurred was one when he could indeed ill afford to lose the counsels of so beloved and so highly esteemed a kinsman. The opinion that the French Revolution was a fearful and unnatural catastrophe, to be shuddered at, and certainly not sympathised with, had become by this time a fixed idea in the rural English mind ; and even before the actual commencement of the Reign of Terror dark rumours of the uncontrollable ferocity of the mob of Paris, the raging in the name of liberty against all the bonds of social order, the

wild defiances hurled to the very heavens against
God Himself, had produced a general attitude of
indignant expectation, not unmingled with alarm
lest some infection of the same madness should,
by any evil chance, visit our own happier shores.
Tom Poole was not the kind of person to reserve
an unpopular opinion, or to be silent when any
of his cherished ideals were attacked or misre-
presented.   His sense of the misery of the French
people through centuries of grinding oppression,
his sympathy with their efforts, however wild and
convulsive, to achieve their just freedom, was
exceedingly deep, and, in season or out of season,
he never scrupled to proclaim what he thought.
He became for a while, and this especially after
the publication of Paine's *Rights of Man* as a
reply to Burke's celebrated *Reflections on the
French Revolution*, a kind of political Ishmaelite
in his own neighbourhood, his hand against every
man, and every man's hand against him.   It was
probably at this time that he made his appearance
amongst the wigs and powdered locks of his
kinsfolk and acquaintance, male and female, without any of the customary powder in his hair ;
which innocent novelty was a scandal to all be-
holders, seeing that it was the outward and visible
sign of a love of innovation, a well-known badge
of sympathy with democratic ideas.   If he did

not find himself literally in a minority of one,
being happy in the comprehension and adherence
of his brother Richard, yet his cousins' journals
show that the household at Marshmill—the little
circle whose support, if he could have obtained it,
would have been grateful to him beyond all others
—bristled with disapproval; whilst the small world
of Stowey and Bridgwater made no secret that
it was very much shocked, and at times almost
inclined to believe that Tom Poole ought to be
denounced as a public enemy.

We will begin with an extract from Charlotte
Poole's journal, the first in which she takes any
notice of her cousin's ' politicks ':—

' *December* 18, 1792.—John dined with Tom Poole,
and from him heard that there was a great bustle at
Bridgwater yesterday—that Tom Paine was burnt in
Effigy, and that he saw Richard Symes sitting on the
Cornhill with a table before him, receiving the oaths of
loyalty to the king, and affection to the present constitution, from the populace. I fancy this could not have
been a very pleasant sight to Tom Poole, for he has im-
bibed some of the wild notions of liberty and equality
that at present prevail so much ; and it is but within these
two or three days that a report has been circulated that
he has distributed seditious pamphlets to the common
people of Stowey. But this report is entirely without
foundation.

' Everybody at this time talks politicks, and is looking

with anxiety for fresh intelligence from France, which is a scene of guilt and confusion.'

On December 23, 1792, Tom himself wrote as follows to his friend Purkis of

'a laughable affair, in which, can you believe it, my dear Purkis, you are somewhat involved, and which I will now relate to you. There is a man at Stowey, an Attorney of the name of Symes, with whom I was heretofore on an intimate footing, but lately, I hardly know for what reason, we have had little intercourse. He is mighty zealous, in his political opinions, for the present establishment, against what he calls Republicans and Levellers, and believes that every man who thinks many things might be mended in the Government of this country, belongs to that class. In consequence of the proclamations his ardour has increased, and those royal mandates have had precisely that effect between him and me which Mr. Grey foretold on the issue of the first ; viz., setting friends and neighbours by the ears, and exciting domestic as well as public discontent where peace had before reigned.

'But to proceed with my story. There is also another man here, a very sensible fellow, a cabinet-maker. In an accidental conversation he lamented the sad alarms which prevailed in the kingdom about the constitution and Thomas Paine ; but withal, expressed a great wish to read his book, and requested me to lend it to him. I accordingly, with some hesitation, lent him a copy I had by me, the only one I ever possessed, *with the leaves uncut*. As the man came out of the house he met Symes, who, seeing what he had in his hand, snatched

it from him, told him it was a very improper book for
him, and in a violent passion tore the book in pieces,
and. stamped it underfoot.   The man was afraid to
return it to me with this story, and I heard nothing of it
for some time.   In the interval, Symes propagated
round the country that I was a violent incendiary in
political matters, that I had a Box of Books from London
which I distributed among the common people, and that,
on the whole, I was a most dangerous person ; in short,
I was stunned with the sound of the Tower, Newgate, etc.
etc., and had really hopes of paying a visit to my Lord
Grenville at least.   On hearing this, you may imagine
the spirit moved me a little, and I seized the first
opportunity of seeing Symes, and I think I never saw a
man more ashamed of himself and his conduct.   The
following conversation passed :—

'*P*. What induced you to report I had a box of these
books from London ?

'*S*. The leaves of the book being uncut, the general
sentiments I have heard you express making it probable,
and I have heard, too, that all your acquaintance in
London, whom you esteem so much, and particularly
the Mr. Purkis who was lately down to see you, are Republicans and Levellers.

'*P*. You have reported and now assert without
foundation that for which you ought to be ashamed.
The first time I read *The Rights of Man* you lent me the
book ; some time after I purchased it myself, but having
read it, I had no curiosity to read it again, and the book
remained in the state in which I had received it from
the booksellers till you destroyed it.   As for my general
sentiments, I believe they have been as loyal and as

consistent with a British spirit as the sentiments of
those who have professed more; and as to my acquaintance in London, they are much above your cen-
sure or your praise, my knowledge of them I consider
to be the happiest event of my life. Mr. Purkis will
laugh at your insinuations, and it is almost beneath me
to tell you that his sentiments on politicks are more
moderate than those of any man I know who thinks
with the ability and disinterestedness that he does. But,
pray, what do you, or any one in this country, know of
the gentleman you have named? Who is your authority?

'At this he boggled a good deal, and at length I found
some one had related to him the transient conversation at
the door of the King's Head, Bridgwater, the Sunday
morning you left that town, in which I ridiculed some
of their Corporation men, but in which, if I recollect
rightly, you bore little or no part. We separated on his
making every apology to me that he could, and on his
promising to contradict all he had said. This was all
the satisfaction I could well have, situated as I am, but
I never had a greater inclination to pull a fellow by the
nose, and I am not certain that I shall not yet put it
into execution. . . .

'You will laugh at this business, and perhaps, too, at
my warmth; and the tale has taken up so much paper I
have no room for half I wish to say. You ask me, dear
Purkis, when I design emigrating.[1] I certainly shall
defer it till the weather gets milder, but my resolution is

---

[1] This is the first allusion that I have been able to find to the
project, afterwards actually carried out by Tom Poole, of seeking
employment as an ordinary workman in some tanyard near London,
and spending some time in that kind of life.

unalterable. Accept my sincere thanks for your kind advice. Now having introduced tanning, I will go on. Pray have you thought of or done anything in the Article for the Scotch Dictionary?[1] If not, I beg particularly that you will. . . .

'Let me know if the Committee propose doing anything in our bark business during the present session; but I fear Government is so taken up with wars and rumours of wars, and so anxious to check the liberty Mad Dogs, they will hardly deign to pay attention, even to one of the first manufactures in the kingdom. I am anxious to hear the event of your expectation of the co-operation of the Corporation of London, in a revisal of the Statutes. If they should be revised, let it be on a broad basis. . . .'

In Charlotte Poole's journal, December 26, 1792, we find :—

' Mr. and Mrs. Lewis and Tom Poole spent the evening here. French politicks are become so very interesting that people cannot take opposite opinions, and continue to converse with temper. We have had an instance of this to-day in the conversation that passed between Mr. Lewis[2] and Tom Poole.'

But 'politicks' did not, as yet, interfere with the cousinly friendship. On December 29 she records :—

'Aunt Thomas and Tom Poole were so kind as to spend the whole day with us, recollecting that it was the

[1] *Encyclopædia Britannica*, third edition, then publishing.
[2] Mr. Lewis was the curate of Over Stowey.

anniversary of my mother's wedding-day. Their being here helped to dissipate the cloud that hung over her.'

In January 1793 she writes :—

'*January* 1.—We heard this morning that Tom Paine was going to be burnt in Effigy at Stowey; but Tom Poole called, and told us he had put a stop to the proceedings, for after what had passed he thought some people might think it was done in opposition to him, and if he appeared in it, others might think it was hypocrisy.

'*January* 15.—Dined at Uncle Thomas's, who was delighted to have us, for they have very little society in Stowey, Sally having left them. Tom can scarcely be called a companion, he is so deeply engaged in his studies; but I think he would be much more amiable if he would endeavour sometimes to amuse his old father and mother.

'*January* 27.—This evening we have been chilled with horror at reading the murder of the King of France.'

The following letter[1] will show what Tom Poole's feelings were in connection with that terrible event and its results :—

'I do execrate as much as any man that unnecessary instance of injustice and cruelty perpetrated in France, and should be happy to see every man who voted for the king's death brought to condign punishment. But 'tis not Louis's death, nor the Scheldt, nor the decree of November, that are the causes of the war. It is a desire to suppress the glowing spirit of liberty, which, I thank

[1] T. Poole to Mr. Gutteridge, a London tanner, February 23, 1793.

God, pervades the world, and which, I am persuaded,
all the powers on earth cannot destroy. . . .

  'Many thousands of human beings will be sacrificed
in the ensuing contest; and for what?   To support three
or four individuals, called arbitrary kings, in the situation
which they or their ancestors have usurped.   I consider
every Briton who loses his life in the war as much mur-
dered as the King of France, and every one who approves
the war, as signing the death-warrant of each soldier or
sailor that falls.   But besides these motives, what shall
we not suffer in other respects?   This country for some
time past may be considered as the workshop of France;
we have been growing rich by their confusion.   And had
Government, instead of the measures they have taken,
promoted a rational reform according to the spirit of the
constitution, we had, indeed, been a happy people.   But
now, adieu to all reform!   There is no alternative
between absolute quiescence or the most violent extrem-
ities.   In the reign of Charles I. France had some
shadow of liberty left; but the artful ministers of Louis
XIV. alarmed the people of that country with the view
of the excesses of parties in England, and induced them
to make their monarch despotick.   I trust in God there
is no similarity between the people of this country and
those of France at that time.   The excesses in France
are great; but who are the authors of them?   The
Emperor of Germany, the King of Prussia, and Mr.
Burke.   Had it not been for their impertinent interference, I firmly believe the King of France would be at
this moment a happy monarch, and that people would
be enjoying every advantage of political liberty.

  'The contemplation of this subject gives me great pain,

and I think your sentiments will in general coincide with mine. The slave trade, you will see, will not be abolished, because to be humane and honest now is to be a traitor to the constitution, a lover of sedition and licentiousness. But this universal depression of the human mind cannot last long. . . .'

Earlier in the autumn—it must have been soon after receiving the news of the September massacres —Poole had already expressed to the same friend his grief and anxiety at the bloody turn that events were taking in Paris. Characteristically enough he begins, not with the madness of the people but with the crimes of kings :—

'Poor Poland, I pity her fate ! Is there no vengeance from heaven for the Empress of Russia? Are her gray hairs to go down to the grave in peace? I trust not. I trust that mankind will be shown that there is a punishment, even in this world, for such abominable tyranny. Louis XIV. succeeded as well as the Empress of Russia, yet he lived to see his power lessened and his pride humbled. But Louis XIV., though he exhausted and desolated his own country, never was guilty of what this woman has done.

'Speaking of a French despot, we naturally turn to French affairs. What are your sentiments on the present crisis? Are all the horrid excesses and cruelties of which we hear necessary?—There is a something, my dear sir, in the character of the French which I thank God Englishmen do not possess. That savage levity which has appeared in this latter revolution, and, indeed, on a review of their history, always did appear in their civil wars, I must abhor; that entire absence of religion and mockery of justice are detestable; but, notwithstanding this, I think they did right in deposing the king, and they have an undoubted right, if they prefer it, to choose a Republican government. But why this disgrace to humanity?—As for Christianity, it is quite out of the question. Had human nature any cause to blush during the glorious Revolution in America?

'The philosophers and friends to mankind that formed the first French constitution I admire and revere, and that constitution, the most beautiful fabrick that was ever erected by the human mind, gained ground and admirers every day; but it is fled like a dream, and I tremble lest the present excesses may not give a greater stab to liberty than the Tyrants of the world who are combined against it. . . .'

Charlotte Poole's complaint that her cousin was so little of a companion to his parents may have been well grounded, for references in later letters show that Tom Poole, at this period of his life, used to spend from four to five hours daily in study. He had brought back with him from London the desire to become thoroughly acquainted with the writings of the above-mentioned French 'philosophers and friends to mankind,' and was working steadily at the acquisition of the French language; and although he had at first no teacher, it appears that he cannot have been very long before he acquired the power of

reading French with tolerable facility. How he
found time for so much reading it is difficult to
imagine, for his uncle's death and his father's
failing health had thrown the chief burden of the
family business on his shoulders, whilst now, as
ever throughout his life, he was constantly engaged
in a variety of local interests ; the Sunday School,
for instance, which he sedulously laboured to keep
going ; the Taunton Hospital, of which the first
stone had been 'laid in 1772 by Lord North,
then Premier of England, the immortal father of
the present minister, with many other persons of
distinction, being present on the occasion.' Now,
twenty years later, the building still remained
unfinished for lack of funds, and it had actually
been proposed that it should be pulled down, and
'the materials sold, in order to discharge expenses
already incurred,' a proposition which Tom Poole
most earnestly endeavoured to combat, both by
writing to the papers and in other ways, entreating
everybody not to be a tame spectator of an event
which, if once accomplished, would certainly become the subject of general, though unavailing
regret.

The Stowey Book Society was also started by
Tom Poole in the beginning of 1793, and his
Copying-book contains a sketch of the rules, and
a copy of the very first list of books ordered to

be delivered 'with all expedition, carriage paid, the volumes in boards and the pamphlets stitched.' I can remember this society as still in existence in my own young days; but it gradually dropped to pieces before the now universal custom of subscribing to a London library. It may entertain readers of the present day to see the kind of books that were ordered; but I must own that I have my suspicions that occasional remonstrances may possibly have been addressed to Tom Poole for sending for too many volumes in which the other members of the society were only very moderately interested. In fact, an instance of something of the kind from his cousin John Poole will in due time find a place in these pages. Here, however, is the list :—

'*Rights of Women*, by Mary Wolstoncraft.
Gillies's *History of Greece;* and also his *Reign of Frederic the Second, with a parallel between that Prince and Philip of Macedon.* In all, 3 vols.
Watson's *History of the Reigns of Philip the Second and Third of Spain.* In all, 3 vols.
Neckar on Executive Government. 2 vols., tr. from the French.
Keat's *Sketches from Nature.*
Robertson's *Disquisition on the Indies.*
The Romance of the Forest.
Pavis Lequel.
Richard's *Songs of the Aboriginal Britons.*

Fox's *Letter to the Electors of Westminster.*
Dowman's *Tragedies.*

And you must send a book of plain writing paper, proper to keep the Society's accounts, of the value of 3s., and on the cover, printed on a piece of red leather, Stowey Book Society.'

The following passage is from a letter to Mr. Purkis, dated February 26, 1793 :—

'. . . It is so long since we have been in correspondence that I hardly know whether we had any particular topicks under discussion. As for politicks, though that subject is now, not as heretofore, a mere matter of conversation, but an interesting concern to all, I will say nothing, for I know we precisely agree in our sentiments. . . . War is a horrid fiend ; and the closer any thinking humane mind approaches him, the more it is astonished at the indifference with which it has been used to contemplate the monster.[1] This is a wonderful instance of the quiescence of the mind, and of its readiness to adopt unthinkingly whatever has been made familiar by habit, and offered to it from its earliest capability of perception : in other words, it shows how little men think on anything for themselves. . . .

'Have you had any further intercourse with Sir Joseph Banks ? My reason for asking is, that a particular friend of mine, Mr. Anstice, has written an essay on the doctrine of the Velocity of Bodies, which, I think,

---

[1] '. . . Boys and girls
And women that would groan to see a child
Pull off an insect's leg, all read of war,
The best amusement for our morning meal.'
COLERIDGE, *Fears in Solitude.*

possesses great merit, and which he wishes to be read before the Royal Society. For this purpose I understand it must be introduced by a member of that body —are any of them within the circle of your acquaintance? Have you heard from the Editors of the Scotch Dictionary, or made any progress in your treatise for that work? In their article on " Mechanics " they have taken in the principal part of a little volume on the Construction of Wheel-carriages, by my friend above alluded to; but they have, in some cases, misstated his doctrine, and he wishes to write to them. Do, in your next, give me their address. . . .'

This Mr. Anstice was a shipowner in the town of Bridgwater, up to which place the muddy waters of the River Parrett are navigable for ships of considerable burden. It is one of those rivers in which the bed seems almost to empty itself at low tide, discovering a brown expanse of soft and shining mud, whilst the water returns in a single great wave, called locally the Bore, the sound of whose approach can be heard a long way off, and as it comes swift and strong round one of the numerous winding reaches, it seems to fill the river in a moment, lifting every vessel, as it lies bare to the very bottom against the sloping banks, with a sudden, peculiar shock. The town of Bridgwater probably originated with the first *bridge* built over this not very fordable river; but there is a ford with an old Celtic name—Combwich—a few miles lower down, where, as Somersetshire antiquaries think, Alfred's army crossed the river on their way from Ailey [1] to Edington, about six miles farther on. Wedmore, where Guthrum was baptized, and Oller, where he was confirmed, are not far distant, and I have heard from my father that it was almost a point of honour with John Poole—Tom's contemporary cousin—to maintain that at this Edington, and not at Edington in Wiltshire, had been fought the battle that decided the fate of England.

Mr. Anstice's house stood facing the river, not very far from the old stone bridge. He was a man of commanding personal appearance, with good means, and much originality and force of character, and was, of course, numbered amongst the principal inhabitants of the town. His name is mentioned as one of those upon whom Clarkson called when he visited Bridgwater in 1787, drawn thither by the fact that the *second* Petition for the Abolition of the Slave Trade ever presented to Parliament (in 1785) came from the town of Bridgwater. The Quaker petition was the first ; [2]

[1] A hamlet near Stowey still bears the name of Ailey Green, and Stowey would really be a long day's march on the way from Exmoor to Edington, *viâ* the ford at Combwich ; supposing the Rock Aegbryhta, the gathering place of Alfred's army, to have been really some well-known rendezvous in Exmoor, as the Rev. John Poole conjectured.

[2] The Bridgwater Petition was presented by the Honourable

it may be that the fact that there were members
of the Society of Friends, who were respected and
wealthy inhabitants, was not without its influence
in the presentation of the Bridgwater petition also ;
and that some of these influential Quakers were
near connections of Mr. Anstice's, was perhaps
the particular circumstance which may have enlisted
his sympathies in the same direction ; for he was
not by nature a reformer.

'Mr. Anstice,' writes one [1] who remembers him,
'was even more self-educated than Tom Poole. His
father, as well as I can make out, had ships in some trade
from Bridgwater, which he commanded himself, and took
his son on one occasion to Italy, where he contrived to
learn Italian, and for many years he kept a journal in
that language. I have seen Italian sonnets of his composition. Like many of the Anstices, he lacked the
impulse which pushes men to the front. Shyness and
a sort of apparent indolence prevented their very uncommon talents from making the mark they ought to
have done.'

My own father has often spoken to me of this

Anne Paulet and Alexander Hood, Esq., then Members for Bridgwater. It begged leave to express a just abhorrence of a system of
oppression, which no prospect of private gain, no consideration
of public advantage, no plea of political expediency, can justify or
excuse. The members reported that there was not the least disposition to pay attention to it. Every one almost said the abolition
of slavery would throw the West Indian islands into convulsions, and
soon complete their utter ruin. 'They will not trust Providence for
its protection in so pious an undertaking.'—*Life of Clarkson*, vol. i.

[1] His grandson's widow, Mrs. Joseph Anstice.

'old Mr. Anstice,' as one of the most noticeable men he ever met, and although the morbid shyness above remarked upon was certainly a family characteristic, one of his grandsons did actually bid fair to achieve very high distinction, but that his brilliant career was cut short by an early death. This was Mr. Joseph Anstice, first Professor of Classics at the London University, who was a college contemporary and friend of Arthur Hallam, Mr. Gladstone, and other distinguished men.

The only thing he had time to publish was a volume of beautiful *Translations from Greek Choric Poetry;* but some of the hymns written during his last illness have found a place in *Hymns Ancient and Modern*, and are well-known favourites. The Harvest Hymn—

> 'Lord of the harvest! once again
> We thank Thee for the ripened grain,'

and the hymn beginning

> 'O Lord, how happy we should be,
> If we could cast our care on Thee,'

may be cited as examples.

This Joseph Anstice's brother Richard suffered from so extreme a form of the family shyness, that his tutor had almost to use force to get him into the schools at Oxford, where on the second day he found in his place a paper, signed by the

examiners, stating that Mr. Anstice had already
done enough to obtain the highest mathematical
honours Oxford could bestow. Both these were
sons of that very Penelope Poole of Marshmill,
for whom Tom Poole cherished such a strong
partiality. Her husband, Mr. William Anstice,
exercised the calling of an ironmaster at Madeley
Wood, in Shropshire. He was much younger
than herself, but the marriage was a very happy
one, and almost all their large family of children
were above the usual average in talent. Her
husband has been described to me as one of the
most fascinating of men, brilliant in wit—all the
Anstices possessed that delightful endowment, a
strong sense of humour—very poetical, very religious and highly principled, and at the same time
a firstrate man of business, and of considerable
scientific acquirements. This was a hereditary
taste. Science, but more particularly advanced
mathematics, was the delight of 'old Mr. Anstice,'
and the favourite employment of all such intervals
of leisure as he could secure from business in those
quieter days when leisure was more abundant
than it is now. Even on his deathbed, at considerably past eighty years of age, he sent to his
grandson Dick (the Richard Anstice before mentioned) some papers in connection with the
squaring of the circle, about which Dick remarked

that though, of course, not really successful, they
contained the nearest approximation that had
ever been made, which was known to mathema-
ticians as the Solution of Archimedes.   He thought
his grandfather must have learnt and forgotten it;
but even if so, this showed that he must have
gone deep into the subject.   It was the last effort
of the old man's brain; he became delirious, and
died in a few days.   The story has been told
here to give some idea what manner of man he
must have been at a much earlier period of his
life, when his grandsons were not yet born, and
their father a mere youth, too young for poor Tom
Poole to regard as yet with jealous eyes, however
frequently he might be seen hanging about that
enchanted spot, the parlour at Marshmill, to which,
indeed, Tom was wont to bring every guest
whom he thought interesting, but where, doubtless,
he would fain have had no one else so intimately
at home as himself.

The next mention of Mr. Anstice in Tom
Poole's correspondence is a very different one, and
must be sought for in another chapter.   It is
discouraging to find, from the following letter to
Mr. Purkis,[1] that the efforts on behalf of the
Hospital were unavailing.

'I thank you,' writes Tom Poole, 'for the trouble

---

[1] T. Poole to S. Purkis, April 17, 1793.

you took about the Taunton Hospital : you have seen
in the papers that the building is to be destroyed. . . .

'The failures at Bristol have been, and continue to
be, melancholy. A great slave merchant was the first
who failed, and in his ruin involved hundreds. Un-
warrantable speculation seems to have been the cause of
these calamities, and indeed may be considered as the
mercantile sin of the age. It arises from a bad principle,
to pursue which would require more room than I can
afford in this letter.

'You say you have done nothing respecting our business before the Lords in Council. I hope you will not
allow it to drop, but at present we are urgently called
to action before a higher court—I mean the House of
Lords, where a Bill is pending which, if I understand
it rightly, will, in its operation, do more harm to the
leather trade than the loss of all the bark exported this
kingdom. Tanners, curriers, cordwainers, all are interested. A most unjust and partial clause is admitted in
a most unconstitutional Bill (the Traitorous Correspondence Bill), by which clause the leather trade is deprived
of the favour extended to other manufactures ; and we are
told that it is high treason to supply the French with a
pair of shoes, whilst you may very innocently sell them
a coat ! I hope our Committee will immediately pay
attention to this subject, and, if we are used unjustly,
spare neither expense nor pains to obtain redress. All
we can do is to lay the business before counsel, and, if
necessary, pray to be heard by counsel at the bar of the
House of Lords. . . .

'I am glad you have so much time allowed to prepare
the article for the Encyclopædia. I recommend you to

begin as soon as you conveniently can, as I am persuaded many new ideas arise in the progress of a work
which we scarcely imagined the subject to be susceptible
of at the commencement.   Besides, it is suicide to the
abilities and an insult to the public to print a crude,
hasty composition, where no concurrence of circumstances prevented mature deliberation.   The only assistance I can give you is through my chemical, tanning
friend at Sherborne, who gives, I think, the best account
I have ever heard of the chemical action of the substances
used in the process. . . .

'With respect to my *Emigration ;* I have fixed it for
the beginning of June.   Wantage seems to be the best
place to select.   I design being *incognito* and *in formâ
pauperis.*   The particulars I will give you in a future
letter. . . .'

This chapter may be appropriately concluded
with another extract from Charlotte Poole's diary:—

'*December* 14.—Amused ourselves with reading Dr.
More's journal while he was in Paris on the dreadful
10th of August ; which sent us to bed in bad spirits,
and not in charity with all mankind, but hating the
French.'

CHAPTER IV

'As generations come and go,
Their arts, their customs, ebb and flow.'
WORDSWORTH.

THE dignified position of the vicars of Stowey
in the estimation of the Stowey neighbourhood
has been already mentioned. It was, no doubt,
partly due to their being also canons of Windsor;
but the circumstance that two or three vicars
successively seem to have been men of some
mark, must be allowed its due weight. Miss
Charlotte Poole said long afterwards to a niece of
hers, who was wondering how, in an age when
female education was little attended to, it had
come in the way of herself and her sisters to
attain to the degree of culture and accomplishment
which they actually possessed, that they owed
much to the *wives* of the vicars of Stowey, who
unconsciously set a standard of refinement and
education distinctly higher than that of the re-

mote little rural world into which their husbands'
duties brought them from time to time.

'We always looked to them, my dear,' said
Miss Charlotte, 'as a civilising element.'

I suppose it is hard for us to understand how
much a civilising element may have been needed
before the great improvement in the means of
communication arrived to bring even the remotest
places into easy connection with the larger world.
The Marshmill family were, of course, not parishioners, but they were always on terms of friendship with the Nether Stowey clergy and their
families ; whilst the Thomas Pooles, father and
son, seem to have acted as habitual helpers to
successive vicars in matters of tithe and glebe, and
other parochial questions, in which the assistance
of a loyal layman, who is also a man of business,
is very essential to a clergyman. The following
letters from the younger Thomas Poole to Dr.
Majendie,[1] in which the formal respectfulness of
the style does not prevent a tolerably free expression of opinion, give a curious picture of the
manners and feelings of a bygone age :—

'REV. SIR—As I have been accustomed to your goodness, I certainly should have intruded on you ere this
had I been able before to procure the little package

---

[1] Vicar of Stowey from May 1790 to April 1793. The letter is
dated December 15, 1792.

which accompanies this letter,[1] and which we beg, with
respectful compliments to yourself and Mrs. Majendie,
you will accept.

'It gave us great concern that we had not the satisfaction of taking leave of you, or of hearing from you,
before you left Stowey. Did you know, dear sir, how
much we were interested in the event then in contemplation—I mean your residence in Stowey—you would
not wonder at this. We have since heard that you have
for the present given up the idea, but we yet hope that a
time will come when you will spend a small portion of the
year in Stowey. I need not, sir, observe that your residence here would correct the manners, mend the hearts,
and strengthen the faith of all your parishioners, and,
I will venture to say, work a very material and desirable
change in the disposition of the most insensible. This
I should not presume to remark did I not know that this
consideration would argue more forcibly in your mind
than any other I could offer. . . . I can only add that
our family would be happy to contribute any means
which may fortunately be in their power to make your
residence at Stowey as convenient as the place will
admit.

'But though, sir, we have not heard from you, we
suspect that you have further claims on our gratitude.
My brother at Sherborne has lately received some atten-
tions from the Admiral and Earl Digby, and perhaps
you have again kindly reminded them of his residence
there. The Admiral honoured my brother with a call,
Saturday, the 20th November; and on the Saturday

---

[1] Perhaps a salmon. That fish abounded in the River Parrett,
and Tom Poole often sent presents of salmon to his friends.

following he was desired to dine at the castle. He
there met the Admiral and his lady, and Mr. and
Mrs. Frome, the only people in Sherborne whom my
lord and her ladyship visit on anything like familiar
terms.   He was received with that condescension,
even from her ladyship, which I must say is unusual
at the castle towards the inhabitants of Sherborne;
and, on taking leave, the Admiral requested my
brother to pay him a visit soon at his house in the
neighbourhood.   These events will give him no in-
considerable *éclat*, and will be, in their consequences,
of solid advantage to him.   We owe them entirely to
you, and can only repeat the thanks we have before
offered. . . .

'We had a short time since a meeting of the subscribers
to the Sunday Schools. We regretted the absence of the
principal supporter of those noble institutions, but trust
he will approve of the measures on which we determined,
which were, to purchase the boys a new coat and hat
each, and the girls a hat to wear Sundays; we hope
to get these clothes ready by Christmas Day.   As a
further inducement, we proposed giving to each child
who attends the schools without one omission, one
penny on the first Sunday in every month.   The expense
will be trifling, and being something in the children's
own pockets, seems to operate very powerfully.   As for
the rest, I believe every desired object of these institutions is answered. The School of Industry, too, is
placed on a new, and, I think, better plan, and we hope
to carry it on in a more spirited manner than we have
hitherto done.   Indeed we should be truly reprehensible
did we not exert ourselves to carry into effect those

institutions to which you, sir, give such liberal, such unprecedented support.[1]

'A more pleasing subject still I have reserved for the end ; it is to congratulate you, sir, on the preferment you have lately acquired, which we see announced in the papers. That this may be only a prelude to that which is yet more solid, and that you may long enjoy all the blessings Providence can bestow, believe to be the sincere hope of, Rev. Sir, your obliged,

'THOS. POOLE.'

The preferment in question was the rectory of Hungerford, to which Dr. Majendie had been presented. In those days of pluralities this did not involve, as a matter of course, the resignation of the vicarage of Stowey, but the two following letters will show that the consciences of the more earnest among the clergy were already beginning to awaken to the evils of non-residence.

'I have both your last letters, but with very different sensations : the former was another instance of your kindness to me, the latter informs me of an event which,

[1] In a subsequent letter the following passage occurs :—'It rejoices me exceedingly that when some men of considerable eminence hold up the most cruel and degrading principles, you, sir, remain unshaken in your conviction of the utility of Sunday Schools. In a political pamphlet which Arthur Young has lately published, containing in general most excellent advice, there are some remarks—particularly in the Appendix—which make me blush for enlightened human nature more than I ever saw occasion for in the whole course of my life. Such doctrines might have been expected from some, but to see them come from Arthur Young must give pain to every feeling mind.'—Thomas Poole to Dr. Majendie, April 1793.

I must confess, I have expected, but which gives me more pain than I can express, and which, perhaps, in its consequences, is a loss to me greater than I can estimate. We had no right, sir, to expect such a man as you long to remain Vicar of Stowey, nor has the treatment which you have experienced here given you any reason to resign the living with regret. I do most sincerely lament those disagreeable circumstances which have occurred during the short time you have presided here, not so much in a pecuniary point of view, as because I fear they have frequently agitated your mind and disturbed your peace. I ardently pray that those amongst whom you are now going may know better how to estimate your worth. My father and mother are equally afflicted by this intelligence, and you may rest assured, sir, that your goodness will be impressed on their minds to the latest hour of their lives. . . .

'You say, sir, wheresoever you may go you will not entirely forget him who is now writing. This, sir, is too much, and I fear I can have very little in future to communicate that will be interesting to you ; but if, at a leisurable hour you will condescend to write to me, it will occupy some of my happiest moments to read and to answer your letters, and should you conceive it ever in my power to render you any personal services, here or elsewhere, your commands would give me the highest pleasure. Hungerford is, I think, situated on the great road from Bath to London ; it is possible I may, some time or other, pay my respects to you there. But I have a hope that we shall see you at Stowey once more before you take a final leave. It would give us the greatest, yet I must say a melancholy, satisfaction. . . .

'At the end of your letter you are pleased to intimate that you will soon inform me more particularly of the circumstances which led to your resignation of this living; I wait anxiously to hear them, and tho' I regret our loss, yet if it adds satisfaction in any manner to you, be assured it gives the sincerest pleasure to, Rev. Sir, your obliged and sincere humble servant,

'THOS. POOLE.

'*P.S.*—Since writing this letter I have been so fortunate as to meet with a brace of woodcocks, which, tho' hardly worth your acceptance, I have added.'[1]

In reply Dr. Majendie seems to have said that he had resigned the living of Stowey principally on account of a conscientious objection to be a non-resident vicar, a reason which met with the warmest approval from Thomas Poole.

'Happy would it be,' he writes,[2] 'for the cause of religion, if every clergyman felt on this subject as you do. Those cavils, and that torrent of abuse, poured out by designing men against the Established Church, had never existed, if all had considered the importance of residence; or, if by peculiar circumstances their own residence was prevented, the importance of chusing a competent representative. Generally speaking, the dignitaries of the English Church do themselves and the sacred religion of which they are the ministers honour. But you, sir, must be aware that very many of the inferior clergy, to whose care large congregations are frequently entrusted, disgrace their profession and violate their

---

[1] The date is January 3, 1793.   [2] March 4, 1793.

religion, not only by the commission and sanction of low vice, but by the neglect of the most positive duties. If on this subject I talk in an unbecoming manner, your goodness will attribute it to no other source than to my ignorance of that propriety of conduct, so difficult sometimes to ascertain; but, in truth, I am led thus to express myself by comparing your most excellent example with the opposite conduct of many whom I now call to mind. . . .

'I write to you, sir, without reserve, and sometimes, I fear, too familiarly, but your repeated assurances prompt me to do it. . . .'

This series of letters may appropriately conclude with one[1] in which Tom Poole expresses his indignation that some one should have reported to Dr. Majendie that his brother Richard is a flaming democrat.

'Rev. Sir—Your last letter informs me of two circumstances which have given me no small uneasiness, and which induce me to take this early opportunity of answering it, tho' I am sensible I ought to apologise for thus frequently intruding on your attention. These are, first, your indisposition, which I sincerely hope is ere now entirely removed, and, in the next place, your having heard that my brother at Sherborne is a *flaming democrat.*

'I most sincerely thank you, sir, for your candour in stating to me what you have heard, and I rejoice that those from whom you receive information at Sherborne condescend to mention any opinions which they suppose my brother to possess, and may, for the moment, dis-

[1] May 27, 1793.

approve. It shows that those, of whom to merit the esteem and approbation will be his highest gratification and honour, do not regard him, or that which may concern his welfare, with indifference.

'When my brother first came to Sherborne politicks were not considered in that serious point of view which they have been since, but were rather recurred to as a matter of conversation, about which men might talk without the least apprehension. They seemed peculiarly well suited to a stranger, who, in a mixed company, with the connections of which he was little acquainted, could scarcely venture to speak of local events, lest he should incur the displeasure of some one or other. With respect to any opinions he may have advanced, I do believe, sir, they were not those of which you would disapprove. When there was a probability of a limited monarchy in France, he applauded some of their measures, but long, very long since, has he viewed with horror and detestation the excesses perpetrated in that unhappy kingdom. He never admired the democratic form of government, nor did he need the fatal experience of French events to convince him of the futility of that splendid theory. With respect to the British Constitution, he always did, and does, revere it as the greatest effort of human wisdom, and would, if necessary, sacrifice everything to its preservation. To say that he does not see some abuses which *in a proper time*, and *in a proper manner*, ought to be amended, would be ridiculous. I believe there is not a Briton but perceives some ravages of time in the splendid mansion of his fathers, in a summer season, and by *competent* and *duly authorised* workmen, he could wish to see repaired.

'I need not, sir, observe to you that frequently, very frequently, the vanity of argumentation induces men to advance what they by no means seriously approve, or wish to be considered as their principles. This idle conduct is often exercised in the discussion of topicks which are considered of small importance, which, in fact, was my brother's idea with respect to his opinion on politicks; but when he found there were those who, perhaps, were jealous of that degree of notice with which, through his friends, and through you, sir, particularly, he was honoured, who carefully propagated any expressions which might fall from him in the juvenile heat of conversation, which they thought would operate to his disadvantage, he became more cautious, and took the only means in his power of refuting those calumnies—by deliberately coming forward among the first to sign the declaration of attachment to the present Establishment in Church and State, which was agreed to by the inhabitants of Sherborne, and patronised by Lord Digby.

'I do not know, sir, what more I can add; but thus much have I said to exculpate him from the charge brought against him, and I entreat you, sir, to undeceive those who informed you of it, as I pledge my honour that what I have asserted is literally and unequivocally true. You will excuse some warmth on my part, as I cannot express how tenderly I feel this circumstance, which strikes so near his best interest, and which may operate to the loss of the good opinion of those whom he loves and honours. I fear, sir, I have tired you with this topick, and will, though reluctantly, change it. . . .'

And then Mr. Tom Poole plunges into parish

matters and questions of rent and glebe. He
concludes as follows :—

'On receiving notice to set out his tithe in kind ——
thought proper to offer ninepence in the pound for his
small tithes ; this is the full value of them if he sowed a
due proportion of corn, which I am thoroughly convinced
he must soon do, to gain anything like the real profits of
his farm.   On this consideration my father advised Dr.
Fisher[1] to accept the proposal. . . . You, sir, have fought
the battle, and your successor receives the fruits of it.
At this I am sure you will not be displeased, but it
embitters my mind when I recollect the pain you were
given during the time that you presided over us.   That
you may never again experience the like usage I hope
and trust. . . . Believe me to be, with sincere respect
and affection, your obliged humble servant,

'THOS. POOLE.'

In connection with the above letter it may be
observed that probably few measures have ever
had a more satisfactory effect in healing heart-
burnings and averting strife than the Act for the
Commutation of Tithes.   I have heard my father
say that, before that Act was passed, there was
scarcely a parish in the kingdom in which the
amount of the tithes was not a fruitful occasion
of disputes and unpleasantness ; whilst in almost

[1] The Rev. John Fisher, D.D., was Dr. Majendie's successor.
He had been tutor to the Princess Charlotte, and was afterwards
Bishop of Exeter.

every instance with which he was personally acquainted, the parson was habitually receiving less than his legal due.

There will be some, perhaps, who will feel a little offended at the extreme deference with which Mr. Tom Poole, in the foregoing letters, writes to 'a dignitary of the Church,' and still more scandalised at the obsequious tone of the reference to 'my Lord Digby.' We must, however, be careful to remember the difference of manners, and understand not only that, in every kind of social intercourse, a degree of form and ceremony was then observed which, in the present day, has entirely gone out of use; but also that, when railways had not as yet brought the whole kingdom into easy connection with London, local centres had a far more definitely marked existence, and the chief personages in every country neighbourhood were far more important potentates than they are now or ever can be again, and were, as a matter of course, approached, and treated, with a deference which is now hardly accorded even to the royal family, and certainly to no one else. Upon the whole, the change of manners has been in the right direction, and means not only a general rise in self-respect, but also a generally higher average of culture and good-breeding throughout all classes, —a sort of *levelling up*, which cannot be thought of without great satisfaction and thankfulness. Of course there is no advance without its attendant drawbacks, and many of us are inclined to think we are now a little in danger of being carried rather too far in the opposite direction, and becoming unmannerly in our unceremoniousness. Perfect ease and freedom, with perfect self-restraint, is the natural atmosphere of good manners ; but perfect free-and-easyness, with as little self-restraint as possible, is vulgarity in principle, and must, sooner or later, become vulgarity in practice.

That Mr. Tom Poole's deference to rank and dignity did not prevent a sturdy pride in his position, may be seen from the following letter,[1] in which he laments the retirement from business of his friend Mr. Purkis, and bewails the tendency which he observes in those around him, to put sons into professions rather than into trade. It was, perhaps, on account of the declining prospects of the tanning trade at that particular time, that the Poole family seem to have generally, though gradually, withdrawn from it. John Poole had been elected Fellow of Oriel a few months before his father's death, and was intending to take orders ; J. Ruscombe Poole, the next brother, and my own grandfather, had, also just before his father's death, been articled to a Mr. Jeffreys, a

---

[1] T. Poole to S. Purkis, undated.   Probably December 1793.

solicitor in Bridgwater, where, in course of time, he
became the founder of a very good business, still,
in the third generation, in the hands of his
descendants ; another brother, Nathanael, died
young.   Tom Poole's other uncles left only female
descendants ; his brother Richard, we know, was
a doctor.   He himself held faithfully to the old
tanyard, putting a degree of feeling into the
matter utterly perplexing to outsiders, whose
general impression cannot but be that nobody can
imagine what place there is for enthusiasm, in
connection with an avocation so undistinguished
and so unbeautiful :—

'MY DEAR PURKIS—You are then really about to
resign trade. I have written to you sincerely my sentiments
on the subject, and I should not have been satisfied had
I not done so.   I bow to your elder judgment, but I
must say a word or two on your sarcastic observations on
what fell from me concerning the dignity of man and
the duties of a member of society.   You say, you could
write pretty periods on these holiday theories not fit for
every-day practice.   Is a man's placing himself in a
situation by which he could do much good to society, by
supporting a number of its members, a holiday theory un-
fit for every-day practice, and a proper subject for pretty
periods?   If a man is conscious of virtues, does not
humanity prompt him to extend the sphere of their influence as far as possible?   And does he do this by
becoming a hermit?   Were all men equally informed,

were the desires of all moderate, were there no room to
alleviate the misfortunes and distresses of some, and to
check the vice and disgusting ostentation of others, then
may the man who feels those things, and thinks of them,
indulge the epicurean desire of living only for himself;
but as human nature is constituted, it seems to my mind
an imperious duty for every such man to extend those
principles which he thinks will tend to correct the extremes of society, and to stand firm to the post at which
Providence has placed him. You may give the epithet,
if you please, of pretty periods to what I now write; but
these are only a very few of the arguments which may be
advanced on this side of the question, and I think they
are sufficient.

'We will now contemplate the subject in another point
of view. . . . In the present state of our community
when a man retires, however contracted be his means, he
is considered a Gentleman. If he has children, the young
mind soon seizes the gilded idea, and they fancy they are
to be fine ladies and genteel gentlemen in their turn;
and, in truth, these fancies only fall in with the depraved
mind of the public, for it is deemed a retrograde motion
of a man in the situation in question, to breed his boys
to trade and his girls to housewifery. What then is such
a man to do to make his children happy, and to keep up
his fancied dignity? "The professions are open." With
respect to the Bar, it has in this country been a splendid
road to preferment, but I am mistaken if its constitution
will not be much altered, before your children or mine
are able to enjoy its abuses. Physick, generally speaking,
does not offer the means of subsistence; and as to the
lower squad of the Law and the Church, they too often

annex disgrace to the characters who fill them. All this proves that the sons of men of middling property ought to be tradesmen,[1] and their girls tradesmen's wives. Every individual, therefore, who loves this class of society will do everything in his power to make it respectable.

'I fear these sounds are harsh gratings to the polished ear; but they are truth.   Trade, properly arranged, admits much leisure, and exercise gives additional zest to the gratifications which leisure offers.   I would wish Tradesmen to be the best-informed part of the community. The idle, debauched, ostentatious great, should look up to their supporters with respect, and come to them for information. But I remember that I talk here of the subject in general *sans* applying anything to you. You, my dear Purkis, are about to retire, and you, I doubt not, will exercise your superior abilities in some way or other for the good of all. This I expect from you. . . .'

Tom Poole goes on to hope that his friend will now write the book about which they have sometimes talked ; after which he adds, inconsistently enough:—

'I wish I had that leisure, which, if you carry your scheme into execution, you will hereafter enjoy.'

---

[1] T. Poole always uses this word in the larger sense of a man engaged in trade, in whatever manner and upon whatever scale.

CHAPTER V

' So was he framed, and such his course of life.'
WORDSWORTH, *The Excursion*, Book I.

THAT Tom Poole did actually, at some period of
his life, carry out his purpose of putting on the
dress of a working tanner, and going forth to seek
employment in some large yard near London, has
always been a well-established tradition in the
Poole family ; but it is well-nigh impossible to
determine with certainty the particular time which
was devoted to this adventure.   The motives which
had prompted him to undertake it were twofold :
first, no doubt, he desired to extend and complete
his knowledge of the methods employed in the
tanning manufacture.   His father's sarcasms had
rankled, and he felt that it would be a satisfaction
to dispose, once and for ever, of the reproach of
being ignorant of the practical details of his own
trade.   But, besides this, he was sharing very
deeply in the social enthusiasm of a time when
Southey repeatedly lamented that his father had

not brought him up to be a carpenter, and
Coleridge was longing to live by the labour of his
hands in the cultivation of the earth.   Tom Poole's
experience of business, and his practical turn of
mind, alike preserved him from the delusion of
visionary extremes ; in him the prevailing impulse
took the form of an eager sympathy with the
labourer and the workman, a deep sense of his own
duty towards them, as an educated man and an
employer of labour, and a determination to set
himself to gain a more perfect knowledge of their
condition, in order that he might understand their
wants and wishes, and how best to help them.
His friend Purkis was his chief, perhaps his only,
confidant.   He must have given, as will be seen
by the following letter,[1] many useful counsels, but
not unmingled with remonstrances, setting forth
the unusualness of his design, and the discomforts
and inconveniences which would be certain to
attend it.

'DEAR PURKIS—I had postponed day after day writing
to you, in hopes of being able to transmit the observations of my Sherborne friend on tanning ; but I find
procrastination is the general sin of mankind, and that
not even a Quaker, whose methodical arrangements and
unimpassioned line of conduct would, I conceived, have
exempted him from this fatal malady, steers entirely free

[1] T. Poole to S. Purkis, June 27, 1793.

of that *death of time* from which most of us have
constantly suffered. . . .

'I have lately been, and indeed am now, much
engaged in our little bark harvest,[1] so that I have not at
this moment time to write you a long letter. . . . I will
only tell you that I shall set out on my peregrinations
some time next week, therefore let me hear from you
immediately, that your letter may reach Stowey before I
leave it. My plan must be to offer myself to some one
in the form of a common workman. This undertaking
is, for me, odd, disagreeable, and romantick enough; yet
I am convinced of the necessity of it, and I certainly
shall attempt it. I expect some curious circumstances
will occur, but I shall feel myself very comfortable under
my mask, as I design not only changing my dress for
the usual habit of a tanner, but my name also to Thomas
Adams. When I am fixed at any place, which I shall
first endeavour to be at Wantage, I shall write to you,
and inform you how I support my new character. Do,
in your letter, give me any hints you think will be useful
to me in the progress of my undertaking, and also inform
me of the yards which you know of in the kingdom, out
of London, at all famous for their manufacture; so that,
in case I should not be admitted in one, I should have
others to apply to.

'Your reflections on my emigration perhaps are various.
First, you will smile at that transition which I certainly
must experience; and, in the next place, you will shake
your head at my having neglected acquiring what it was
long since my indispensable duty to acquire. But I

---

[1] Oak underwood is, I am told, barked once in every sixteen
years.

must tell you if my ideas were only to carry on the trade
in the manner my father has done, I need not incur the
risque of this adventure. My hope is to encrease his
trade; and I wish to see every variety of the manufacture, that I may appropriate to myself that which I
conceive best.   Having now a little leisure, and health
and strength enough, I do not think I shall spend a few
months unprofitably by applying them to this main
object.   At the close of my peregrinations, when I have
washed my hands clean, and by due ablutions am fit to
stand before you, I shall call at Brentford, and then I
hope you will find I have not contaminated either mind
or manners, by intercourse with those in the society of
whom I necessarily must be; but that I have only
stooped a little to acquire useful experience, and also to
obtain a greater knowledge of that class of life, of which
it is our duty to know most, inasmuch as that class most
requires our assistance and protection.   God Almighty
bless you.   With kind compliments to Mrs. Purkis, and
health to you, to her, and your little ones, believe me,
ever yours,   THOS. POOLE.'

'MY DEAR FRIEND—Perhaps you will be surprised at
seeing me date from this place,[1] and you will accuse me
of unkindness in not having written to you before.
You, who, I believe, know the operations of the mind as
well as most, will easily conceive the reluctance I felt in
writing to you again from Stowey, for after a plan had
been laid down to you with so much formality, I could
not find it in my heart to tell you that it was in the
power of any circumstances to frustrate it.   This sensation

---

[1] T. Poole to S. Purkis, Stowey, August 13, 1793.

certainly arises from pride and disappointment; I hope
they are not bad principles excited on such an occasion.
I told you in my last that I should leave Stowey the first
week in July.   I had my clothes packed, and everything
ready.   Two days before my intended departure my
father was seized with a bad fit of the gout; 'twas
impossible I could leave home.   He got tolerably well;
I was again about to start, when he was attacked with a
pleurisy, in so violent a manner that we thought he
would have died.   Within this fortnight he has been
tolerably recovered, and I should have been at Wantage
ere this, but fortune seems determined to thwart me in
all my plans, for an aunt of mine, the wife of that little
old man you saw at Stowey, was about ten days ago, on
a visit to a friend in London, taken seriously ill, and is
since dead.   My uncle has been in London with her,
but returns to-morrow; 'tis necessary, for prudential
reasons, that I remain at home a week or two to arrange
his affairs, as, his wife being dead, he designs altering
entirely his plan of living.

'You now ask me if I have abandoned my plan.   No.
I do intend, if fate is willing, to set off on my peregrinations from Bristol Fair.   Thank you for the instructions
and hints contained in your last letter.   With respect to
my travelling name, I had some reasons for choosing
Adams, and should have taken care of the marks on my
linen; but as you propose that of Pope, I will accept it,
though at first I revolted at it, for I hate the sound.
But on consideration that my plan savours a little of
deceit, I think it characteristick, and shall adopt it.[1]

[1] Notwithstanding much friendly intercourse with French
Roman Catholic priests, Tom Poole cherished, in the abstract, the

Mention to me in your next letter in what manner a common fellow comes and asks you for work, and what you say to him, and how he is received in the yard by the workmen—whether he has any footing to pay, etc. etc. The work in the yard I can go through tolerably well. You will laugh at my caution, but I so much dread the support of anything like a feigned character, that I have my fears how I shall go through with it. . . .'

The letter concludes with one of those sorrowful, indignant references to the state of Europe, and to the part taken by England in the disturbed drama of continental politics, which, occurring as they do in almost every letter he writes, betoken clearly enough how much Tom Poole's mind was pre-occupied with this subject, and how strongly he felt about it. Thus, in writing to another friend [1] he says, at the end of a letter of thanks for civilities shown to his sister, then making a round of visits in London, Isle-worth, Windsor, etc :—

'With respect to the tanning and bark business, I imagine it is pretty much at a stand, both publick and private ; indeed, in our publick business I scarcely know what can be done, yet I think something should—if only to remind Government that though they have neglected everything in their power to preserve the trade,

strongest possible prejudice against what he would have called 'Popery.'

[1] T. Poole to Mr. Gutteridge, June 7, 1793.

the tanners are still in being, and have grievances to complain of. As for our private business, I believe there never was such an alteration. Do let me know in your next how your markets are for raw tanned and bark, and *what your opinion is concerning the future state of the trade.* This is not a pleasant subject to dwell on, and if I turn to politicks, nothing presents itself that can give satisfaction to a benevolent mind. If the French conquer, will licentiousness instead of liberty prevail ? If the French are conquered, Europe is enslaved. I had rather run the risque of the former, than bear the burden of the latter. Yet I trust in God that there is, and I think there is, a medium ; I think that the French will neither conquer nor be conquered, but that they will have strength enough within themselves to establish independently that government which the majority of the people wills—for woe be to that nation whose government is dictated by despots ! Poor, helpless Poland justifies this exclamation. There is no word in our vocabulary sufficiently expressive of my detestation of the conduct of the tyrants of Russia and Prussia towards that unoffending nation. But these tyrants are our allies ! If there be any event in the annals of this country which should make an Englishman's cheeks burn with shame more than another, it is that the government under which he lives should continue and cherish an alliance with those who had thus acted. . . .'

' I am weary of thinking of European politicks,' he says again ;[1] 'America seems the only asylum of peace and liberty—the only place where the dearest feelings of man

[1] In a letter to Purkis, June 1793.

are not insulted; in short, the only spot where a man
the least humane and philosophical can live happily.
The event of the struggle in France is doubtful, and,
should it end victoriously, it cannot end yet. Besides,
the vice, deeply rooted in France, will prevent it ever
being what America is. England is a declining country,
and now too guiltily leagued with despots to obtain an
object at which a Briton ought to blush. Few of its
inhabitants who feel as their ancestors felt, can have
much affection for it; the mind shrinks with melancholy
detestation from contemplating the conduct of most of
the crowned heads in Europe, particularly that of Russia.
This is a painful topick; let us change it. Since I saw
you I have thought much on the subject, the result you
shall have when we meet. I will only say now that I
consider the Supreme Being indulgent in allowing man
the felicity he enjoys, whilst he, by most of his institutions, has counteracted the decrees of the Almighty, his
own happiness, and the first feelings of nature. You
perhaps will think me gloomy, but I am not so. Yet I
should be happy to hear explained some hints in your
last letter on the subject of religion. I hope and think
there is no material difference in our creeds. Adieu,
my dear Purkis.—Believe me, most truly yours,

'THOS. POOLE.'

After this exposition of his sentiments we cannot greatly wonder if we find that the free expression of Tom Poole's opinions was getting
almost beyond what the Stowey mind, immovably
fixed at the opposite point of view, could endure
without exasperation, even from an old neighbour's

son and a cousin of one's own, in whom the divergence could be treated as a simple aberration of the
intellect, his goodness of heart being too well known
to admit of the slightest suspicion that he would
like to introduce a Reign of Terror in England.
Nevertheless we are not surprised to find Charlotte
Poole entering in her journal : [1]—

'Tom Poole drank tea with us. I wish he would
cease to torment us with his democratick sentiments ;
but he is never happy until the subject of politicks is introduced, and, as we all differ so much from him, we
wish to have no conversation about it.'

On the same occasion her brother John confided to *his* journal that he had been 'a little '—
Charlotte and her sisters had perhaps been not a
little—' warm and irritated ' when Tom, after tea,
' produced some of his republican ideas;' and that
he was sorry for it afterwards, and 'did not
approve of this anger towards a person who, in
his last illness, was perhaps the cause of his life
being preserved.'

As Charlotte observed, Tom usually did talk
' politicks' whenever he came to Marshmill, and he
usually ' had all against him.' Not even when he
and John went out woodcock-shooting together
could he altogether refrain, but John notices that
on that November day when Tom came in to fetch

[1] January 12, 1794.

him to go out with him, and Nathanael, the delicate younger brother who afterwards died of consumption, joined them too, 'and shot his first woodcock,' Tom talked politicks indeed, as usual, but 'was very temperate,' and in the evening sat down tranquilly to play cards, whilst John read the *Life of Franklin*, and admired him as 'a great friend of mankind in many respects,' and above all, 'useful in showing in his own life the good effects of industry and exertion,' though perhaps in some respects 'not all a wise man would wish to be.'

This was on November 27, 1793. It is therefore clear that on that day Tom Poole was certainly in Somersetshire, so that, if he started on his 'peregrinations' any time during the summer or autumn of 1793, he must have returned home before the end of November. But it will have been observed that his last letter to Purkis was dated August 13, and that in it he states his intention of starting from Bristol Fair, which was always held in September. This would allow little more than two months for the entire enterprise, and it may be well to mention that family tradition has assigned it to a later date. One version of the story which has been related to me as a legend handed down from an older generation, supposes a dramatic disappearance on the very day of his father's funeral, in July 1795 ; and,

in support of this view, it might be observed that
there is not a single entry in his letter-book between July 24 and September 6, 1795. But the
same thing is to be noticed in 1793. The letter
that follows the letter to Purkis of August 13, is
a letter to Dr. Majendie, dated December 7, and
in this a sudden return home on account of his
father having been taken ill is mentioned. 'I
was much mortified that I could not spend a day
or two at Windsor,' he says, 'but my father's indisposition was such that I was obliged to hasten
home as soon as possible.'

It is clear that, whether in 1793 or in 1795,
Poole cannot have been absent from Stowey for
much more than two months, and I think the
balance of probability is in favour of the year
1793. He must have recounted his experiences
to Purkis in a personal interview, as, indeed, he
had said he would, for there is no further allusion
to the matter in any letter that I have been able
to discover. The tradition runs that the finding
of a Latin Classic, lying on his bench during the
dinner hour, discovered to his employers that
he certainly was not a *common* workman; and,
further, that when he parted from them, he warned
them against an extensive system of waste and
pillage, by which they were the unsuspecting losers
of some hundreds of pounds every year, and at

the same time suggested some very simple method whereby matters might easily be placed upon a better footing.

Many years later, when his services in connection with the Parliamentary Inquiry into the Working of the Poor Laws had brought him into a good deal of notice, and made him acquainted with many men of mark and influence, he was walking one day in the streets of Bath in company with Lord Lansdowne, when he recognised, in an old waggoner, driving by with his team, a man who had been a carter in the yard where he had worked. He excused himself to Lord Lansdowne, and walked across the road, holding out his hand to his old acquaintance. The waggoner stared at him for a moment, and then at last, seizing the offered hand, he delightedly burst forth: 'Sure, 'tis never our Tummas! Well, I did always think thee was summat above the common.'

There is another tradition connected with this episode in Tom Poole's life which cannot altogether be passed by without notice. The daughters of that Thomas Ward who was a youth, living with Tom Poole as his articled apprentice, at the time when S. T. Coleridge was in Stowey, and who afterwards became his partner, and was ever his attached and intimate friend, are still living in the Stowey neighbourhood, and, indeed, in that very house at Marshmill which has been so often mentioned as the home of the John Pooles. One of these Miss Wards declared to me quite positively, when I saw her about two years ago, that she could distinctly remember hearing from her father, not once but often, that the very first time S. T. Coleridge and Tom Poole came across one another was in some inn, whether in London or elsewhere she could not be sure, but she thought in London, Coleridge in the guise of a private soldier and Poole in that of a workman, when the soldier was as much astonished at the workman's attainments as the workman was amazed at the conversation of the soldier. ' I cannot have dreamt all this,' she concluded ; ' I am perfectly certain that I am telling you the tale as 'twas told me by my father.'

This sounds like good authority ; and yet, when we come to compare dates and documents, it appears to be manifestly impossible that the incident can ever actually have happened. The time that S. T. Coleridge spent as a private soldier was from December 3, 1793 to April 1794, and it seems undeniable that during the whole of that period Tom Poole was at home at Stowey. Of course, *if* Poole had been working at Wantage whilst Coleridge was in the barracks at Reading, they would not have been far apart, and a chance encounter might very easily have come to pass ; and this, I think, is the direction in which we must look for a solution of the difficulty. Perhaps Coleridge and Poole may sometimes have amused themselves with imaginations of what so very nearly might have been, until conjectures gradually shaped themselves into a real history, and became a sort of household word, not easily distinguishable from actual fact, especially if sometimes deliberately employed for the mystification of the boy Ward himself.

CHAPTER VI

'The privilege of talking and even publishing nonsense, is necessary in a free state; but the more sparingly we make use of it the better.'
                                   S. T. COLERIDGE, *The Friend*.

THE year 1794 was to be a memorable year in Tom Poole's life, for it is the year of his first acquaintance with S. T. Coleridge. It opened, in Stowey, with the annual meeting of the Book Society. The cousins, John and Ruscombe Poole, Tom Poole himself, and 'the greater number of the members of the society,' dined together at the Globe Inn on New Year's Day. 'We had a pleasant meeting,' writes John Poole, 'and matters were, in general, conducted very amicably. About eight the auction began, and I purchased Russell's *View of the History of Modern Europe* and Gillies's *History of Greece*. Ruscombe purchased Robertson's *Disquisition, etc.* We stayed till ten, and went to supper at Uncle Thomas's.' The ordering of fresh books seems to have been left in the hands

of Thomas Poole, who asked John to assist him in
the task.

'He had drawn out a list which he showed me,' John
writes,[1] 'but I found in it some books that appeared to
me very improper to be circulated among the members
of our society.   I objected particularly to a work of
Volney's, which, from some extracts I had seen in the
Review, I knew to be strongly tinctured with infidelity.
I objected likewise to the introduction of any of those
political pamphlets which may be either the vehicles of
the present fashionable principles or the occasion of
contention and ill-will among the members.   I must
own that T. Poole readily came in to my wishes, and
told me he was not acquainted with Volney's principles
with respect to religion, nor did he, he said, think it
right to circulate books of that description amongst
us. . . .'

John Poole was at this time living principally
at home, at his mother's house at Marshmill, and
reading for Holy Orders.   From time to time
he paid short visits to Oxford, when he used to
ride to and fro on his own horse, 'Pud,' over whose
comfort and well-being he is very properly solici-
tous, noting in his diary with special praise the Inn
at Swindon—his first stage on the homeward route
—which was 'equal to any inn with respect to
comfort, and with respect to stable discipline,
superior to all he ever frequented.'   The journey

[1] Journal, January 4, 1794.

took him about three days. Like his cousin Tom, though very unlike him in most other respects, John Poole was bent upon a life of usefulness. To him the 'end of his being,' which a man should have ' always before his eyes,' was ' to follow, either directly or obliquely, at all times, the melioration of his nature, the good of others, and the glory of God.' He had a high ideal of what a clergyman ought to be, and his whole heart was set upon realising it in his own career. The course of study that he had laid down for himself centred in a thoughtful and painstaking reading through of the whole Bible, beginning with the Old Testament in the Septuagint, as well as in the Authorised Version. Hebrew, at this time, he did not know, though he learnt it later. He accompanied this study of the Scriptures themselves by the careful reading of a constant succession of books bearing upon the Scriptures, and of well-written sermons, amongst which he particularly notes Bishop Wilson's, as being ' formed on that plan which in my mind best suits a country congregation.'[1] John Poole must have been at this period of his life a tall, fair-complexioned young Oxford don, a true

---

[1] I have heard my father say that in after years his Uncle John's sermons were models of simplicity and clearness. He used to aim at ' preaching in Saxon,' and carefully struck out every word of Latin origin for which it was possible to find an old English equivalent.

reformer at heart,[1] but after a sober and temperate fashion, having a constitutional distrust of everything spasmodic and extreme, and being in manner somewhat precise and formal, and so much accustomed to meeting with deference from all around him, that anything like an obstinate assertion of opposite opinions must have given him a sort of shock by mere force of unusualness. He loved field-sports and country pursuits, and even followed the hounds occasionally, but never after he took Orders, notwithstanding that he lived in the age of hunting parsons. But his favourite relaxation was botany. I, who remember him only in old age, remember most clearly how fond he even then was of the study of flowers, how he knew the exact *habitat* of every rare plant in the neighbourhood, and showed me, then a child, the place where Solomon's Seal was to be found, and the one spot where the Narcissus might yet be seen growing wild. In his diary the remarks on the books he is reading are constantly intermixed with notices of the blossoming of plants :—

'. . . I observed *caltha palustris* in flower for the first time this year. . . .'

'. . . Walked round Ruxford Meadow, where I met with the pistilliferous flowers of the Dog's Mercury. . . .'

---

[1] *e.g.* He writes February 18, 1794 : 'I was glad to find Mr. Y. was an advocate for the abolition of the slavish duties affix'd to the office of servitors, Bible-clerks, etc.'

It is scarcely possible to turn over three pages without coming to some entry of this sort, and whenever he was in Oxford he was a constant visitor of what was then called the 'Physic Garden.'

In disposition he was very unimaginative and matter of fact, but capable of deep and lasting enthusiasm for the cause to which he principally devoted his life—namely, education, and especially the education of the poor. He was a born teacher, and delighted in the exercise of his gift ; and when Tom Poole asked him to read Latin with him he most readily consented, indeed he had persuaded his younger brother Ruscombe also—the articled clerk—to become his pupil, and read *Selecta è veteri Testamento* and Cæsar's *Commentaries* with him, finding him 'better acquainted with the language than he expected.' Tom Poole had already, by solitary study, made himself master of the elements. What he now desired was to begin something like a real acquaintance with Latin literature ; and we find from John Poole's journal that during the following twelvemonth there were meetings at least as often as once a week, and the two cousins read together Horace's *Ars Poetica*, his first and second *Satire*, and his *Odes ;* Cicero's *Dream of Scipio, De Amicitia*, and *De Senectute ;* and Virgil's *Æneid.* 'Tom Poole,' wrote his cousin Charlotte in April, 1794, ' is now, with an industry and perseverance that does him honour, acquiring a knowledge of Latin, and has put himself under my brother John's tuition, so that we shall often have the pleasure of seeing him. . . .' For they were, after all, very fond of poor Tom, notwithstanding his unaccountable opinions, in relation to which their view, being strongly modified by natural regard and great personal respect for their own kinsman, was certainly milder and more tolerant than that of the neighbourhood generally, as will be seen by a letter to Mr. Purkis, dated August 23, 1794, which is also interesting for the account of Tom Poole's studies with which it opens :—

' MY DEAR PURKIS—I wrote a letter to you some time ago, which I hope you received, and I must acknowledge that I expected an answer ere now ; not that I had any right so to do, but I rather built on your former goodness in similar circumstances. Besides, I know when you have leisure you feel as much pleasure in writing as in reading, which is not at present the case with me ; for in truth I should scarcely take a pen in hand, were I not stimulated either by necessity in matters of business, or, when I write to my friends, by the regard I bear them. You, I can say from experience, do not want this latter stimulus, but in you it is not counteracted by any other affection, but rather assisted by the love, which is so natural, of exercising that faculty in which we excel. Your love of writing, and my aversion to it, may be accounted for by the particular circumstances of our reading. .You seldom read any language for pleasure except the English; and this you read with such rapidity that, in a very small portion of your leisure period of the day, the mind collects as much as it can conveniently bear off. You naturally fill up the remaining portion, or, at least, feel no aversion so to do, with writing.

' I, wishing to be perfectly familiar with French, and to increase my knowledge of Latin, seldom read a book out of one or the other of those languages; and, indeed, I find nothing on those subjects in which I most delight so well written as in Latin. But then to read these languages, particularly the latter, costs me much more time, and I find I can, without the consciousness of having read too much on account of the matter of fact contained in what I read, read four, five, or six hours in the day; but this I am sure I could not do with any profit in the English language. This consideration consoles me for the time I have spent in acquiring some knowledge of these languages, for perhaps in the very act of acquiring a language, if proper books be chosen, the mind acquires as much information as it can well digest, and after having attended three or four hours, rises, as it were, from a banquet, rather with a satisfied than with a satiated appetite. Thus then I conclude :—we both wish to get a knowledge of the various regions of literature ; you choose a vehicle which carries you with rapidity through that part you wish to contemplate, and leaves you much leisure at the end of every post—I choose one which enables me to view the country with more attention, and attains prospects

which yours can only show you at a distance. But
then mine requires my whole time.   As this is not your
case, is there anything unreasonable in a friend's request-
ing you to fill up a small part of this leisure in writing
oftener to him, than he, who has little or no leisure,
writes to you?   But you will justly remark this cannot
be the case of him who is writing, for the present letter,
beyond most others, seems the effort of a mind that
knows not how to employ itself.   I write corrected.
Well, then, my dear friend, a curious circumstance,
added to the pleasure I always feel in writing to you,
has perhaps now induced me to write.

'Last Thursday, at Bridgwater, a very particular
friend of mine, Robert Anstice, whom I have often
mentioned to you, desired me to call on him, as he much
wished to talk with me on a subject of consequence.   I
called.   He began by saying he hardly knew how to
begin the subject he wished to speak on, but proceeded
to say that a person whose sources of information were
the very best had told him that I was considered by
Government as the most dangerous person in the county
of Somerset, and, as it was well known that this part of
the country was disaffected, the whole mischief was, by
Government, attributed to me.   I laughed—thinking he
meant to *hum* me ; he assured me he was serious.   He
said it was not only on account of my unusual violence
in speaking, but also on account of what I had written.
I said I had never written a word that had been
published.—Never anything in letters? said he.
Certainly I had mentioned politicks in letters, but I
believe all the world might see what I had written.   He
said he did not know how it happened, but certainly such

was the idea of Government, and he thought it probable
that they had intercepted some of my letters and opened
them.   He concluded by exhorting me by the regard I
had for myself, for my family, and for my friends, to
be in future particularly cautious both in speaking and
writing.

'I was differently affected during this recital.   At first
it flattered the vanity of a *petit* tanner of Stowey to be
thought of consequence by the Government of an empire
which holds half the crowned heads of Europe as
pensioners.   Next, I felt the ridiculous falsity of the
story, and could not help laughing.   But I assure you,
my dear Purkis, the last sensation I experienced, and
which still remains with me, was a melancholy one.   It
was a recollection of what we were, and what we now
are.   It was a recollection of the boast an Englishman
was wont to make that he could think, speak, and write
whatever he thought proper, provided he violated no
law, nor injured any individual.   But now an absolute
controul exists, not indeed over the imperceptible
operations of the mind, for those no power of man can
controul; but, what is the same thing, over the effects of
those operations, and if among those effects that of
speaking is to be checked, the soul is as much enslaved
as the body in the cell of a Bastile.   The man who once
feels, nay, fancies, this, is a slave.   It shows as if the
suspicious secret Government of an Italian Republic had
replaced the open, candid Government of the English
laws.

'I can hardly imagine, according to his suspicions, that
anything so unaccountably ridiculous has happened as
that a letter of mine has been opened; if any has in

which politicks were found, it must have been one to you, for you are almost my only correspondent, and I am sure the only one to whom I talk of politicks.

'With respect to my future conduct: as I have done no more than every man ought to do, I shall continue to act as before. Indeed, I have been uncommonly cautious. I have made a rule never to begin the subject of politicks with any one. If the topick be started, I give my opinion if I choose it, and ever will, on every subject, as long as I live. I would fight to the last drop for this privilege, and if the globe were to fall under the dominion of tyranny, would cheerfully die [1] defending the last six feet of ground by two, which should grow green by my ashes, where this principle should be maintained. Is this sedition? I glory in it. I know what the English constitution is, and the measure of happiness it professes to give to each individual. Shall I be a passive instrument in lessening my own happiness, and a guilty one in abridging that of my posterity? A man's soul must be all *Earth* who would subscribe to such notions. With respect to encreasing the advantages of our political state *I am not prepared to say this is the proper time.* All I ask, at any time, is a reform in our House of Commons; and on this the People are Fools if they don't insist, immediately after the termination of the war, should we, as a nation, survive it. Our constitution, thus reformed, is the only

---

[1] The rather heroic phrases that Tom Poole was wont to use exposed him to a certain amount of ridicule. Once, when he wound up an excited period by declaring that 'for these opinions he would willingly go to the tower.'—'The tower, indeed!' said Mr. Anstice—'I should think Ilchester Gaol would do for you.'

one suitable to our state of society.   But enough.   God
bless you, my dear friend.   Remember me kindly to
Mrs. Purkis and to Mary.[1]—Yours most truly,

'T. P.

'*P.S.*—What think you of the death of Robespierre?'

The question in the postscript is one of the
links which enable us to fix to a day the exact
date of Coleridge's first visit to Stowey.   We find
in a letter, dated September 22, 1794, that Tom
Poole had at that time seen Coleridge, whom he calls

---

[1] Another curious instance of the intolerance of the time is to be
found in John Poole's journal, *March* 19, 1794.   He has been
reading 'part of *Scipio's Dream*' with T. Poole, who 'stay'd
supper, and during it he shew'd us a letter from Mr. Purkis, containing a copy of the Article Tanning, which he has written for a
new Encyclopædia.   He mentions in his letter his having receiv'd a
rather unpleasant answer from Sir Joseph Banks, to whom he had
written for leave to consult his library for books treating of the
article above mentioned.   Sir Joseph seemed to suspect Mr. P.'s
political principles, which arose probably from his having withdrawn
his name from an " Association " in his neighbourhood, in consequence
of their having adopted, as he thought, violent " resolutions."   Upon
Mr. P. making a disavowal of any principles inimical to the present
constitution, Sir Joseph sent a very candid and liberal answer, and
Mr. P. in consequence consulted his library, where he met with every
convenience and accommodation worthy of the President of the
Royal Academy' (surely a slip of the pen for Institution).   The
article on Tanning is again alluded to on *May* 10, 1794 :—' T. Poole
called before breakfast and bro't with him a paper, containing an
account of the Art of Tanning, etc., written by Mr. Purkis, and designed for the *Encyclopædia Britannica*.   T. P. has subjoined his
observations on it.   He read it to me, and desired my remarks on
the language, which I corrected in one or two instances.   He
breakfasted with us, and we afterwards read the first part of
Cicero's *De Amicitia*.'

'Coldridge,' and Southey, once only, and that for but a few hours. In this letter, which is addressed to a gentleman[1] who had asked for information respecting the Pantisocratic Scheme, he gives his first impressions of both ; and it will be observed that, even in that one interview, he has not failed to recognise the extraordinary abilities of Coleridge, as well as the entirely different calibre of his otherwise highly cultivated and very clever young companion. He writes as follows :—

'DEAR SIR—I received your obliging letter a day or two ago, and will with pleasure give you all the information I can respecting the emigration to America to which you allude. But first, perhaps, you would like to have some idea of the character of the projectors of the scheme. Out of eight whom they informed me were engaged, I have seen but two, and only spent part of one day with them; their names are Coldridge and Southey.

'Coldridge, whom I consider the Principal in the undertaking, and of whom I had heard much before I saw him, is about five and twenty, belongs to the University of Cambridge, possesses splendid abilities— he is, I understand, a shining scholar, gained the prize for the Greek verses the first or second year he entered the University, and is now engaged in publishing a selection of the best modern Latin poems with a poetical translation. He speaks with much elegance and energy, and with uncommon facility, but he, as it generally

[1] Mr. Haskins.

happens to men of his class, feels the justice of Providence in the want of those inferiour abilities which are necessary to the rational discharge of the common duties of life. His aberrations from prudence, to use his own expression, have been great; but he now promises to be as sober and rational as his most sober friends could wish. In religion he is a Unitarian, if not a Deist; in politicks a Democrat, to the utmost extent of the word.

'Southey, who was with him, is of the University of Oxford, a younger man, without the splendid abilities of Coldridge, though possessing much information, particularly metaphysical, and is more violent in his principles than even Coldridge himself. In Religion, shocking to say in a mere Boy as he is, I fear he wavers between Deism and Atheism.

'Thus much for the characters of two of the Emigrators. Their plan is as follows :—

'Twelve gentlemen of good education and liberal principles are to embark with twelve ladies in April next. Previous to their leaving this country they are to have as much intercourse as possible, in order to ascertain each other's dispositions, and firmly to settle every regulation for the government of their future conduct. Their opinion was that they should fix themselves at—I do not recollect the place, but somewhere in a delightful part of the new back settlements; that each man should labour two or three hours in a day, the produce of which labour would, they imagine, be more than sufficient to support the colony. As Adam Smith observes that there is not above one productive man in twenty, they argue that if each laboured the twentieth part of time, it would produce enough to satisfy their wants. The produce of their industry is to be laid up in common for the use of all; and a good library of books is to be collected, and their leisure hours to be spent in study, liberal discussions, and the education of their children. A system for the education of their children is laid down, for which, if this plan at all suits you, I must refer you to the authors of it. The regulations relating to the females strike them as the most difficult; whether the marriage contract shall be dissolved if agreeable to one or both parties, and many other circumstances, are not yet determined. The employments of the women are to be the care of infant children, and other occupations suited to their strength; at the same time the greatest attention is to be paid to the cultivation of their minds. Every one is to enjoy his own religious and political opinions, provided they do not encroach on the rules previously made, which rules, it is unnecessary to add, must in some measure be regulated by the laws of the state which includes the district in which they settle. They calculate that each gentleman providing £125 will be sufficient to carry the scheme into execution. Finally, every individual is at liberty, whenever he pleases, to withdraw from the society.

'These are the outlines of their plan, and such are their ideas. Could they realise them they would, indeed, realise the age of reason; but, however perfectible human nature may be, I fear it is not yet perfect enough to exist long under the regulations of such a system, particularly when the Executors of the plan are taken from a society in a high degree civilised and corrupted. America is certainly a desirable country, so desirable in my eye that, were it not for some insuperable reasons, I would certainly settle there. At some future period I perhaps may. But I think a man would do well first to see the country and his future hopes, before he removes his connections or any large portion of his property there. I could live, I think, in America, much to my satisfaction and credit, without joining in such a scheme as I have been describing, though I should like well to accompany them, and see what progress they make. . . . I shall be happy to hear from you soon, and to learn your opinion of this scheme. Should you wish for further information, I will get you Coldridge's address, and pave the way for your writing to him. . . .'[1]

Only a month or two before this letter was written Coleridge had come to Bristol for the first time to join Southey, Lovell, Burnett, and the other young enthusiasts who were bent upon devoting themselves to the carrying out of the dazzling, but impracticable scheme to which Coleridge had given the name of Pantisocracy or Asphetism. Nothing is easier now, than to see that the entire plan was the baseless fabric of a vision ; but it was different then, to those eager young hearts spell-bound by Coleridge's eloquence, and to Coleridge himself, fairly intoxicated with hope, and full of faith in the impossible. Most likely it was as the apostles of Pantisocracy, and

---

[1] It may be noted that this is the most detailed account we have of the Pantisocratic Scheme.

in search of recruits and converts, that he and
Southey first made their appearance in Stowey,
and spent that half day with Tom Poole, which
we clearly understand from the foregoing letter to
have been the *only* occasion upon which Tom Poole
had seen either Coleridge or Southey *before* September 23, 1794.   But there is a story connected
with their names, and with this period, that carries
us much closer to the actual day, which we perceive
must have been coincident with the very time
when the news of the death of Robespierre had
but just reached Stowey, and when, therefore,
every one was talking about it.   John Poole, the
story begins, had brought the tidings of the death
of Robespierre home with him from Oxford ; but
this is manifestly impossible, as we find by his
journal that he arrived at Marshmill from Oxford
on July 18, and Robespierre did not die till
July 28.   However, it is, of course, easily to be
supposed that he *may* have brought the intelligence
home from Bridgwater or Taunton.   On his way,
according to one tradition, he stopped at his uncle's
house in Nether Stowey to tell his news ; according
to another it was at Marshmill itself that he found
his Cousin Tom, in company with two young men,
introduced to him by the names of Coleridge and
Southey, who not only did not show the feelings
any right-thinking people might have been expected

to manifest at such a piece of intelligence, but one of them—Southey—actually laid his head down upon his arms and exclaimed, 'I had rather have heard of the death of my own father.'

So runs the tale as it has been told to me, more often, I think, than any other story that I have ever heard of Coleridge's life at Stowey; indeed my own father and other members of the family of the same standing, have repeatedly assured me that *they have themselves heard it related by Mr. John Poole himself.* And yet all who remember how little sympathy either Coleridge or Southey had with the Jacobins, how deeply they felt the 'murder of Brissot,'[1] how simply the dramatic fragment on the death of Robespierre relates, but does not lament, his overthrow, must feel that there is something here that requires explanation. Of John Poole's general character some idea will have been formed from the account given in the beginning of this chapter. It may be added that he was a person of the most punctilious veracity, liable, no doubt, to be warped by prejudice, but habitually free from exaggeration, and quite incapable of inventing a sensational story either for fun, or from any other motive. Therefore, making whatever allowance we may for the effect of time in altering the features, and confusing the details,

[1] Southey's *Letters.* See also the *Watchman* on Brissot, p. 308.

of whatever may have been the original history,
we cannot escape the conclusion that we have here
the genuine impression of some real incident that
actually did happen during that short first visit of
Coleridge and Southey to Stowey ; and, if so, it is
also clear that that visit must have taken place at
some time in the month of August.

So far I had arrived by independent reasoning
when John Poole's journals for the year 1793-
1798 came into my hands, and the interest with
which I opened them, and found the year 1794,
may easily be imagined. My hopes that there
would be something that would throw light upon
the matter amongst the entries for the month of
August were not disappointed. In that particular
month it so happened that John Poole was keeping
his journal in Latin, a practice which certainly had
the advantage of preventing most people from
reading his diary, if he chanced to leave it lying
about, but which otherwise, besides being trouble-
some to posterity (but, happily, he did not think
of posterity, or he might have burnt his journal),
has a certain tendency to the grotesque, so oddly
do the names and arrangements of modern English
life figure in this classical disguise. Turning
slowly over the pages, and somewhat laboriously
spelling through the Latin, very illegible sometimes,
in the faint, brown ink, and with the quaint, un-

expected contractions, we presently come to the very thing we are looking for, which I give here, as follows :—

'18vo. Surgo horâ 2^{dâ}. Post jentaculum ad domum D^{ni} Lewis eo ; et *Vitam Johnsonianam Boswelli* ab eo mutuam accipio. Horâ fere 7^{mâ} Thos. Poole, et frater Richardus, Henricus Poole, et duo juvenes ei familiares huc veniunt. Duo isti ignoti, intelligo, è Cantabrigiâ exierant ; et totam fere Walliam peragraverant. Unus Oxoniensis Alumnus ; alter Cantabrigiensis. Uterque verò rabie Democratica, quoad Politiam ; et Infidelis quoad Religionem spectat, turpiter fervet. Ego maxime indignor. Tandem verò, horâ fere 8^{vâ}, omnes discedunt. Post prandium ego me ad *Vitam Johnsonianam* confero. Horâ ferme 1^{mâ} D^{ns} Reekes Stoweiâ venit ; multum indignatur propter malitiam odiosam et detestandam juvenum istorum, quibus, apud Avunculi mei Thomae occurrerat. Illi plus videntur cogitationes suas, quam apud nos, illic indicâsse. Sed de talibus satis. . . .'

Which may be thus translated :—

'Rise about eight. After breakfast go to Mr. Lewis's and get the loan of Boswell's *Life of Johnson* from him. About one o'clock, Thomas Poole and his brother Richard, Henry Poole, and two young men, friends of his, come in. These two strangers, I understand, had left Cambridge, and had walked nearly all through Wales. One is an undergraduate of Oxford, the other of Cambridge. Each of them was shamefully hot with Democratic rage as regards politics, and both Infidel as to religion. I was extremely indignant. At last, however, about two

o'clock, they all go away.   After dinner I betake myself
to the *Life of Johnson.*   About seven o'clock Mr. Reekes
comes from Stowey ; he is very indignant over the odious
and detestable ill-feeling of those two young men, whom
he had met at my Uncle Thomas's.   They seem to have
shown their sentiments more plainly there than with us.
But enough of such matters. . . .'

'*Ego maxime indignor !*'   Here, no doubt, we
have the germ of the whole history, though John
Poole unluckily omits to record the particular
nature of the utterances which so strongly moved
him to wrath.   '*Sed de talibus satis,*' he contemptuously breaks off, without the faintest presentiment
of the very different point of view from which
another generation would regard the incident.
But putting this and that together, it is easy to
understand that the death of Robespierre was
certain to be mentioned as an awful event and
the leading topic of the day, and that the talk of
isti duo ignoti was wild enough to be the origin of
the most extravagant rumours, as it became em-
bedded in fragments in the gossip of a scandalised
neighbourhood ; where it was soon 'well known' that
one of Tom Poole's literary friends [1]—was it the
young man Coldridge, or the young man Southey ?
they were not quite sure ; but it was certainly one of

[1] Related to me by Miss Ward in perfect good faith.   She herself
had always heard it, and it had never occurred to her to entertain
any doubts as to the correctness of the tradition.

them—had positively said that *Robespierre was a ministering angel of mercy, sent to slay thousands that he might save millions.* Let us be accurate. It was *not* positively certain whether the words were hundreds and thousands, or thousands and millions ; but that Robespierre had been called a 'ministering angel of mercy' everybody knew for a fact.

This is quite simple ; but what is really perplexing is to imagine how Coleridge, or even Southey, who, according to Tom Poole, was, on that occasion, 'the most extreme' of the two, could have said anything so apparently opposite to their own convictions. I believe the solution is to be found in the mischievous enjoyment that they both experienced in the state of superlative indignation into which they provoked John Poole—especially Southey. Let us remember that he was an Oxford undergraduate, and a very insubordinate one, who had already amused himself by making remarks on the 'waste of wigs and want of wits' to be observed amongst the university authorities ; the very sight of John Poole, serious and scholarly, with powdered locks, and precise attire, and a certain air of expecting every one to mean what he says, and to be reasonable, may have been quite enough to make him set himself, with that peculiar kind of wrongheadedness which is a not uncommon

characteristic of very early manhood, to parade
outrageous opinions, and to say whatever came
into his head as most likely to shock a very proper
young Don's sense of fitness.[1]

Usually large allowances are made for this sort
of nonsense ; but the temper of the times was
grave, the horror which the deeds of the Jacobins
had excited was too recent and too genuine to be
trifled with ; and nobody except Tom Poole made
any allowance at all.   Shocking people is, as
every one knows, an amusement which gathers zest
as it succeeds, and we are not surprised to learn
that the evening visitors at Marshmill, who had
encountered those strangers later in the day,
reported conversation even more detestable than
that which had horrified John Poole.   It really
seems as if they had been trying their very best
to scandalise the entire neighbourhood.

And if so, they certainly succeeded ; and the
incident was not without its consequences.   It
determined the direction of popular opinion, and
certainly had its share, perhaps no very small one,
in producing that attitude of incurable suspicion
and mistrust which was adopted towards Coleridge
and Wordsworth when, a little later, they attempted

---

[1] Compare S. T. C.'s letter to Sir George and Lady Beaumont
(*Coleorton Memorials*, i. 12) on the subject of Emmett's death, and
of the extravagance of his own language and opinions when he, too,
was but twenty-four.   The passage is too long to quote.

to make their home under the shadow of the Quantocks. For the popular mind cannot take the trouble to be pedantically accurate. What did the name matter? Wordsworth, too, was certainly 'one of Tom Poole's literary friends.'

CHAPTER VII

'. . . Turning
The servile dust of opportunity
To gold. . . .'

WORDSWORTH.

DURING the whole of the autumn of 1794 Tom
Poole was very much out of health—a fact never
mentioned in his own letters, but clearly traceable
by frequent references in his Cousin John's diary.
It seems to have been a long, lingering, nervous
illness, which sometimes confined him to his room
for days at a time. In October he went to his
brother's at Sherborne for change of air, and, calling at Marshmill on his return, he 'said he was
better ;' but a very few days later, on November
4, he is 'very ill' again, and, on November
27, we find John Poole begging him to seek
further advice : 'I persuaded him to go and consult Dr. Dunning on his long illness, which I
believe he did.'

But, notwithstanding this illness, Tom Poole

seems to have kept up all his usual activities; except that, after the letter to Mr. Haskins on September 23, there is no other letter entered in his Copying-book till the following January. On October 9, when John Poole came to Nether Stowey to read *Virgil* with him, he showed him the 'new anti-friction steam rollers' invented by his American friend, Mr. Garnett, which he had introduced into his father's yard; and in January 1795 we find him making his Cousin Charlotte even more angry than usual by what John Poole calls '*noves ejus sententias.*'

'Tom Poole would force politicks into notice,' she complains, 'and was, in consequence, very disagreeable. Since he has adopted these sentiments his mind seems to be enveloped in gloom, and though he preaches liberty, his conduct often contradicts his precepts.'

It is curious to observe that even here, as in the writings of Burke and of other contemporaries, the word *sentiments* is almost always employed where, in the present day, we should say *views* or *opinions*. This is a subtle instance of the far-reaching influence of the writings of that school of French philosophers of whom Rousseau is the chief example, in producing a habit of mind in which feeling—the subjective effect upon the individual—is the ultimate test of every principle, whether political, moral, or religious.

It may be that there was a tinge of personal feeling in the 'gloom' that Charlotte Poole noticed in her cousin, at a time when the visits of a college friend of John Poole's and his courtship of Penelope,[1] must have been gradually making the knowledge that she would never return the affection with which he himself regarded her, more and more unmistakable ; but it is much more certain that the disappointment of his enthusiastic hopes, by the dark and terrible turn that events had taken in France, and, in general, the lowering aspect of the political horizon, weighed heavily upon his spirits, and that a strain of despondency is traceable in almost every letter he wrote to any intimate friend.   A painful impatience of his surroundings, a subdued but continual longing to get away, to put himself, by some means or other, into a new framework, seems to have been the almost habitual state of his mind at this particular period, and contrasts remarkably with the steady contentment with his own place in life, the singular absence of any craving after personal distinction, and the strong determination to make the best of his actual position and opportunities, which were his most noticeable characteristics in after years.   But these were dreary days.   His

---

[1] They became engaged for a short time, but the engagement was broken off.

home life was marred by the increasing irritability
of his father's temper, and by the self-reproach he
experienced when he allowed himself to be drawn
into contentions with him ; and though he was
more constantly than ever at Marshmill, the atmosphere of contradiction and disapproval that he
found there, can scarcely have had a soothing
effect on his ruffled spirits.[1] The one resource
and refuge that never disappointed him was his
love of books ; even when he was really ill he
tried to go on [2] with his Latin reading, and early
in 1795 he was able to show his Cousin John his
'new book-room,' where he was already pleasing
himself with the arrangement of the small beginnings of that fine collection of books which, twelve
years later, was noticed with so much admiration
by Mr. De Quincey. The day was Shrove Tuesday,
and, as the two cousins went out for a turn, it is

[1] In connection with the disapproval Tom Poole excited when he
cut his hair short and ceased to wear powder, it is amusing to meet
with an entry in Charlotte Poole's journal, March 3, 1795, alluding
to the operation of that Hair Powder Tax, which was the subject of
one of S. T. Coleridge's early lectures, and which was shortly to
shake the powder out of the hair of even the firmest supporters of
'the present establishment in church and state.' 'We walked to
Stowey,' she says, 'and found all the girls had taken the powder
out of their hair, to see if they could avoid the tax without any diminution of their beauty ; but they were so little pleased with themselves
they resolved to continue to wear it.'

[2] John Poole's journal : 'September 10. Again to see T. P. Not
much better, but read a little *Cicero* together. September 13. T.
P. recovering, read *De Senectute.*'

characteristic of the times that they 'happened to meet some men carrying a hen up the street with the intention of *squalling*[1] at her.' It was also characteristic of Tom Poole that he immediately put a stop to the brutal amusement ' by purchasing the hen.' Then returning to the house, they ' read *Cicero* together.' His love for French literature, already mentioned in his letter to Purkis, may be further illustrated by the following extract, which is part of a letter addressed to a neighbouring clergyman, together with a parcel of ' Book Society books.'

' As for Brissot's book, I have read it in French; the translation has as much of the spirit and beauty of the original as a translation can possess, and as you, with Mrs. Clark, are fond of French literature, you will, I trust, be pleased with it, not only on account of its being French, but more particularly as every page is the picture of a benevolent heart. If you think him on some occasions too enthusiastick in the cause of liberty, you must recollect what he suffered under despotism. Brissot was, by the caprice of a French minister, doomed to languish some years in the cells of the Bastile. 'Twas there his indignant soul, brooding over its sufferings, conceived and enlarged those ideas which you will see depicted in his book, and which were realised by his

---

[1] *Squalling* or *Squailing*. Usually the ' fat hen ' was ' thrashed,' and it was the wretched cock that was set up as a mark for throwing sticks at on Shrove Tuesday. This cruel custom is very ancient. See Brande's *Popular Antiquities.*

conduct during his subsequent life. Thus it is that despotism makes patriots, and patriots destroy despotism. Happy had it been for France had all her leaders been like Brissot.[1] . . .'

Having experienced the comfort and advantage of studying Latin under a good tutor, Tom Poole naturally turned his mind to the obtaining of similar assistance in French. Already, in September 1794, he had by some means made the acquaintance of a French ecclesiastic, *e patria sua pulsis*, whom John found sitting with him one day when he walked into Stowey *post prandium*—and who gave them a short account of the dangers that had attended his escape. He was a priest from Brittany, and seems to have found a refuge at a religious house belonging to his own communion, which then, as now, existed at Cannington, a

[1] Brissot's temperament was more congenial and, therefore, more comprehensible, to English people than that of other French patriots. Clarkson visiting Paris found him 'a man of plain and modest appearance. His habits, contrary to those of his countrymen in general, were domestic. In his own family he set an amiable example as a husband and father ; on all occasions he was a faithful friend. He was particularly watchful over his private conduct. From the simplicity of his appearance and the severity of his morals he was called the Quaker in all the circles I frequented. He was a man of deep feeling. He was charitable to the poor as far as a slender income permitted, but his benevolence went beyond the usual bounds. He was no patriot in the ordinary acceptance of the word, for he took the habitable world as his country, and wished to consider every foreigner as his brother.'—*Life of Clarkson*, I. chap. ii.

village about four miles from Bridgwater, where the old English Roman Catholic family of Clifford has property, and although his name is not mentioned, I think he must be identical with the Mr. Pains with whom we shall find Tom Poole in correspondence early in the following year. But there was also a M. Perceval, another French refugee, whom he came across at Sherborne, and whom he invited to spend the Christmas vacation with him, when his 'foreign manners, so different from ours,' were a source of some amusement to the Marshmill sisters, of whom Charlotte took lessons from him. The two following letters are addressed to Mr. Pains :—

'My dear Sir,[1]—Knowing that every moment of your time, at least during the hours when I am in Bridgwater, is particularly engaged, I have refrained from calling on you. When we last saw each other you kindly offered to correct any little exercise, which, from time to time, I may send you. You see I have here taken you at your word, and send you the beginning of a translation which I have attempted of Cicero's *Dream of Scipio*. You will perhaps be surprised at the choice I have made, but I was led to it both for profit and pleasure ; profit, because I wished to keep and to perfect the knowledge which I have of Latin, even while learning French ; pleasure, because there is no little piece to be found, the contemplation of which, and the dwelling upon every period and

[1] T. Poole to Mr. Pains, February 1795.

every word of which, could give me more sincere
delight. . . . Many objections you may justly make to
my translating Latin into French. You will say that by
writing French through the Latin idiom, which, perhaps,
is nearer the French than the English, I shall be at a loss
to express my ideas—conceived, of course, in English—in
the French language. This would be a consideration for
him who is familiarly acquainted with the Latin tongue,
but for myself, I believe the sense of most passages is
abstracted into English in my mind before I attempt
rendering it in French. You will say it may be Latinised
English. Probably so. These objections I state for your
advice, by which I shall be governed. If you approve
the plan I have attempted, I will go through with the
little piece in hand, and afterwards any others which you
may recommend. I have left a margin for corrections
and remarks. If you see I have mistaken the sense of
my author, correct it; for I have had few opportunities
of assistance in difficulties, in any literary pursuit. Thus
you see I trespass on your goodness and expose my
inability. But—

"Cur nescire *pudens pravè* quam discere malo?"

When shall I see you at Stowey? I will send a horse
when you can spare a day. . . .'

On March 17, 1795, Tom Poole writes again
to Mr. Pains to thank him for his corrections, and
to send him 'another exercise.' The letter concludes as follows :—

'I hope you received S. Pierre. I am now reading
the fourth volume. As a moralist he is divine, but as a

natural philosopher certainly fanciful, though doubtless he elicits bright sparks from whatever he touches—sparks from which men of more patient heads and cooler hearts may perhaps fan a flame which may enlighten the world. . . .'

In after years it seemed wonderful to a younger generation that not only Tom Poole, but even the less impressionable household at Marshmill, and more particularly the cool-headed and rather didactic John Poole himself, so greatly admired S. Pierre, as they certainly did. How could they tolerate such sickly sentimentality? it was asked. But John Poole was, as we know, an ardent botanist, and taking down a volume of S. Pierre, he showed the intolerant niece who raised the objection so beautiful, and at the same time so accurate a description of a strawberry plant, that she was instantly touched with a new comprehension of the charm of a writer once so popular and now so little appreciated.

Monsieur Pains was the son of a Norman farmer. He had a friend and fellow-student, the son of another farmer, in the same part of Normandy, in a certain Abbé Barbey, who, having escaped the September Massacres, had taken refuge in England. Perhaps it was Tom Poole's persistent desire to obtain instruction in French, which inspired Monsieur Pains with the idea that his friend might find both a resting-place and a means of livelihood, at the remote little town of Stowey. Accordingly, some-what later in the year, the Abbé Barbey arrived, and soon became quite a favourite in the neigh-bourhood, teaching French in all the principal families, and usually dining and spending the evening at the house where he gave his lesson. Many old prejudices crumbled away in the general pity for the victims of the Reign of Terror, and I have been told that English Roman Catholics trace a distinct mitigation of the feeling of hostile intolerance with which their clergy had so long been regarded, to the esteem and sympathy felt for so many of the French priests who sought a shelter in England in that day of difficulty and distress. 'Creed and test vanished before the unreserved embrace, of Catholic humanity,' wrote Wordsworth, noting that very circum-stance.

But in speaking of the Abbé Barbey I have anticipated a little ; for it was not till the autumn of 1795 that he came to settle in Stowey, and I must go back to speak of the death of the elder Thomas Poole, which occurred in the July of this same year. His son, whose tenderness in times of sickness and sorrow I have already noticed, himself attended upon his sick-bed, and held him in his arms when he breathed his last.

Yet Charlotte Poole, visiting the bereaved household on July 20, and finding them 'calm and tranquil,' observes that

'Tom seemed the most gloomy, but the recollection of his father is, I doubt not, embittered by the thoughts of their former petty dissensions, though the blame belonged as much to my uncle as to him.'

Tom himself, writing some years later to Mr. Garnett, speaks of the abiding depression into which he was apt to be plunged by any great strain upon his emotions—a dull, brooding condition very difficult to shake off. 'Such scenes,' he wrote, 'are equal to seven years' ordinary experience and evaporation of youthful thoughtlessness.' A letter written to the same friend [1] very shortly after his father's death, seems to show that the idea of emigration to America had really at one time seriously occupied his mind :—

'MY DEAR SIR—You ask me whether my ideas of America are the same as when we parted. My ideas are the same; but my situation is strangely altered. I have cause to regret not having seen America during my father's life. . . . I hardly think I can now go on a *visit of observation.* The business left me by my father would be destroyed by my absence; but a stronger reason than this is the objection my dear mother would make, whose state of health is such that she cannot, I fear, live long. I could not happily leave her, and

[1] T. Poole to Mr. Garnett, July 24, 1795.

wherefore should I make two miserable? However, circumstances and my views of things may change much by the ensuing spring. I acknowledge that I now see everything through a gloomy medium. I should be most happy if, when you were at Bristol, you would come down for a few days and see how I am situated, and weigh well with me the chance of happiness in my present situation against the enjoyment of that which I have reason to expect in America.

'When I say this I do not mean to damp the ardour even of my own mind on the subject. Weigh the advantages of competence, consistent with moderate desires: of a country delightful by nature; of being loved by my relations, and I hope not disesteemed by my neighbours; of a business which is in itself particularly independent, producing exercise enough for health, and leisure enough for other pursuits. Weigh these things against those: against political independence, including the full enjoyment of the rights of man; the absence of a proud aristocracy, creating and patronising inhuman and unjust wars; and of a load of taxes; and of the risque of those political convulsions which seem just at our doors.[1] . . . The side the balance will preponderate in our minds is not difficult to determine.

'But here I must be fixed for the present, and while I am here I shall endeavour to improve my business, and make my situation as pleasant as I can. This will be profitable in any event. In the line of business I think I shall have one of your bark-mills, which on many accounts are admirable, though I have my doubts

---

[1] T. Poole has drawn his pen through this part of the letter, which probably never went beyond his Copying-book.

whether the bark is sufficiently lacerated to give out its properties.   I am at present making some experiments to ascertain this point, which you will allow is very important.   A few weeks since I saw and admired Coxe's mill, and brought home some bark ground by it. . . .'

The letter concludes with a detailed recommendation of a Stowey lad of fifteen, intelligent and well behaved, and possessing a good knowledge of arithmetic, who is 'badly off at home, and longs to meet with some situation where he may get his bread.'   It will give Tom Poole 'great pleasure,' if Mr. Garnett can find an opening for him.   Below the signature comes a short postscript :—

'If I go, I must get the best observations I can from some one in whom I can confide—then close my affairs in this country and finally depart.'

But in that very year, 1795, Tom Poole, disappointed and unexpectant, fretted by the contrarieties and limitations of his life, yet loyally convinced that the bonds that held him to his post were ties of love and duty which he would never have the heart to disregard, was in the very act of turning the leaf of a new chapter in life—a chapter in which the commonplace, comfortable brown house, with the tanyard at the back, and the long garden, from which there was indeed a view of the hills, but which otherwise had manifestly the air of a garden devoted to use rather than to enjoyment, was to become for a short but brilliant period a very centre and focus of the best thought, the truest poetry, the strongest intellectual activity of his time.   It is remarkable, almost startling, to observe how exactly Tom Poole had prepared himself for a chance in life, which would have been no chance at all, and indeed must have slipped by absolutely without recognition, if he had not been so strangely and admirably ready to know what to do with it, but which, being ready both in mind and heart, he enthusiastically embraced, to the wide enlargement of his horizon, and the far-increased happiness and usefulness of his life.

The first letter of his to S. T. Coleridge that has been preserved is dated October 10, 1795, and is a warm outpouring of congratulations on his marriage.   It is chiefly remarkable for the ardent expression of faith in Coleridge's powers which it contains :—

'I do congratulate you—most heartily I do.   I wish I knew Mrs. Coleridge—remember me most kindly to her.   May you both long, long be happy, and may the lowering morning of your days precede a meridian serenely bright and cloudless, leading in due time, naturally, to the soft close of a tranquil evening.   I cannot tell you, my dear friend, for such I am sure I

may call you, how much I am interested in everything
which concerns you.   The world is all before you ; your
road seems yet to choose.   Providence has been pleased,
if I may so express myself, to drop you on this globe as
a meteor from the clouds, the track of which is undetermined.   But you have now, by marrying, in some
sense fixed yourself.   You have created a rallying point.
It is the threshold of your life.   It is the epocha from
which you must date every subsequent action.   You
now begin to live.   Let us then consider your future
prospects :—

'You have given up the Magazine.   This I am not
sorry for.   I never liked the plan ; you were not born
to be a compiler.   Your friends augur higher things, and
don't, don't disappoint us.   The Cambridge plan does not
strike me ; it *must* have many inconveniences.   As for
the Imitations, as you have so long neglected them, you
should not now regard them ; they never could be very
popular.   They may, it is true, give you the reputation
of learning, but simply learned men are not very scarce
—*original* works of genius are your forte.   Think not I
wish to damp for a moment your extending your literary
knowledge, or your improving yourself by the most pro-
found speculations.   No—what I mean is, that you
should set yourself about some work of consequence,
which may give you a reputation, whether it be in poetry
or prose ; in treating it, delight and improve us all, and
remove the prejudices by which we are poisoned, not by
an electric spark to which nine out of ten will fear to
have recourse, but by those fascinating strains which
suspend, and finally destroy, the venom of the serpent's
bite.   You can shock—you can charm—but the wise

physician and the friend of human nature will prefer that prescription which all his patients will swallow. You see that I treat you as a friend in speaking freely. If too freely, forgive me. 'Tis the head, not the heart, which errs. . . .'

The letter concludes with an outburst of sentiment, a kind of thing which we nowadays all live far too habitually under the fear of being absurd ever to indulge in for one moment. And then there is a postscript that 'My dear mother begs to say she wishes you all the good that man can know.'

It is plain that the acquaintanceship has made rapid progress since that letter to Mr. Haskins written a little more than a year earlier. Probably Tom Poole had often journeyed to Bristol to hear Coleridge lecture, perhaps to listen to the course of which I find a prospectus, with some nonsense verses of S. T. C.'s written on the back, laid away among his papers. It may even be that he was the friend at whose particular request the lecture on the Slave Trade was delivered.[1] At any rate it is certain that Coleridge had already begun to be a visitor at Stowey, and had been taken, as Tom Poole always loved to take his friends, to Marshmill. We cannot trace that he was recognised as one of the two young strangers of the

---

[1] The only contribution of T. Poole's that appears to have been actually published in the *Watchman* is on this subject.

year before, but we find him noted down by
Cousin Charlotte, in her keen, epigrammatic way,
on September 19, 1795.

'Tom Poole,' she writes, 'has a friend with him of
the name of Coldridge : a young man of brilliant understanding, great eloquence, desperate fortune, democratick
principles, and entirely led away by the feelings of the
moment.'

A very different record of the same visit remains
in a rude and halting copy of verses, placed in my
hands by the kindness of Mr. Ernest H. Coleridge,
in which Tom Poole struggles to pour forth his
enthusiastic delight in the recognition of his
friend's genius. The paper, folded into a small
compass, perhaps to suit the size of a pocket-book,
is worn and tattered and soiled. The verses are
quite unpolished ; evidently Coleridge laid hands
upon them and carried them off just as they were,
with all the corrections and erasures, and the
verse about 'Sarah' added as a kind of footnote
to the rest ; but such as they are, I give them, for
however conventional the phrasing, they are no
mere abstract burst of imperfectly expressed admiration ; *they describe Coleridge*—and Coleridge
as he was in the first early freshness of the dawn
of his marvellous powers :—

1

‘ Hail to thee, Coldridge, youth of various powers !
    I love to hear thy soul pour forth the line,
To hear it sing of love and liberty
    As if fresh breathing from the hand divine.

2

‘ As if on earth it never yet had dwelt,
    As if from heaven it now had wing’d its way;
And brought us tidings how, in argent fields,
    In love and liberty blest spirits stray.

3

‘ I love to mark that soul-pervaded clay,
    To see the passions in thine eyeballs roll—
Their quick succession on thy weighty brow—
    Thy trembling lips express their very soul.

4

‘ I love to view the abstracted gaze which speaks
    Thy soul to heavenwards towering—then I say,
He’s gone—for us to cull celestial sweets
    Amid the flowerets of the milky way.

5

‘ And now at home, within its mortal cage,
    I see thy spirit pent—ah me !—and mourn
The sorrow sad, that weighs it down to earth,
    As if the Cherub Hope would ne’er return.

6

'And then I mark the starting tear that steals
    Adown thy cheek, when of a friend thou speak'st,
Who erst, as thou dost say, was wondrous kind,
    But now, unkind, forgets—I feel and weep.

7

'I hear thee speak indignant of the world,
    Th' unfeeling world crowded with folly's train;
I hear thy fervent eloquence dispel
    The murky mists of error's mazy reign.*

8

'And thou, Religion, white-robed Maid of Peace,
    Who smil'st to hear him raise his voice on high
To fix thy image on the Patriot's breast—
    Remove the bitter tear, the fearful sigh.

                            'T. P.

'*September* 12, 1795.'

---

* 'Anon thy Sarah's image cheers thy soul,
    When sickening at the world, thy spirits faint;
Soft balm it brings—thou hail'st the lovely maid,
    Paint'st her dear form as Love alone can paint.'

CHAPTER VIII

' Friendship is a sheltering tree.'
COLERIDGE, *Youth and Age.*

THE time when Charlotte Poole made the entry
in her diary was exactly a fortnight before Coleridge's marriage ; and probably no one ever took
that important step in life in more blissful ignorance of the responsibilities that he was assuming,
or with less practical idea of the importance of
a regular income, or of the way in which, if he set
himself to keep a family upon literature, he would
have to clip the muse's wings and teach her to
walk in a daily groove.

What is more surprising is that none of his
friends, neither Cottle nor Thomas Poole, nor, for
anything that can be discovered, any one else, seems
to have even thought of putting in a word of
warning or of counselling delay. I do not know
whether any belief is to be given to a story told
me by a relation of mine, who received it from

some of the Marshmill family, that the marriage
was believed to have been rather hurried on, in
consequence of some hostile breath of rumour that
had arisen in connection with the Misses Fricker,
caused partly by the unconventional manner in
which they were constantly to be seen walking
about Bristol with two such remarkable and well-
known young men as Coleridge and Southey, and
partly from the impression that Pantisocracy
meant a system of things which dispensed with
the marriage-tie.   When this disagreeable gossip
came round to the ears of those most nearly con-
cerned, the result was a generous impatience for
immediate marriage on the part of the two poets.
Southey, as we know, left his wife at the church
door, making, however, careful provision that she
should live with the Cottles, and did not claim
her companionship till he was able to see his way
to something like a regular income ; Coleridge,
more impetuous, and much less worldly wise, took
his bride home to the cottage at Clevedon, and to
the enjoyment of a honeymoon that seems to
have been like a brief dream of perfect happiness
in the midst of the shifting clouds of a troubled
and uncertain life.

But the glory faded.   A remote village such
as Clevedon then was, proved to be too inac-
cessible a residence for a young man ' of desperate

fortune,' compelled to be on the look-out for a career. The distance from Cottle the publisher, from his friends, and from the Bristol library, seemed daily more inconvenient ; and he returned to Bristol, to live, most uncomfortably, in the very centre of a large town, at the house of his wife's mother on Redcliff Hill. And here, of course, it is needful to remember how exceptionally gifted a man Coleridge was, and to picture to ourselves the position of such a nature in the midst of the ordinary surroundings of a family of the narrowest possible means, belonging to the lower middle class. Probably few people ever make *enough* allowance for the continual jar of the commonplace against the consciousness of those, whose habitual region of thought is, as it were, the mountain air of the soul. It is true they would say that they are—and they are—ready to be cheerfully content with the utmost simplicity of life ; but this means, in their imaginations, a large and tranquil simplicity, in which the natural antithesis to few wants is few cares. A life of sordid limitations, thronged with interruptions, and crowded with little anxieties, is almost death to them ; it paralyses their faculties, and torments them with a perpetual difficulty in breathing freely.

Coleridge drooped and pined on Redcliff Hill,

and his friends saw that it was so ; but his uneasiness was soon relieved by a welcome invitation
from Tom Poole, asking him to bring his wife
and come and spend some time at Stowey.   The
visit left a deep impression upon Coleridge's mind
—an impression as of a haven of rest and sympathy to which he could not but long to return.
He studied gardening, with a plan working in his
mind of which we shall hear more hereafter, wrote
Reviews, and 'gave every moment he could
spare' to the congenial task of revising and preparing for the press his *Religious Musings*, which
he was 'extremely anxious to have as perfect as
possible.'

Early in 1796 he returned to Bristol, but
this time to the definite work of superintend-
ing the issue from the press of his first volume
of poems ; whilst one of the many projects
that followed each other in rapid succession
through his mind took form and reality in the
publication of the *Watchman*, of which the first
number appeared on March 1, 1796.   It was in
February 1796, and therefore very shortly after
the visit of Mr. and Mrs. Coleridge to Stowey,
that Tom Poole addressed the following curious
letter to a lady whom he must have met whilst
staying with his brother at Sherborne.   She and
her sisters were the mistresses of a very good

school for girls in that town, and were all of them highly esteemed by Tom Poole ; whilst with ' the admirable Miss Henrietta,' as he sometimes calls her, he seems to have been on terms of friendship, which, however stiff and formal in the estimation of the present day, might reasonably have been expected to ripen into a warmer feeling, but apparently never did so. John Poole, who visited Sherborne in 1794, describes Henrietta Warwick as ' remarkably clever,' but ' not at all hand-some,' and looking much older than her real age, which was then scarcely twenty. He found her, however, a very agreeable companion, and ' had no objection to make the best use of the short time he was in Sherborne to converse with the most sensible woman there. . . . She seemed,' he says, ' to have a masculine understanding, with-out any diminution of feminine softness.'[1] The following letter[2] is printed from the rough copy preserved in Tom Poole's Copying-book :—

'You reproach me, Henrietta, I understand, for a breach of promise. It is true I agreed to write to you ; but you will remember that no particular time was speci-fied, and did you know my numerous avocations, you would, in candour, hesitate to blame me. I have con-cerns of my own and concerns of others which, though, per-haps, of small individual importance, serve in the aggregate

[1] Journal, May 4, 1794.
[2] T. Poole to Henrietta Warwick, February 6, 1796.

to fill the fleeting moment as effectually as the sublime pursuits of a Cook, or the pernicious politicks of a Pitt. There was a time when I had much leisure, when I should have been happy to have written long, very long letters, to such a one as you; but now, if you find me irregular even in answering your letters, I must implore you to attribute it to no want of inclination, or of interest in the topicks which I am sure will be the subject of our correspondence, but to such causes as you yourself, were I to trouble you by reciting them, would deem sufficient. Thus, you see, at the threshold of our intercourse I am making terms for myself. This I deem necessary, as I foresee it will in future prevent my blotting much of that paper with apologies for apparent neglect, which ought to be more profitably employed.

'The main design of our correspondence is mutually to instruct and amuse each other, and not, as is too often the case, to exaggerate the value of any talents we may possess, and to foster that vanity which is so natural to the human head. I know you too well to imagine you require such homage, though it were just; and I should lessen you in my mind were I to attempt offering it. I shall write to you frankly and sincerely, and on whatever subject we speak, I shall give you my undisguised sentiments. Perhaps I may be at times too frank; if so, pardon it, and be assured that the head not the heart will err. You will observe a trivial example of this when I simply address you—Henrietta. The truth is, I know of no appropriate epithet which I could add with sincerity to your name, without incurring the risque of great singularity. I therefore avoid any.

'Thus much for introductory matter. I have heard

with pain from my sister Mrs. Wolstonecraft's story. . . .
It is a sublime though melancholy instance of the justice
of Providence, that we seldom see great talents, particularly that class which we peculiarly denominate genius,
enjoying an even tenour of human happiness. A
continuation of the rapturous intellectual delights which
beings of this description often experience would be
inconsistent with that looking forward, which is certainly
a duty, to a state of superiour existence. Their souls
seem, at times, to start from the flesh, and to mingle
with their native skies. But on their return, as if wearied
by the exertion, they feel more bitterly the sad weight
which surrounds them, and seem sunk even below the
common standard of human nature. Doubtless he who
can, with calmness, and most frequently, abstract himself
from the body, and come home again with becoming
dignity, is of human beings the most perfect. But it be-
hooves him who possesses this faculty, so nearly allied
to superiour spirits, to keep ever a strong guard over his
feelings, to consider that he is at present connected
with a mortal part that is earthly, low, has passions and
appetites which must be, in a certain degree, indulged.
The neglect of this consideration seems to me the great
rock against which men of genius are wrecked. In their
moments of mind, if I may be allowed the expression,
they form plans which would be practicable only if those
moments were of continued duration; but in their
career they feel like other mortals the sad burdens of
mortality, and these being overlooked in their scheme of
life, in the form of various passions they enter the
fenceless field, making unbounded havoc.

' What a striking instance of this is Mrs. Wolstonecraft !

What a striking instance is my beloved friend Coleridge !
Spenser, Milton, Dryden, Otway, and last of all, the
"sweet Harper of time-shrouded minstrelsy," Chatterton,
were the same.   This is a sad retrospect, Henrietta,
but, alas, a true one.   What shall we then say ?   Is
genius a misfortune ?   No.   But people of genius ought
imperiously to command themselves to think *without*
genius of the common concerns of life.   If this be
impossible—happy is the genius who has a friend ever
near of *good sense*, a quality distinct from genius, to fill
up by his advice the vacuity of his character.   Indeed I
think a good book might be written entitled Advice to
Men of Genius.   But a truce to this subject ; it ought
not to have been undertaken in a letter, so much may
be said on it.

'Let me hear from you as soon as you can conveniently write, and inform me, as far as a platonick friend
may be informed, of your principal pursuits.   Propose
any subject you think proper for our conversation, for I
deem letter-writing conversation.   It is for you to propose
topicks ; fortunate will it be if I, though in an imperfect
manner, may be enabled to assist you in discussing them.
Adieu.   My sister is very well.   My dear mother, I
thank God, is better.—Believe me, your sincere friend,

'THOS. POOLE.'

Amongst the various avocations spoken of in
the foregoing letter, a constant and ever-deepening
interest in the condition of the poor must be
reckoned.   Bread was almost at famine price in
the year 1795, and in that very month of Sep-

tember, when Coleridge was staying at Stowey,
we find Poole in conference with his aunt at
Marshmill on the subject of the various experiments then making with a view to obtaining a
cheaper loaf.

'Tom came up,' writes his Cousin Charlotte, 'and
brought two pieces of bread as patterns ; one was made
with wheat, barley, beans, and potatoes, and nobody
can wish to eat better bread.   The other is made with
wheat, barley, beans, and turnips, and that is likewise
good ; but the turnips give it a particular taste which
some persons may dislike.'

Mrs. John Poole seems to have set to work to
test the practical value of these combinations, for
we find another entry[1] recording that her ' Mother
has been employed all day in preparing some
bread to sell to the poor.   It is composed of a
bushel of wheat flour, one peck of barley flour,
one peck of potatoes, peeled, boiled, and rubbed
into the flour, and a small quantity of bean flour.
Unfortunately Nancy Jones did not quite understand her oven, and by not heating it sufficiently
spoiled the bread.'

Let us hope Nancy Jones did not do it on
purpose !   But every one who has ever tried the
experiment knows only too well the dislike, almost
approaching to resentment, with which the unedu-

[1] November 23.

cated are apt to receive an attempt to persuade them to eat anything to which they are not accustomed.

But however ready the family at Marshmill might be to co-operate with Tom in his philanthropic schemes, their dislike to his political opinions was as unmitigated as ever. Imagine, therefore, the point of view from which they would regard his intercourse with Coleridge. To the cousins Tom's 'democratick sentiments' were becoming no mere eccentricity of vision that might be pitied and tolerated, but a great moral divergence which they were bound to condemn.

'Tom Poole came up in the evening,' writes Miss Charlotte on March 15, 1796; 'he is never happy till he has introduced politicks, and as usual he disgusted us; for he has no candour, and there seems to be so much venom, bitterness, and determination in his whole conduct that it quite shocks me. He endeavours to load the higher class of people indiscriminately with opprobrium, and magnifies the virtues, miseries, and oppressed state of the poor in proportion. If he does not stand up as the advocate of the French enormities, he endeavours to palliate them, and I am sure, from his conversation and conduct, he would be glad to see all law and order subverted in this country. What can be the cause of such conduct? Certainly pride and the love of power; for though the democrats so eloquently talk of the wickedness of the world, and declaim against tyranny, I do not find that their lives are more spotless, and I am

sure in their own little concerns they display a great deal
of tyranny.   In short, his mind is poisoned—I fear
irrecoverably poisoned.'

But if rebuffed and disappointed at Marshmill,
Tom had at least the comfort of finding himself
ardently supported in his own household.   The
sympathy of tastes and convictions of which I have
already spoken as existing between him and his
brother, is well illustrated by the following letter,
addressed by Richard Poole to S. T. Coleridge on
May 3, 1796 :—

'MY GOOD FRIEND—Having lately been at Stowey,
and seeing at my brother's several numbers of your
Watchman, with which I was much delighted, I will
trouble you to send me in future two of the numbers
weekly, one for myself, the other for a friend here ; we
have a newsman, who goes direct to Bristol, whom I
shall direct to call at Mr. Cottle's. . . . If you have the
numbers from the beginning, I will thank you to send
them, as the set will be then compleat.   I will either
transmit you the money by the newsman, monthly or
quarterly, as you may wish.

'Your volume of Poems I have likewise read with
rapture.   Many of them I had seen, or before heard you
repeat.   Some passages of the *Religious Musings* are
exquisitely sublime ; I only regret that you write not more
to the level of common understandings ; you yourself
have been much engaged in metaphysical pursuits and
studies ; what probably therefore appears easy of comprehension and familiar to your mind, is either unintelligible

to the generality of your readers, or requires so much exertion of the understanding as to give pain and embarrassment instead of pleasure.

'I have likewise read your two lectures. If the last were less passionate, I should like it better. The cause of truth and reason never wants violence or invective for its support; sober argument and rational investigation are alone necessary to convince the unprejudiced and disinterested. As for the herd of interested and luxurious bawlers that every way abound around us, leave them to themselves and the awakening of British freedom and energy. I would avoid all harsh and irritating epithets (of which, by the bye, you are so fond), and steadily inculcate what is right, with temper and philosophy. Leave the rest to Truth.

'Your goodness, I am sure, will excuse the above remarks; they are simply dictated by the wish to see you arrive at that pinnacle of fame to which your writings give you so just a claim, and from a lively interest I take in everything that concerns you. I was sorry to hear from my brother that Fortune, that fickle jade, is not yet tired of playing her slippery tricks towards you. I sincerely hope, however, you keep up your spirits amidst all your difficulties. Your friends are numerous, and I have no doubt will do anything reasonable to serve you. If you persevere in the *Watchman* I think it will be necessary for you fully to give your opinions on Government, and to support those opinions by cool and dispassionate argument. The man who constantly rails at the establishments that exist, and proposes nothing in their stead, can only be styled an Anarchist, a character which I know you hold in sovereign contempt. If I

mistake not, you are warmly attached to the principles of
the British Constitution for this country.   The people
here are certainly much prejudiced in favour of monarchy ;
to reinstate, therefore, the constitution to its former state
of purity should, in my opinion, be your constant theme.
Mr. Yorke, whom I have lately seen in Dorchester Bastile,
and of whom I will speak more when next I write to
you, contends that Annual Parliaments was formerly
the law of the land, however, it is certain the general
principles of liberty were well understood at least by our
ancestors, if not practised.   I would wish you very much
to turn your attention to the character of Alfred ; he
certainly has not been sufficiently attended to by writers
on our Constitution.   The research would be useful on
two accounts, as I hope to see him the hero of an Epic
Poem by S. T. Coledridge.   May heaven bless and preserve you.—Yours fraternally,   Richd. Poole.'

Not a few readers may smile at the calm
confidence in his own opinion with which Richard
Poole, whilst asking Coleridge to send him the
Watchman, scruples not to volunteer his advice as
to the subjects and style both of that publication
and of Coleridge's other compositions.   Not so
Coleridge himself.   There is a time in the lives
of most great men, when, disheartened by the
slowness of an unresponsive public to recognise any
gift in the utterances of one whose name is as yet
unknown to fame, and whose pretensions clash with
their accustomed standards, they suffer very cruelly
from depression and self-distrust.   At such a

moment no cordial is of such unspeakable value
as one word of genuine appreciation from a friend
whose judgment is worth having.   In a literary
point of view there may not be much in Richard
Poole's letter ; but it does express that perfect
faith in Coleridge's powers, that undissembled
expectation of great things to be accomplished by
him, which was as the breath of life to him at that
particular moment.

'This morning' [May 5], he writes to Thomas Poole,
'I received a truly fraternal letter from Richard Poole of
Sherbourne, containing good and acceptable advice.   He
deems my *Religious Musings too metaphysical for common
readers*.   I answer, the poem was not written for common readers.   In so miscellaneous a collection as I
have presented to the public *singula cuique* should be
the motto. . . .'

'With regard to my own affairs,' he continues, in a
well-known passage, part of which must, nevertheless, be
transcribed here, 'they are as bad as the most Trinitarian
Anathematizer, or rampant Philo-despot could wish in
the moment of cursing. . . . It is not pleasant, Thomas
Poole ! to have worked fourteen weeks for nothing—*for
nothing !* . . . "O Watchman, thou hast watched in
vain," said the Prophet Ezekiel, when, I suppose, he
was taking a prophetic glimpse of my sorrow-sallowed
cheeks. . . .'

Indeed it would appear that, but for a happy
thought, which seems to have originated with Tom

Poole, Coleridge must have found himself at this particular moment absolutely without resources. Of course it is easy to show that the *Watchman* was foredoomed to failure. That it might avoid the newspaper stamp duty, it was arranged to appear with systematic irregularity, every eighth day, to the discomfiture of all ordinary arrangements for receiving periodicals ; and instead of consulting the taste of the public who were expected to take it in, its aim was to improve and instruct their minds ! Yet upon this unbusiness-like project Coleridge was depending for ‘that vulgar commodity yclept Bread,’ of which marriage was teaching him ‘the wonderful uses.’ He had conceived the plan with enthusiasm ; he had thrown himself into it with all the ardour of his nature. We know, by his success afterwards in the *Morning Post*, that he did really possess, in a very high degree, the special kind of aptitude which is needed by a successful writer for the public press, but—the *Watchman* failed ; only a few appreciated his poems ; many people, even many good people, (and how hard to bear is the condemnation of the good !) were utterly offended at them ; what foundation had he for believing that he ever would succeed in anything else ? Succeed, that is, in the sense of achieving a popularity that would pay. When the last number of the *Watchman* appeared, on

May 13, 1796, he must have been almost desperate, being either penniless or very nearly so, and entirely without any certain prospect of being otherwise.

But even as early as March 28, the rough sketch of the following letter had been drafted in Tom Poole's Copying-book; already the plan had been communicated to a few of Coleridge's friends, and 'acted on,' says Tom Poole, 'by I think seven or eight,' and a small sum of £35 or £40 (a small sum, but how great a relief to one who has come within sight of his last sixpence!) was awaiting Coleridge's acceptance, and that in the honourable form of a testimonial, offered by his admiring friends, as a token of their esteem and appreciation. With the tender forethought and considerateness that belongs to real affection, Tom Poole contrived that the letter should be received on the very day on which the last number of the *Watchman* was issued.

[In the *Biographical Supplement* the project is alluded to as a plan for buying an annuity which was never put into execution. This, it will be seen, is not exact. It is true that the scheme so enthusiastically described was only partially carried out; namely, on the present occasion, and once again in 1797. It may have been thought that the Wedgwood annuity removed all further necessity for going on with it.]

'It has occurred to the undersigned sincere Friends and ardent Admirers of the Author of the "Monody on the Death of Chatterton," and of various other pieces in verse and prose of unusual merit,—it has occurred to these to deposit five guineas each in the hands of John Cruikshank,[1] to be by him immediately sent to the person above alluded to. They further purpose annually, for the six succeeding years, in the week preceding Lady Day, each of them to transmit the like sum to the said John Cruikshank, to be immediately after the receipt thereof applied to the same use as the first deposit now made. And this they pledge themselves to each other to perform, in full confidence that a benevolent Providence will enable them, with unabated cheerfulness, to fulfil their engagement. It is their pride and their pleasure, if it seemeth good to S. T. Coleridge, to offer him this trifling mark of their esteem, gratitude, and admiration: esteem generated from a knowledge of his heart; gratitude for instruction and delight received by his writings and conversation; admiration produced by contemplating the extraordinary marks of sublime genius with which he is endowed.

'They are also irresistibly impelled to make this offer by recollecting the disinterested traits in his character; by recollecting that he has abandoned all, even the most seducing allurements, for a situation which leaves him only the triumphs of an honest heart, which are in truth exquisite, and the power to retain and disseminate those principles which he believes to be true, and to tend to the happiness of man. He also united himself to her he

---

[1] Mr. Estlin, not Mr. J. Cruikshank, seems to have eventually become the treasurer.

loves, regardless of every other consideration.   It is thus
that, lifted above the cupidity almost inwoven in the
hearts of all who live in such a society as ours, he presents in himself an object which awakens every tender
and noble sensation of the soul.

'His friends have now only to exhort him to proceed
with a steady and unceasing ardour in the career which
he has entered ; to exert with kindness his argumentative
powers, his forcible eloquence, his keen satire, his learning, in the support and dissemination of what he honestly
believes to be the truth; but above all, to invóke that Muse
who is the source of his highest delight, who will effectually assist him to that end, and who while she instructs
the ignorant, will not cease to charm and elevate the wise.

'They cannot better close this testimony of their
mutual regard for him than by the fond wish that all
anguish of mind may be removed from his dwelling, and
that he may in peace enjoy the most perfect domestic
felicity, added to every intellectual delectation, until the
awful moment when the curtain shall be withdrawn, and
to his soul shall be disclosed that relation existing between
man and the great Invisible, which, during his residence
here, his ardent eye had often sought in vain.

'*March* 28, 1796.'

Coleridge's reply was that 'burst of affectionate
feeling' which has already been printed in the
Biographical Supplement.

'Poole !' Coleridge wrote, 'the Spirit, who counts the
throbbings of the solitary heart, knows that what my
feelings ought to be, such they are.   If it were in my
power to give you anything which I have not already given,

I should be oppressed by the letter now before me.
But no! I feel myself rich in being poor; and because
I have nothing to bestow, I know how much I have
bestowed.   Perhaps I shall not make myself intelligible,
but the *strong, and unmixed affection* which I bear to you,
seems to exclude all emotions of *gratitude*, and renders even
the principle of *esteem* latent and inert.   Its presence is
not perceptible, though its absence could not be endured.

'Concerning the scheme itself I am undetermined.
Not that I am ashamed to receive;—God forbid!   I
will make every possible exertion; my industry shall be
at least commensurate with my learning and talents; if
these do not procure for me and mine the necessary
comforts of life, I can receive as I would bestow, and in
either case—receiving or bestowing—be equally grateful
to my Almighty Benefactor.   I am undetermined therefore, not because I receive with pain and reluctance,
but because I suspect that you attribute to others your
own enthusiasm of benevolence; as if the sun should
say—"With how rich a purple those opposite windows
are burning!"   But with God's permission I shall *talk*
with you on this subject.   By the last page of No. X.
you will perceive that I have this day dropped the
Watchman.   On Monday morning I will go per caravan
to Bridgwater, where, if you have a horse of tolerable
meekness unemployed, you will let him meet me.

'I should blame you for the exaggerated terms in
which you have spoken of me in the Proposal, did I not
perceive your motive.   You wished to make it appear an
offering, not a *favor*, and in excess of delicacy, have, I
fear, fallen into some grossness of flattery.   God bless
you, my dear, very dear friend. . . .'

VOL. I   L

Whether or no the meek horse was sent to
meet him we cannot say ; but in that year 1796
Tom Poole's house was a harbour of refuge,
always open to poor Coleridge in his many trials ;
and certainly, three days later, Charlotte Poole
met him in Stowey, and made the following rather
savage entry in her diary.   On that particular
afternoon, May 15, she was drinking tea with
her 'Aunt Thomas,' and 'in the evening who
should arrive but the famous Mr. Coldridge!'

Oddly enough, she again writes as if she had
entirely forgotten ever having seen him before.
'I cannot form an opinion of him in so short a
time,' she says, 'but could have discovered, if I
had not before heard it, that he is clever, and a
very short acquaintance will unfold that he is
extremely vain of it.'

It is strange to read these sharp judgments
from the pen of one who has left behind her in
the memory of the nephews and nieces, with whom
she was a favourite and much-loved aunt, nothing
but traditions of kindness, geniality, sweetness of
temper, and great practical sense and benevolence.
It can only be accounted for by remembering how
extremely harsh and crude is the colouring that
political prejudices lend to the mind.   Perhaps,
too, the sentence was not wholly at fault, for it
is precisely in times of failure that characters

conscious of power, and perplexed to account for their own want of success, are apt to silence the bitter promptings of self-distrust, to vent the irritation caused by the stings of disappointment, and to express their defiance of an unjust world, by the wildest outbursts of self-assertion. None of us, I think, has ever sufficiently realised the prolonged agonies of defeated hope, and only too well-grounded anxiety, which must have been the portion of poor Coleridge at this period of his life.

He stayed one fortnight with his friend, and returned to Bristol on May 29, by coach from Bridgwater, where, arriving 'too early for the caravan,' which did not start till nine, he gives some proof of recovered spirits by penning a nonsensical letter to Tom Poole, recalling the 'honey pie' that he had eaten at Stowey,[1] and relating how he had passed away the time, partly by eating a tremendous breakfast, and partly by wandering along the muddy banks of the Parrett, which, he remarked, 'looked as filthy as if all the parrots in the House of Commons had been washing their consciences therein,' and indulging in tender recollections of the 'dear Gutter of Stowey.'[2]

[1] In 1796 the Bill for the Abolition of the Slave Trade having been thrown out, friends of the cause all over England were mutely protesting by abstinence from all slave-grown luxuries, and especially sugar.

[2] A straight gutter bordering the street in Stowey, through which a running stream passes.

CHAPTER IX

'Ah me !   Literary adventure is but Bread and Cheese by chance.'
Coleridge to Thelwall, 1796.

IN spite of the comical letter sent back to Tom
Poole, it is not difficult to understand that neither
the heartfelt sympathy that he had found at
Stowey, nor even the substantial aid so delicately
pressed upon him by Poole and others, could
altogether relieve the burden of anxious care
which must still have weighed on Coleridge's mind
as he returned to Bristol.   True, if he did not pay
it away to Cottle for the debts the *Watchman* had
left behind it, he had a sufficient sum of money in
his possession to provide for the necessities of
many weeks to come.   But afterwards, what then?
He was perfectly aware of the transcendent
character of his own powers, but the experience
of disappointment and failure, the strangling,
unrelaxing pressure of domestic responsibility, led
him very often, in hours of despondency, to doubt

whether his abilities were of the marketable kind,
and to conceive harassing suspicions of his own
incapacity to earn an income. A young and
untrained wife, fond of him indeed, but perplexed
by ways and gifts entirely beyond her small experience, and no doubt tempted to feel both irritated
and alarmed at the total absence of what commonplace people call 'prospect,' is more to be pitied
than blamed if she clung and cried when she
ought to have encouraged and comforted, and
could neither be very hopeful nor very helpful in
the desperate condition of her husband's affairs.
To keep out of debt, and to make such small
sums of money as drifted irregularly into her
hands last as long as possible, must have been to
her the one subject of absorbing interest and
difficulty ; and if she was, upon the whole, fairly
successful in accomplishing this task, must not
this have been no unimportant assistance to
Coleridge in his struggle with adverse circumstances ?

But the struggle was a very hard one, and
Coleridge a man of more than ordinary sensitiveness. His letters during the latter half of the
year 1796 are not to be read without pain, so
full are they of sadness, disappointment, and
suffering. Not till six weeks after his return from
Bristol did Tom Poole even hear from him.

'Suspense,' he then wrote, 'has been the real cause of my silence. Day after day I have confidently expected some decisive letter, and as often have been disappointed—"Certainly I shall have one to-morrow noon, and then I will write." Thus I contemplated the time of my silence in its small component parts, forgetful into what a sum total they were swelling. . . .'

An opening had, indeed, presented itself, and one that offered a sufficient prospect of 'regular compensation adequate to the maintenance of himself and Mrs. Coleridge,' but it was a proposal to remove to London, and write for the *Morning Chronicle*, and the idea of writing for a newspaper was at that time most unwelcome to him. He talked of hiring a horse for two days and 'galloping down' to Poole to have his advice, but the thing seems to have come to nothing, except that Coleridge may actually have gone up to London about the matter, for the following note from Purkis is evidently an answer to a letter from Tom Poole introducing his friend. It would seem that the ride to Stowey must also have been accomplished ; for the letter is so evidently written entirely under the influence of Coleridge's own idea, that to be what he calls 'a hackney writer for a newspaper' would be a melancholy expenditure, in ephemeral tasks, of powers that were meant to produce something lasting, that we are

inclined to think the spell of his presence and conversation must have been upon Poole when he
penned it.   Purkis treats the subject from a cooler
and far more business-like point of view :—

'MY DEAR POOLE—I have this moment received
your letter, and as it may be some days before I see
your friend Coleridge, I scratch a line in haste to say I
shall rejoice to know him, both for your sake and his
own.   Of his abilities I entertain the very highest opinion,
and of his heart I cannot but be favourably impressed
by your partiality and affection.   To pity him would be
an insult, but I cannot help feeling a kind of indignation
that *such* a mind should be doomed to wander through
the world, and drudge to-day, in order to make provision
for the bread of to-morrow. . . .

'But to leave this strain.   Be assured, dear Poole, that
my heart will be open to receive your friend ; and though
he will not profit much by any information or advice
that I can give him, yet he will at least have the satisfaction of knowing that *one more* in the world admires
his genius, and sympathises with his misfortunes. . . .

'With respect to an engagement with an editor of a
newspaper, I do not see it in that contemptuous point
of view in which you paint it.   I allow that Coleridge
has talents beyond it, but if Perry will pay him liberally,
he may not be uselessly employed.   He may benefit
himself and his country, perhaps, at the same time.
The influence of a well-conducted newspaper on the morals
and politics of a nation is beyond what may be at first
imagined, and as Raphael did not disdain to paint cups
and vases, I think Coleridge may display his taste and

genius in a paragraph or an essay. I just know Perry
by sight, and have heard him much praised; but to me
he seems to have a spice of puppyism. However, that
is nothing to your friend. I hope they will agree on
terms. . . .—Yours most faithfully,   S. PURKIS.'

But the idea of settling in London passes completely out of sight, and in its stead the name of
Mrs. Evans of Darley comes to the front, a widow
lady of culture and sensibility who is eager to
entrust the education of her sons to Coleridge.
Everything is arranged. Coleridge is delighted to
undertake the charge; Tom Poole is happy in the
thought that his friend's uncertainties are about to
be comfortably concluded, when an incoherent, re-
gretful note from Mrs. Evans overthrows the entire
scheme. Her boys have guardians, and so strong
are their remonstrances that she has been compelled to yield up her own wishes. Tom Poole's
indignation at the feminine weakness that had in-
flicted so severe a disappointment upon his friend,
is almost amusing in its vigour :—

'MY DEAR, VERY DEAR COLERIDGE—I read with heart-
sickening anguish, though not with surprise, your packet
by Bob.

'My dear fellow, you are schooled to disappointment.
I hope you bear this with steadiness. You say you do,
and never tell me what is not true. The delusion, however painful the discovery that it was a delusion, has
produced solid advantages. You are reconciled to your

friends ;[1] write to them, I pray you, and tell them that
the curtain is withdrawn from before your eyes, and that
behind is nothing ! I write immediately, to ease my
own heart, for it fears that you may be impatient to be
sure that it feels as you feel, and I am in hopes also
that it will reach you before you leave Darley. You
said that if you had not remained with Mrs. Evans you
might have got pupils at Derby. I would have you inquire before you leave the neighbourhood concerning
this. Could you get any to take with you down to
Bristol, or to come to you at any fixed period there ?
Or perhaps, by settling at Derby, time and your conduct
may soften the ferocious opposition made to her plans ;
or, at any rate, by the friendship of such a woman you may
gain much. I still say such a woman, though she has
lamentably betrayed that she knew not that she was
woman. I am now convinced of what I doubted before,
that woman is inferiour to man. No man who is capable
of willing as ardently as she willed, who had the heart
and head she possesses, and understood the object to
be attained so well, would vacillate. Woman, thou wast
destined to be governed. Let us then bow to destiny.

' In even mentioning your settling so far off, I sacrifice
every selfish feeling to integrity. For I should think
myself dishonest if I allowed you to pass a hair that
would prop you, though it should lead you far from me.
But if, watching anxiously as you beat along the road
for some green path which may lead you to a fixed abode,
none such be to be found, I shall, I confess, after having

[1] During the year 1796 Coleridge had visited Ottery, and had
been affectionately received by his mother and brothers.—*Estlin
Letters*, printed by the Philobiblon Society.

discharged my conscience, rejoice at the fruitlessness of
the search.   My dear, dear boy, God Almighty bless
you and assist you.   Adieu! adieu!

'THOS. POOLE.

'Write! write!

'*August* 8.'

The negotiation appears to have gone so far
between Coleridge and Mrs. Evans that he and
his wife seem to have been actually on their way
to Darley, to make final arrangements.   The poor
lady met them with much agitation and embarrassment, but Coleridge hastened to relieve her.

I told her—he writes to Poole—'to feel nothing
on my account.   I cannot be said to have lost
that which I never had, and I have gained what I
should not otherwise have possessed, your acquaintance and esteem.'

'Say rather,' she exclaimed, 'my love and
veneration.'   And the visit which began under
such awkward and disappointing circumstances
accomplished its course pleasantly enough.   Coleridge, writing from Stowey to Thelwall in 1797,
remembers those five weeks spent by himself and
Mrs. Coleridge at Darley as 'a sunny spot in their
lives.'   By the time that Tom Poole's letter of
sympathy reached Darley, the tact and delicacy of
his hostess, and his real enjoyment of the beauty of
the Derbyshire scenery, had so taken the edge off his
disappointment that he could sincerely write :—

'Indeed, my very dear Poole, I wrote to you the whole truth. After the first moment I was perfectly composed, and from that moment to this have continued calm and light-hearted. I had just quitted you, and I felt myself rich in your love and esteem. You do not know how rich I feel myself. "O ever found the same; and trusted and beloved!"

'The last sentences of your letter affected me more than I can well describe. Words and phrases which might, perhaps, have adequately expressed my feelings, the cold-blooded children of this world have anticipated and exhausted in their unmeaning gabber of flattery. I use common expressions, but they do not convey common feelings. *My heart has thanked you.——* In preaching on Faith yesterday,[1] I said that Faith was infinitely better than Good Works; as the Cause is greater than the Effect, as a fruitful Tree is better than its Fruits, and as a friendly heart is of far higher value than the kindnesses which it naturally and *necessarily* prompts. It is for that *friendly heart* that I now have thanked you. . . .'

A month later, September 24, 1796, he has been in Birmingham again, staying with the family of Charles Lloyd.

'MY DEAR, VERY DEAR POOLE,' he writes—'The heart thoroughly penetrated with the flame of virtuous friendship is in a state of glory; but "lest it should be exalted above measure, there is given it a Thorn in the Flesh." I mean that when the friendship of any person forms an

---

[1] At Birmingham, on his way home from the North.

essential part of a man's happiness, he will at times be
pestered by the little jealousies and solicitudes of
imbecile humanity.   Since we last parted I have been
gloomily dreaming that you did not leave me so affectionately as you were wont to do.   Pardon this littleness
of heart, and do not think the worse of me for it.
Indeed my soul seems so mantled and wrapped round by
your love and esteem that even a dream of losing but
the smallest fragment of it makes me shiver—as though
some tender part of my nature were left uncovered and
in nakedness. . . .'

He goes on to say that Lloyd's parents having
given their joyful concurrence to their son's residence with him, but particularly wishing to see
him for a few days, Mrs. Coleridge had advised
him to go, declaring herself not likely to be laid
up for three weeks to come ; but 'on Tuesday
morning' he had been surprised by a letter,
announcing the birth of his firstborn Son.   (SON
in the largest possible letters.)

'I was quite annihilated,' he adds, 'with the sudden-
ness of the information, and retired to my room to
address myself to my Maker ; but I could only offer up
to Him the silence of stupefied feelings. . . .'

Of course he hastened home ; whether it seemed
equally of course to Mrs. Coleridge that, at such
a moment, Charles Lloyd should accompany him,
may be questioned.   But at all times Coleridge

was as social as Wordsworth was segregative in his tendencies, and to congenial guests his house stood ever open, with a comic, heedless indifference to the limitations of size, or the ins and outs of domestic convenience.

'When I first saw the child,' he continues—it is the thought that he afterwards embodied in a sonnet—'I did not feel that thrill and overflowing of affection which I expected. I looked on it with a melancholy gaze. My mind was intensely contemplative, and my heart only sad. But when, two hours after, I saw it at the bosom of its mother, on her arm, and her eye tearful and watching its little features,—then I was thrilled and melted, and gave it the kiss of A FATHER. . . . The baby seems strong, and the old nurse has overpersuaded my wife to discover a likeness of me in its face . . . its name is DAVID HARTLEY COLERIDGE. I hope that ere he be a man, if God destines him for continuance in this life, his head will be convinced of, and his heart saturated with, the truths so ably supported by that great master of *Christian* Philosophy. . . .'

The letter goes on to speak of Charles Lloyd, of his qualities of mind and heart, and his gratitude to heaven for the opportunity of living with Coleridge. His father, a member of the Society of Friends, has declared that if he sees his son forming habits of severe economy, he will not insist on his adopting a profession :—

' My dearest Poole, can you conveniently receive us in the course of a week ? . . . I have much, very much to say to you and consult with you about,—for my heart is heavy respecting Derby, and my feelings are so dim and huddled that, though I can, I am sure, communicate them to you by my looks and broken sentences, I scarcely know how to convey them in a letter. And Charles Lloyd wishes much to know you personally. . . .'

Then follow two sonnets of Charles Lloyd's, of which the following one alludes ' to the conviction of the truth of Christianity, which he had received from Coleridge, for he had been, if not a Deist, yet quite a Sceptic : '—

' LLOYD'S SONNET.

' If the lone breathings of the poor in heart,
    If the still gratitude of Wretchedness
    Reliev'd when least expecting, have access
    To Thee, th' Almighty Parent ! thou wilt dart
    Thy loving-kindness on the offering meek
    My spirit brings, opprest with thankfulness
    At this lone hour : for Thou dost ever bless
    The stricken mind, that sighs and cannot speak.

' Omniscient Father !   I have been perplex'd,
    With scoffers link'd ! yea, called them my Friends
    That snare the Soul.   But Doubt and black Despair
    Are past !   My heart, no longer sorely vex'd,
    May now unshroud itself—its arm extends
    To Heaven !   For Thou, my best Friend ! dwellest
        there ! '

The letter concludes with messages to Poole's family circle. 'Give my kind love to your sister and dear mother, and likewise my love to that young man with the soul-beaming face, which I recollect much better than I do his name. . . .'

This was a youth named Thomas Ward, whose family belonged to the Sherborne neighbourhood, and who had, some little time before, been brought to Stowey on a visit by Richard Poole. He was then a boy of fifteen, intelligent and thoughtful beyond his years, and destined by his friends for the medical profession. But Thomas Ward had never before seen any one like Mr. Poole ; and he attached himself to him with a sudden fervour of boyish enthusiasm and admiration, which was actually powerful enough to alter the whole course of his life. Returning home he had announced that he did not want to be a doctor, and he did not care about going to the university ; the one thing he did desire was to be apprenticed to Mr. Poole. To live in his house and to learn his business, seemed to him a lot in life to be preferred and chosen before every other that could be offered to him.

It is always such a comfort to have to do with a boy that knows his own mind, that we are not at all surprised to learn that Thomas Ward was allowed to have his own way. Some time in

1795 or 1796 he was duly articled, and found
that a nearer and more intimate acquaintance
only increased and deepened the love and veneration that he had conceived for Mr. Thomas Poole,
who, fully responding, gradually learnt to look
upon his articled pupil more and more in the light
of a son, and, in later years, he took him into
partnership.   They were great companions even
from the first; and there is a tradition that one of
their favourite amusements was to play chess
together, and that when the primitive customs of
the household, or Mrs. Poole's motherly solicitude
for the lad's health, interrupted their game earlier
than they approved, they would sometimes continue
it in the dark from their respective bedrooms,
shouting the moves across the passage into which
their doors opened.   To play a game of chess
without seeing the board strikes one as a rather
unusual intellectual feat on the part of a boy of
sixteen or seventeen ; but then Ward was certainly
no common boy.   He married and spent all his
life in Stowey ; and I have already mentioned that
many of the traditions and reminiscences alluded
to in these pages have come to me from his
daughters.

The following was Tom Poole's reply to the
foregoing letter :—

'My dearest Friend—the friend held dearest by me.

I say it thinkingly—and say it as a *full* answer to the first part of your last interesting letter. By you, Coleridge, I will always stand, in sickness and health, in prosperity and misfortune; nay, in the worst of all misfortunes, in *vice* . . . if vice should ever taint thee —— but *it cannot*.

' My dear, I came an hour ago from Sherborne, where I have left my mother and sister. On my arrival I met your letter.

' I congratulate you on becoming a father—the father of David Hartley; on the health of his mother, to whom remember me tenderly. When I have a son, his name shall be John Hampden. If either of them should feel, what a coronet he will have to support !

' I have now two or three buzzing round me, and I can only simply answer your letter. I am happy Mr. Lloyd is with you; I shall be more happy to see him. Come both directly. I am all alone. And we will *live*. Yes : I hope we will live.

' I have only ran over the poetry. When we meet we will talk of all things.

' Give me a line by return of post, just mentioning the day—nay, I will send horses to Bridgwater—only mention the day and the time of the day. They shall be there.—Adieu most kindly,   Thos. Poole.

' *September* 26, 1796.'

CHAPTER X

'That polish of style, that smoothness of versification, and that
harmony of periods, which demands labour, and labour only,
are incompatible with the strong and rapid combinations of
Genius. Restlessness of thought, power superior even to will,
ardent but indefinite hope—these constitute the great elements
of that feeling which always has something above the common
habits of thought ; has been, as it were, supernaturally infused
into the mind, or self-born in it,—which, though derived from
the senses and feelings, bears very little relation to them,—which
is, as it were, matter converted into mind, spirit animating
thoughts and feelings, embodied in reasoning.'—From a Note-
book of Sir H. Davy.

COLERIDGE'S visits to Stowey, Coleridge's letters,
Coleridge's perplexities, and the constant question
how best to help and counsel him, these were,
beyond all doubt, the leading interests in Tom
Poole's life during the year 1796.   But contemplative philosopher as Coleridge might be by
nature, the main tendency of every line that he
wrote, the entire bent of his teaching, was ever to
awaken that sense of responsibility to God, and
brotherhood with man, which is the master-impulse
of activity and service, and no one ever came

within the sphere of his influence without being quickened to fresh hope, and, as it were, new-born to fresh energy. When the two friends first met Tom Poole was suffering under a load of depression and discouragement, personal and political, which was destroying all his zest in life, and had even affected his health. The mere contact with Coleridge's genius, the delight and stimulation of intercourse with one so highly gifted, was as a draught of clear spring water to a man whose energies were paralysed by thirst. It was a great increase to his happiness to begin with, and increased happiness soon showed itself in increased vigour, and renewed confidence in himself and his purposes.

It is true that the habit of reading Latin with his cousin, John Poole, had been dropped. Some unexplained coolness arose between Tom and the Marshmill family during the earliest weeks of the year; and although the report of an illness of Tom's mother's brought John Poole instantly to the door, to wonder why they had not heard of it before, after which the intercourse between the two households became almost as frequent as ever, yet signs are not wanting that it was not quite upon the old footing, and there is no more dropping in *ante jentaculum* to read *Horace*, or *Cicero*, or *Virgil.* That unlucky occasion when John Poole

wrote '*maxime indignor*' in his journal, seems to
have established a first impression, never to be removed, of the characteristics of Tom's new friends,
and the chilling disapproval with which he
knew his growing intimacy with Coleridge to be
regarded at Marshmill, must have created a painful
feeling of restraint between him and his cousins.
His mother, however, had become in the highest
degree sympathetic.   John Poole, calling once when
Tom was out, was perhaps rather amazed at the
vigour with which she repeated and maintained
her son's favourite sentiments.   'Aunt Thomas
was exceedingly violent against the War, Ministers,
etc. etc.,' he complains.   Whether Sarah Poole,
engaged to be married to a Bristol merchant who
was certainly no democrat, shared the same views,
is not apparent.   She was, like her brothers and
her cousins, a person of cultivated understanding,
knowing 'from cover to cover,' she is once reported to have said, her Bible and her Shakespeare,
and many messages of 'fraternal remembrance'
addressed to her in Coleridge's letters, seem to
show that no prejudices, political or otherwise,
prevented her from making herself pleasant to her
brother's friends.

A leading feature in the occupations of the
year, at Marshmill as well as at Stowey, was
learning French of the Refugee Abbé already

spoken of.   He had arrived in Stowey in August
1795—'a good old man in appearance, and
speaking but little English.'   John Poole bridged
over the difficulty by conversing with him in Latin,
where, one would imagine, the insular eccentricity
of English pronunciation may have been rather
a bar to mutual comprehension, but the very next
day the Abbé was at Marshmill, giving John and
his sister Charlotte—the journalising Charlotte—a
lesson in French, and, from that day forwards, he
was so constantly either there, or at Tom's house
at Stowey, that continual practice must soon have
developed the power of conversing with him as
freely as any one could wish in his own tongue.
Happily for the fulfilment of Tom's desire to
become acquainted with French literature, the
Abbé was evidently a lover of books.   Exile as
he was, and reduced to live by teaching his own
language, there is, among the many mentions of
his name in the Pooles' journals, only one notice
in which it is observed that the Abbé Barbey
seemed depressed and out of spirits ; and then
John Poole found that the news had just reached
him, indirectly, through Monsieur Pains, that his
library had been sold in the course of the preceding year.   'Most of his other property was
safe, he having consigned it to his brother.'
Emigré and royalist as the Abbé might be, he

could scarcely be a Frenchman and not be acquainted with the French philosophical writers of
the day, or, at any rate, with the foremost amongst
them, and any book that he might mention as
worth reading would, doubtless, soon be added
to Tom Poole's collection.   The following letter[1]
will show both his enthusiasm for the study of
French, and also the manner in which the half-
philosophical, half-sentimental problems of French
revolutionary thinkers worked also in English
minds, but without the same ferment, and without
the dangerous tendency to extremes in thought
and action.

'I sincerely thank you, my amiable friend, for the excellent letter you sent me, and notwithstanding my long
delay in answering it, permit me to assure you that I
highly value your correspondence, and anticipate its
progress with no small satisfaction.   The account of the
progress of your own mind highly interested me.   There
is a celebrated maxim of La Bruyère which says if "Man
is not as good as he should be, it is the fault of his
education "; with respect to the dispositions of the heart
there is, I believe, a great deal of truth in this adage;
but ask yourself, without fearing the imputation of self-
complacency, if the most spirited education could have
given to many of your pupils those quick perceptive
powers you must be conscious of possessing.   In truth,
you, my fair friend, may be what you think proper; you

[1] T. Poole to Henrietta Warwick, April 2, 1796.

have only to *will* ardently, and the object is attained. And, as you have condescended to ask my opinion concerning your future pursuits, I would recommend you, as you anticipated, first, to *will* that you will acquire a thorough knowledge of the French language. Were I a woman of superiour mind I should bless myself that the tyranny of prejudice had not hitherto proscribed my sex this truly useful and elegant attainment. To be sincere, I cannot consider a woman passably educated without a knowledge of it ; and I am sure I could not, without reproof, hear her complain of any monopoly of learning on the part of the Man, whilst she herself had neglected this, —in the present moment certainly the first branch of learning. . . . I have never felt any delights in reading English literature comparable to those which I have experienced in reading French. L'Émile de Rousseau, for example—what a book is there ! " *Comme il pense et comme il fait penser*," as has been well said ; but not only this book but many others which I could recommend you, if you read French. I have lately perused with much delight *La Citoyenne Roland*. Learn French, I pray, and you may make even your learning the language the vehicle of much solid instruction. . . . I never retain so much as when I read in a language with which I am not familiar.

'I can spare no more of this letter for this subject, as I wish to say a word or two on your question : Is the perfectibility of Man in this world compatible with the comfortable doctrine that our existence here is but antecedent to a better ?—

'I have never read Godwin's work ; but I fear in pampering the mind, he has destroyed the heart. How he answers your question I know not, but the question seems to me as if it would bound the benevolence of God. I believe that Man, by physical and moral discipline, may attain perfection as Man; a perfection of which we have, perhaps, no adequate idea, or which, at any rate, we see but dimly. Yes, I can conceive that his body and mind may be so improved that the former may be more durable, and the latter susceptible of infinitely higher enjoyments than at present; in short, that the age of gold, as it is called, of which there is a tradition with every People, may be renewed—an age when Man, fresh from his Maker's hands, and strongly impressed with a recent revelation, lived over centuries, enjoying a mind and being as yet undisturbed by passion or vice. The transition from this state to our present condition is, perhaps, the truth shadowed out by our Scriptural allegory of the Fall of Man. The very expressions seem to prove it; the tree of knowledge meant worldly knowledge, *i.e.* vice. Vice produces death, *i.e.* shortens life, etc. etc. There was a renewal of this blissful state immediately after the flood—no wonder, after such a lesson; and, at this moment, the awful process going on in Europe, added to the present energetic search after truth, induce me fondly to hope that Mankind is now, though slowly, advancing once more to this, the most perfect state of earthly felicity.

'Surely in believing this I can by no means conclude that God designs me to die! No. The more perfect I am here the more worthy I shall be to live hereafter; in such a state I am, indeed, worth preserving. I conceive, then, that after being satiated with all earthly happiness, we are, by that crisis in our nature which we call death, simply introduced to a new scene, offering a beatitude of which Man, even in his most perfect state, may be incapable of forming an idea. Here we may, with abundant gratitude, rest and be satisfied; but I do not think that the benevolence of God will rest. I doubt not but hopes more elevated will be there excited; and they will not be excited in vain; but we shall, ever in a progressive state of mind, proceed from heaven to heaven, to all eternity, still approaching the great source, and still adoring. . . .

> " " 'Tis such delights, such strange beatitudes,
> Seize on my young anticipating heart,
> When that blest future rushes on my view."
>
> COLERIDGE.

'It is thus that I think the perfectness of Man will prepare him for immortality. I can say no more. The bounds of a letter are unequal to this subject. Adieu.

'I trust your admirable sister is better. Where talents are employed as hers have been, the welfare of many is involved in her state of health. . . . How interesting— nay, if the expression may be permitted, how sacred is the work of education. Oh, that it were throughout the world in such hands as at your house. God bless you.   THOS. POOLE.'

The composition, and then the copying out, of such an epistle as the above, must have absorbed rather a considerable share of the time which it had been, for years, Thomas Poole's daily habit to devote to what may be called the things of the mind. It must not be forgotten that, in the practical affairs of life, the management of his business, the cultivation of his farm, the local interests of the little place in which he lived, he was as energetic, and capable and industrious, as if he never spared a thought to anything else. And yet he had time to go out woodcock-shooting with his cousin in the shooting season, sometimes even to follow the harriers, and time, too, for social, friendly inter-course with all the large circle of acquaintance and connections living in and about his native place. We are reminded of the common ex-perience that it is only busy people who can be relied upon for finding time for additional work ; idlers never appear to have any leisure, they are too completely occupied in idling.

We have seen him in eager consultation with his aunt in October 1795 about cheap bread for the poor ; in November of the same year John Poole found him trying to introduce an improved way of planting wheat upon his farm.

'Went to Baker's Land,' he says, 'where I found T. Poole overlooking his work-people. Some women were planting wheat. There was one man and three boys dibbling it after the Norfolk method, a description of which has been sent to him by Dr. Fisher, with a sketch by himself.'

In fact, Tom was making improvements in

every direction—'taking down useless hedges, clearing ditches, planting, etc.,' and, in his business, leading the way in the use of improved machinery. He had, even then, 'opened a quarry for stones at Castle Hill Gate,' and was building 'a new house for grinding bark'; and in April 1796, John Poole saw the 'new bark mill' at work, which Tom's American friend, Mr. Garnett, had invented, and records that it 'answered perfectly.' The novelty of the new bark house has departed long since; but there it still stands, and there, when I last visited Stowey, I saw a woman grinding bark at a mill of perhaps very much the same construction, and was told of the local tradition that Mr. Coleridge used to take a great deal of interest in the putting of it up.

It is probable that this must have been a later mill erected in 1807,[1] but one thing is certain, namely, that the practical aspect of his friend's life had always a wonderful fascination for Coleridge. Abstract thinker as he was by nature, his ideal of life at all times, but most especially at this period, was a life in which contemplation, whether in the form of reading, study, or meditation, should rest upon a basis of *manual* industry, by which the necessaries of life should be provided. To sell the highest intellectual gifts

[1] *Life of William Baker*, p. 23.

for bread was always repugnant to him, and, indeed, in the painful straitness of which he had had so harassing an experience, he was acquiring a conviction that pearls of great price are not very saleable commodities ; inferior jewels find pur- chasers much more easily.

In Tom Poole he saw for the first time the actual combination of highly cultivated literary tastes and quick intellectual sympathies, with a no less high degree of practical vigour and utility.   The gentle and gifted Charles Lloyd was set apart by infirm health from the active business of life ; Estlin was a Unitarian minister and a schoolmaster ; an older and dearer friend, Charles Lamb, certainly never handled any instrument of labour but a pen ; but Tom Poole actually was, what he delighted to call himself, a *tradesman.*   He belonged, definitely and not indirectly, to the class of *producers*, and earned his living in what even the most advanced of social reformers would allow to be an entirely satisfactory way, by the manufacture of an article of primary necessity.   Not only this, but he had land, which, as has been seen, he farmed himself ; and the actual cultivation of the soil is not only the very example and archetype of productive industry, but is capable of being celebrated as such in poetry, which can hardly be said of the humble avocation of tanning.   Nor did Tom Poole lead, as many people do lead, a sort of double existence, being, as it were, one man in his book-room and another in his business. His life was eminently all of one piece. Duty and service were alike his watchwords whether he were reading French with Abbé Barbey, or overlooking his work-people on the farm or in the tanyard. Literature was never to him, either

'a couch, whereon to rest a searching and restless spirit; or a terrace for a wandering and variable mind to walk up and down with a fair prospect; or a tower of state for a proud mind to raise itself upon; or a fort or commanding ground for strife and contention; or even a shop, for profit and sale; and not a rich storehouse, for the glory of the Creator and the relief of man's estate.[1] . . .'

'To give a true account of the gift of reason, to the benefit and use of men,' had ever been, and ever was, 'the last and furthest end' to which the entire course of his studies was directed.

It is not very wonderful that admiration of Tom Poole's calm, well-ordered life, together with the peace and freedom and perfect toleration, which Coleridge knew awaited him, the moment he could get inside the door of that plain, old-fashioned house, with the tanyard and the garden at the back, and the sight of tranquil rustic labours, and cheerful country

[1] Bacon's *Advancement of Learning*, Book I.

pursuits, all combined to make Stowey seem to Coleridge's imagination the one happy resting-place where he might be safe from all his cares amongst those who loved him. No doubt some expression of longing to live there may have often crossed his lips during his frequent visits to his friend, but it is not till November 1, 1796, that we find the subject started in his letters. There was a small house at Adscombe, close to Stowey, which belonged to Lord Egmont, and which, it would seem, Coleridge hoped to be allowed to rent.

'I am frightened at not hearing from Cruikshank,' he writes (Cruikshank was Lord Egmont's agent). 'Has Lord Thing-a-my-bob—I forget the animal's name—refused *him*? Or has Cruikshank forgotten *me*?'

How eagerly his mind was set upon the plan is easily to be seen by the following passage from the beginning of the same letter :—

'. . . I have seen a narrow-necked bottle so full of water that, when turned upside down, not a drop has fallen out. Something like this has been the case with me. My heart has been full, yea, crammed with anxieties, about my residence near you. I so ardently desire it that any disappointment would chill all my faculties, like the fingers of death. And entertaining wishes so irrationally strong, I necessarily have *day*-mair [1]

---

[1] Day-*mair* is S. T. C.'s spelling. As in the *Ancient Mariner*, ' The night-*mair* death-in-life was she.'

dreams that something will prevent it, so that, since I quitted you, I have been gloomy as the month which even now has begun to lower and rave on us. . . .'

Four days later [1] he wrote again, in answer to a letter from Tom Poole which has not been preserved.

'Thanks, my heart's warm thanks to you, my beloved friend! for your tender letter. Indeed I did not deserve so kind a one; but by this time you have received my last. To live in a beautiful country, and to enure myself as much as possible to the labours of the field, have been for this year past my dream of the day, my sigh at midnight; but to enjoy these blessings *near you*, to see you daily, to tell you all my thoughts in their first birth, and to hear your's, to be mingling identities with you, as it were!—the vision-weaving Fancy has indeed often pictured such things, but *Hope* never dared whisper a promise. Disappointment! disappointment! dash not from my trembling hand this bowl which almost touches my lips! Envy me not this immortal draught, and I will forgive thee all thy persecutions. . . . I am anxious beyond measure,' he concludes, 'to be in the country as soon as possible. I would it were possible to get a temporary residence till Adscombe is ready for us. I would that it could be, that we could have three rooms in Bill Poole's large house for the winter. . . . Tell me whether you think it at all possible to make any terms with him. You know I would not wish to touch with the edge of the nail of my great toe the line which should

[1] November 5.

be but half a barleycorn out of circle of the most trembling delicacy. . . .'

This last sentence is surely a caricature of some one. William Poole was an uncle of Tom Poole's. He farmed a good deal of land and was popularly known in Stowey as 'Prophet Poole,' on account of his astonishing sagacity in predicting the course of the weather. Coleridge's poem beginning—

> 'Why need I say, *Louisa* dear !
> How glad I am to see you here,
> A lovely convalescent ;'

was addressed to his daughter Lavinia, afterwards Mrs. Draper. Nothing came of the above suggestion, but this letter of November 5, 1796, is remarkable amongst Coleridge's letters and papers, as being the very earliest in which, years before opium became his tyrant, recourse to a narcotic is mentioned. Months of wearing anxiety, and of expectations alternately raised and thrust down, acting on a highly sensitive nature could not fail to produce precisely the same kind of physical breakdown which the same causes almost invariably do produce, even in natures far tougher and far less finely strung than Coleridge's, at the present day. In the wilderness of disappointment, and amid the arid wastes of heart-aching care,

Neuralgia, persistent and relentless, dogs her victims, waiting only, like some beast of prey, until the depressing atmosphere has done its work, and the strength is brought too low for resistance.

'I wanted such a letter as your's,' writes poor Coleridge, 'for I am very unwell. On Wednesday night I was seized with an intolerable pain from my right temple to the tip of my right shoulder, including my right eye, cheek, jaw, and that side of the throat. . . . It continued from one in the morning till half-past five, and left me pale and fainty. It came on fitfully but not so violently several times on Thursday, and began severe threats towards night, but I took between sixty and seventy drops of laudanum and *sopped* the Cerberus just as his mouth began to open. On Friday it only *niggled;* as if the Chief had departed from a conquered place, and merely left a small garrison behind . . . but *this morning* he returned in full force, and his name is Legion! Giant-fiend of an hundred hands! With a shower of arrowy death-pangs he transpierced me, and then became a Wolf, and lay gnawing my bones. I am not mad, most noble Festus! but in sober sadness I have suffered this day more bodily pain than I had before a conception of. . . . My medical attendant decides it to be altogether nervous, and that it originates either in severe application, or excessive anxiety. My beloved Poole, in excessive anxiety I believe it might originate.

'I have a blister under my right ear, and I take twenty-five drops of laudanum every five hours, the ease and *spirits* gained by which have enabled me to write you this flighty but not exaggerating account. . . . Your letter is dated November 2.   I wrote to you on November 1.   Your sister was married that day, and on that day, several times, I felt my heart overflowed with such tendernesses towards her, as made me repeatedly ejaculate prayers in her behalf.   Such things are strange.   It may be superstition to think about such correspondences ; but it is a superstition which softens the heart, and leads to no evil. . . .'

Two days later he wrote that he was better ; for the greater part of a whole day he 'had enjoyed perfect ease,' and though 'totally inappetent of food, and languid, even to an inward perishing,' had found energy to write 'a short note of congratulatory kindness' to Mrs. King. 'I shall be eager to call upon her,' he adds, 'when LEGION shall have been thoroughly exorcised from my temple and cheek.'

CHAPTER XI

'An angry letter, but the breach was soon healed.'
Thomas Poole's Memoranda.

'I am not fit for public life; yet the light shall stream to a far distance, from the taper in my cottage window.'—*Coleridge to Thelwall*, December 1796.

IT is not clear why, or in what manner, Coleridge was disappointed of his hope to be allowed to rent the house at Adscombe. A week passed by, during which perhaps Tom Poole hardly knew what to say to him, for we find Coleridge writing on 'Tuesday, November 15, 1796—half-past five '—

'MY DEAREST POOLE—Since the receipt of your last letter I have written you *twice;* and for this week past I have been punctually at the door of the post-office every evening at five o'clock, anxiously expecting to hear from you. My anxieties eat me up. I entreat you write me, if it be only to say you have nothing to write. Have you thought concerning my suggestions in the letter I wrote during my illness? Yes! I am sure you have. Let me know the result of your reflections. . . .

'If I should be likely to find out any temporary residence near you, I would immediately walk down to
Stowey and look for it.

'But write!'

In reply Tom Poole seems to have told his
friend that the one only house which it was likely
to be in his power to take was the unattractive
cottage directly facing the street, which in the
end Coleridge actually did inhabit.   Tom Poole's
doubts whether it could possibly be considered a
fit abode for his friend were answered by the
following impetuous note :—

'MY BELOVED FRIEND—Pardon the childish impatience which I have betrayed. The sailor who has
borne cheerily a circumnavigation may be allowed to
feel a little like a coward when within sight of his
expected and wished-for port.

'We shall be more than content to live a year in the
house you mention.   It is not a beauty, to be sure, but
its vicinity to you shall overbalance its defects.   Pray
take it for us for a year.   I would it were possible that
we could get into it in three weeks, for we must quit
our house on Christmas Day, and it will be awkward to
take lodgings for a week, and expensive.

'I will *instruct* the maid in cooking.'

The above letter is undated, but was evidently
written some time in the last days of November.
Tom Poole had, perhaps, expected a different
answer to a letter in which he would seem to have

dwelt, rather uneasily, on the disadvantages and drawbacks of the house in question. Business, however, called him up to London, and it was not till his return home, ten days later, that a feeling of alarm at the thought that he might be doing anything but an act of friendship in leading Coleridge to bury himself in a remote corner of the world, where he must perforce make his home in a mean and unsuitable cottage, together with the fact that some more advantageous residence had offered itself at a place called Acton, within a short distance of Bristol, or perhaps even, as Coleridge himself seems to have suspected, some instance of local prejudice and intolerance, making him feel a little dread as to what might be his friend's reception amongst the inhabitants of Stowey, caused him to write and advise Coleridge after all to think whether he had not better give up the Stowey plan. The chance of renting Adscombe seems to have entirely come to nothing ; and the cottage really would not do—he could never be comfortable there.

But these prudent counsels were crossed by another enthusiastic note from Coleridge. The account of the dinner at the Kings', with his disgust at Mrs. King's retrogression in the matter of hair-powder, reminds us that the mode of wearing the hair was then a political Shibboleth, and the bride's powdered locks were a visible sign of backsliding from her brother's opinions.

'MY BELOVED POOLE—The sight of your villainous handscrawl was a great comfort to me. How have you been diverted in London? What of the theatres? And how found you your old friends? I dined with Mr. King yesterday week. He is *quantum suff:* a pleasant man, and (my wife says) very handsome. Hymen lies in the arms of Hygeia, if one may judge by your sister; she looks remarkably well! But has not she caught some complaint in *the head?* Some *scurfy* disorder? For her *hair* was filled with an odious white Dandruff. ('*N.B.*—Nothing but powder,'—a feminine hand has added here in pencil.)

'About myself I have so much to say I really can say nothing. I mean to work *very hard*—as Cook, Butler, Scullion, Shoe-cleaner, occasional Nurse, Gardener, Hind, Pig-protector, Chaplain, Secretary, Poet, Reviewer, and *omnium-botherum* shilling-Scavenger. In other words, I shall keep no servant, and shall cultivate my land-acre and my wise-acres as well as I can. . . . I wish that little cottage by the roadside were gettable? That with about two or three rooms—it would quite do for us, as we shall occupy only two rooms. I will write more fully on the receipt of yours. God love you and

'S. T. COLERIDGE.'

So wrote Coleridge on Sunday morning, December 11, 1796; and on the very same day, or perhaps on the Saturday, Poole, as we have seen, was writing too—a letter that fell like ice on the state of ardent expectancy in which his friend had been living for weeks, and threw him into an agitation which found immediate vent in a vehement and resentful letter, written at the Bristol Library on his way home, and followed by the extraordinary outburst of wounded feeling and pathetic remonstrance, which, by the kind permission of Mr. Ernest Coleridge, I here print *in extenso.* It is written as closely as possible on a sheet of paper of the very largest size, larger than ordinary foolscap ; and, it may be observed, it was one of the few papers kept back by Poole when, in 1835 or 1836, he placed the greater number of the letters he had received from S. T. Coleridge at the disposal of his family for biographical purposes.

Perhaps the vivid picture, undesignedly given here, of a man of genius, endowed with high and singular gifts, and intended to be a leader of national thought, face to face with the narrowest penury, whilst inexperienced as a child in the ordinary concerns of life, may go some way to explain, if it cannot excuse, the inconsistencies and shortcomings which wrecked his later career. It illustrates also the sensitive excitability and vehement impulsiveness which doubtless caused him to be the more beloved by those who loved him ;

but must, also, have often tried the patience, even of those who loved him best.

The first letter [1] begins tranquilly enough :—

'You tell me, my dear Poole, that my residence near you would give you great pleasure, and, I am sure, that if you had any objections on your own account to my settling near Stowey, you would have mentioned them to me. Relying on this, I assure you that a disappointment would try my philosophy. Your letter did indeed give me unexpected and most acute pain. I will make the cottage do. We want but three rooms. . . .

'As to Acton, it is out of the question. In Bristol I have Cottle and Estlin (for Mr. Wade is going away) willing and eager to serve me ; but how they can serve me more effectually at Acton than at Stowey, I cannot divine. If I live at Stowey, you indeed *can* serve me effectually, by assisting me in the acquirement of agricultural practice. If you can instruct me to manage an acre and a half of land, and to raise on it, with my own hands, all kinds of vegetables and grain, enough for myself and my wife, and sufficient to feed a pig or two with the refuse, I hope that you will have served me *most* effectually, by placing me out of the necessity of being served. . . .

'But whence this sudden revolution in your opinions, my dear Poole? You saw the cottage that was to be our temporary residence, and thought we might be *happy* in it, and now you hurry to tell me that we shall not even be *comfortable* in it. You tell me I shall be so far from my *friends, i.e.* Cottle and Estlin, for I have no other

[1] Undated. Endorsed December 12, 1796.

in Bristol. In the name of heaven, *what can* Cottle or
Estlin [do] for me? They do nothing who do not teach
me how to be independent of any except the Almighty
Dispenser of sickness and health. . . . My habits and
feelings have suffered a total alteration. I hate company,
except of my dearest friends, and systematically avoid
it, and when in it keep silence as far as social humanity
will permit me. Lloyd's father, in a letter to me
yesterday, inquired how I should live without any companions? I answered him, not an hour before I received
your letter :—

'"I shall have six companions: my Sara, my babe,
my own shaping and disquisitive mind, my books, my
beloved friend Thomas Poole, and lastly, Nature, looking
at me in a thousand looks of beauty, and speaking to
me with a thousand melodies of love. If I were capable
of being tired with all these, I should then detect a vice
in my nature, and would fly to habitual solitude to
eradicate it."

'Yes! my friend! while I opened your letter my heart
was glowing with enthusiasm towards you. How little
did I expect to find you earnestly and vehemently
persuading me to prefer. Acton to Stowey ! . . .

'On Wednesday week we must leave our house, so that
if you continue to dissuade me from settling near Stowey,
I scarcely know what I shall do. Surely, my beloved
friend ! there must be some reason which you have not
yet told me which urged you to send this hasty and
heart-chilling letter. I suspect that something has passed
between your sister and dear mother, in whose illness I
sincerely sympathise with you. I have never considered
my settlement at Stowey in any other relation than its

advantages to myself, and they would be great indeed. My objects (assuredly wise ones) are to learn agriculture (and where should I get instruction except at Stowey?) and to be where I can communicate in a literary way. I must conclude.   I pray you let me hear from you immediately.   God bless you and

'S. T. COLERIDGE.'

There is a tone of rising passion in the latter part of this letter, which gathered volume as he hurried homewards, and poured out its full tide when, later in the evening, he again snatched pen and paper, and began a second time to write a reply to Poole.[1]

'*Monday night.*

'I wrote the former letter immediately on receipt of your's, in the first flutter of agitation.   The tumult of my spirits has now subsided, but the Damp struck into my very Heart; and there I feel it.   O my God! my God! when am I to find rest!   Disappointment follows disappointment, and Hope seems given me merely to prevent my becoming callous to Misery!   Now I know not where to turn myself.   I was on my way to the City Library, when I found your letter at the Post-office—I opened it at the Library, and wrote an answer to it there. Since I have returned I have been poring into a book, as a shew for not looking at my Wife and the Baby.   By God, I dare not look at them.   Acton!   The very name makes me grind my teeth!   What am I to do there?

'"You will have a good Garden; you may, I doubt

---

[1] Postmark Bristol.   Endorsed December 12, 1796.

not, have ground." But am I not ignorant as a child
of everything that concerns the garden and the ground?
And shall I have one human being there who will instruct
me? The House too—what should I do with it? We want
but two rooms, or three at the furthest. And the country
around is intolerably flat. I would as soon live on the
banks of a Dutch canal! And no one human being
near me for whom I should, or could, care a rush! No
one walk where the beauties of nature might endear
solitude to me! There is one Ghost that I *am* afraid
of; with that I should be perpetually haunted in this
same cursed Acton—the hideous Ghost of departed
Hope. O Poole! how could *you* make such a proposal
to me? I have compelled myself to reperuse your letter,
if by any means I may be able to penetrate into your
motives. I find three reasons assigned for my not
settling at Stowey. The first, the distance from my
friends, and the Press. This I answered in the former
letter. As to my friends, what can they do for me?
And as to the Press, even if Cottle had not promised to
correct it for me, yet I might as well be fifty miles from
it as twelve, for any purpose of correcting. Secondly, the
expense of moving. Well, but I must move to Acton,
and what will the difference be? Perhaps three guineas.
. . . I would give three guineas that you had not
assigned this reason. Thirdly, the wretchedness of that
cottage, which alone we can get. But, surely, in the
house which I saw, *two* rooms may be found, which, by
a little green list and a carpet, and a slight alteration in
the fireplace, may be made to exclude the cold: and
this is all we want. Besides, it will be but for a while.
If Cruikshank cannot buy and repair Adscombe, I have

no doubt that my friends here and at Birmingham would, some of them, purchase it. So much for the reasons: but these cannot be the real reasons. I was with you for a week, and then we talked over the whole scheme, and you approved of it, and I gave up Derby. More than nine weeks have elapsed since then, and you saw and examined the cottage, and you knew every other of these reasons, if reasons they can be called. Surely, surely, my friend! something has occurred which you have not mentioned to me. Your mother has manifested a strong dislike to our living near you—or something or other— for the reasons you have assigned tell me nothing except that there are reasons which you have not assigned.

'Pardon if I write vehemently. I meant to have written calmly; but bitterness of soul came upon me. Mrs. Coleridge has observed the workings of my face while I have been writing, and is intreating to know what is the matter. I dread to shew her your letter. I dread it. My God! my God! what if she should dare to think that my most beloved friend has grown cold towards me!

'*Tuesday morning*, 11 *o'clock.*—After an unquiet and almost sleepless night, I resume my pen. As the sentiments over leaf came from my heart, I will not suppress them. I would keep a letter by me which I wrote to a mere acquaintance, lest anything unwise should be found in it—but my friend ought to know not only what my sentiments are, but what my feelings were.

'I am, indeed, perplexed and cast down. My first plan, you know, was this—My family was to have consisted of Charles Lloyd, my wife and wife's mother, my infant, the servant, and myself.

'My means of maintaining them—Eighty pound a

year from Charles Lloyd, and forty from the Review and
Magazine : my time was to have been divided into four
parts.   1. Three hours after breakfast to studies with
C. Ll.   2. The remaining hours till dinner to our Garden.
3. From after dinner till tea, to Letter-writing and
domestic quietness.   4. From tea till prayer-time to the
Reviews, Magazines, and other Literary Labors.

'In this plan I calculated nothing on my garden but
amusement.   In the meantime I heard from Birmingham
that Lloyd's father had declared that he should insist on
his son's returning to him at the close of one twelvemonth.
What am I to do then?   I shall be again afloat on the
wide sea, unpiloted and unprovisioned.   I determined
to devote *my whole day* to the acquirement of practical
horticulture, to part with Lloyd immediately, and live
without a servant.   Lloyd intreated me to give up the
Review and Magazine, and devote the evenings to him,
but this would be to give up a permanent for a temporary
situation, and after subtracting £40 from C. Ll.'s £80
in return for the Review business, and then calculating
the expense of a Servant, a less severe mode of general
living, and Lloyd's own Board and Lodging, the remaining
£40 would make but a poor figure.   And what was I
to do at the end of the twelvemonth?   In the meantime
Mrs. Fricker's son could not be got out as an apprentice—
he was too young, and premiumless, and no one would
take him ; and the old lady herself manifested a great
aversion to leaving Bristol.   I recurred therefore to my
first promise of allowing her £20 a year; but all her
furniture must of course be returned, and enough only
remains to furnish one bedroom and a kitchen-parlour.

'If Charles Lloyd and the servant went with me

I must have bought new furniture to the amount
of £40 or £50, which, if not Impossibility in person, was Impossibility's first cousin. We determined
to live by ourselves. We arranged our time, money,
and employments. We found it not only practicable, *but easy*—and Mrs. Coleridge entered with enthusiasm into the scheme. To Mrs. Coleridge the
nursing and sewing only would have belonged; the rest
I took upon myself, and since our resolution have been
learning the practice. With only two rooms and two
people—their wants severely simple—no great labour
can there be in their waiting upon themselves. Our
washing we should put out. I should have devoted my
whole Head, Heart, and Body to my Acre and a half of
garden land, and my evenings to Literature. Mr. and
Mrs. Estlin approved, admired, and applauded the
scheme, and thought it not only highly virtuous, but
highly prudent. In the course of a year and a half I
doubt not that I should feel myself independent, for my
bodily strength would have increased, and I should have
been weaned from animal food, so as never to touch it but
once a week; and there can be no shadow of a doubt
that an acre and a half of land, divided properly, and
managed properly, would maintain a small family in
everything but cloathes and rent. What had I to ask of
my friends? Not money—for a temporary relief of my
wants is nothing, removes no gnawing of anxiety, and
debases the dignity of the Man. Not their interest—what
could their interest (supposing they had any) do for me?
I can accept no place in State, Church, or Dissenting
Meeting. Nothing remains possible but a School, or
Writer to a newspaper, or my present plan. I could not

love the man who advised me to keep a school, or write
for a newspaper. He must have a hard heart! What
then could I ask of my friends? What of Mr. Wade?
Nothing. What of Mr. Cottle? Nothing. . . . What of
Thomas Poole? O! a great deal. Instruction, daily
advice, society—everything necessary to my feelings
and the realization of my innocent independance. You
know it would be impossible for me to learn *everything*
myself. To pass across my garden once or twice a day,
for five minutes, to set me right, and cheer me with the
sight of a friend's face, would be more to me than hundreds. Your letter was *not* a kind one. One week only
and I must leave my house, and yet in one week you
advise me to alter the plan which I had been three
months forming, and in which you must have known by
the letters I wrote you, during my illness, that I was
interested even to an excess and violence of Hope. And
to abandon this plan for darkness, and a renewal of
anxieties which might be fatal to me! Not one word
have you mentioned how I am to live, or even exist,
supposing I were to go to Acton. Surely, surely, you do
not advise me to lean with the whole weight of my
necessities on the Press? Ghosts indeed! I should be
haunted with Ghosts enough—the Ghosts of Otway and
Chatterton, and the phantasms of a wife broken-hearted,
and a hunger-bitten Baby! O Thomas Poole! Thomas
Poole! if you did but know what a Father and a Husband
must feel who toils with his brain for uncertain bread!
I dare not think of it. The evil face of Frenzy looks at
me. The Husbandman puts his seed in the ground, and
the goodness, power, and wisdom of God have pledged
themselves that he shall have Bread, and Health, and

quietness in return for industry, and simplicity of wants, and innocence. The AUTHOR scatters his seed—with aching head, and wasted health, and all the heart-leapings of anxiety; and the folly, the vices, and the fickleness of man promise him Printers' Bills and the Debtors' Side of Newgate as full and sufficient payment.

'Charles Lloyd is at Birmingham. I hear from him daily. In his yesterday's letter he says: "My dearest friend! everything seems clearing around me. My friends enter fully into my views. They seem altogether to have abandoned any ambitious views on my account. My health has been very good since I left you; and I own I look forward with more pleasure than ever to a permanent connection with you. Hitherto I could only look forward to the pleasures of a year. All beyond was dark and uncertain. My father now completely acquiesces in my abandoning the prospect of any Profession or Trade. If God grant me health, there now remains no obstacle to a completion of my most sanguine wishes." Charles Lloyd will furnish his own Room, and feels it his duty to be in all things his own servant. He will put up a Press-bed, so that one room will be his bedchamber and parlour; and I shall settle with him the hours and seasons of our being together, and the hours and seasons of our being apart. But I shall rely on him for nothing except his own maintenance.

'As to the Poems, they are Cottle's property, not mine. There is no obstacle from me—no new poems intended to be put in the volume, except the "Visions of the Maid of Orleans." . . . But Literature, though I shall never abandon it, will always be a secondary object with me. My poetic Vanity and my political *Furor* have been exhaled ; and I would rather be an expert, self-maintaining Gardener than a Milton, if I could not unite both.

'*My Friend,* wherein I have written impetuously, pardon me! and consider what I have suffered, and still am suffering, in consequence of your letter. . . . *Finally, my Friend ! if your opinion of me, and your attachment to me, remain unaltered, and if you have assigned the true Reasons which urged you to dissuade me from a settlement at Stowey, and if indeed (provided such settlement were consistent with my good and happiness) it would give you unmixed Pleasure, I adhere to Stowey, and consider the time from last Evening as a distempered Dream. But if any circumstances have occurred that have lessened your Love, or Esteem, or Confidence ; or if there be objections to my settling in Stowey on your own account, or any other objections than what you have urged, I doubt not you will declare them openly and unreservedly to me, in your answer to this,* which I shall expect with a total incapability of doing, or thinking of, anything, till I have received it. Indeed, indeed, I am very miserable. God bless you and your affectionate

'S. T. COLERIDGE.

' *Tuesday, December* 13, 1796.'

The italics are S. T. C.'s, as is also the employment of capital letters as a minor means of conveying emphasis.

There is a passage in Cottle's *Reminiscences* which would lead one to suspect that some of Coleridge's Bristol friends were a little aggrieved at the prospect of losing him, just when a hope

had dawned that he really was settled among
them.   He had removed from Redcliff Hill to a
more comfortable house at Kingsdown.   Charles
Lloyd was to live with him, and to 'contribute
liberally' to the expenses of the household.
'Friends were kind and numerous.   Books of all
kinds were at his command.   Of the literary
society in Bristol he had expressed himself in
terms of warm approval.'   This, Cottle thought,
'looked like permanence,' and if 'the promise was
fallacious,' whose was the fault but Mr. Poole's,
who, 'desirous of obtaining Mr. C. as a neighbour,'
had 'recommended him to take a small house at
Nether Stowey, then to be let at seven pounds a
year, which he thought would well suit him.'

It may be that representations may have been
addressed to Tom Poole, by Cottle and others,
desiring him to consider whether, in encouraging
his friend to settle in Stowey, he was advising him
for his good, and enumerating all the advantages
he would lose by leaving Bristol, and that the
epistle which threw Coleridge into such indignant
grief, the 'hasty and heart-chilling letter,' was
simply the result of some such remonstrances
having awakened in Tom Poole's mind a sense
that it was a duty to put the reverse side of the
question very emphatically before his friend's mind.
It is also possible that he was himself uneasy at

the impracticable nature of Coleridge's plan for living by the labour of his hands, and dreaded the disappointment certain to arise should he ever attempt to realise it. Or else, as Coleridge thought for he tosses all the apparent objections aside like cobwebs, and fastens upon the point that there is certainly something else which has not been allowed to appear—something had been said or done in Stowey to make Tom Poole anxious and doubtful whether Coleridge had better come at all. Seeing, however, that his whole heart was ardently fixed upon this one thing, what could Poole do but just let him have his way, and give all the help he could?

The latest letter of the year[1] is written by S. T. Coleridge as it were in the very act of starting for Bristol :—

'MY DEAR POOLE—I wrote to you with improper impetuosity; but I had been dwelling so long on the circumstance of living near you, that my mind was thrown by your letter into the feelings of those distressful dreams where we imagine ourselves falling from precipices. I seemed falling from the summit of my fondest desires, whirled from the height just as I had reached it.

'We shall want none of the Woman's furniture; we have enough for ourselves. What with Boxes of Books, and Chests of Drawers, and Kitchen Furniture, and Chairs, and our Bed and Bed-linen, etc., we shall have enough to

[1] Undated. Endorsed December 1796.

fill a small Waggon, and to-day I shall make inquiry among my trading acquaintance whether it would be cheaper to hire a Waggon to take them straight to Stowey, than to put them in the Bridgwater Waggon. Taking in the double trouble and expence of putting them in the Drays to carry them to the public Waggon, and then seeing them packed again, and again to be unpacked and packed at Bridgwater, I much question whether our goods would be good for anything.

'I am very poorly, not to say ill. My face monstrously swollen; my recondite eye sits quaintly behind the flesh-hill, and looks as little as a tomtit's. And I have a sore throat that prevents me eating aught but spoon-meat without great pain. And I have a rheumatic complaint in the back part of my head and shoulders. Now all this demands a small portion of Christian patience, taking in our present circumstances. My Apothecary says it will be madness for me to walk to Stowey on Tuesday, as, in the furious zeal of a new Convert to Economy, I had resolved to do. My wife will stay a week or fortnight after me; I think it not improbable that the weather may break up by that time. However, if I do not get worse, I will be with you by Wednesday or Thursday at the furthest, so as to be there before the Waggon. Is there any grate in the house? I should think we might Rumfordize one of the chimneys. I shall bring down with me a dozen yards of green list. I can endure cold, but not a cold room. If we can but contrive to make two rooms *warm* and *wholesome*, we will laugh in the faces of Gloom and Ill-lookingness.

'I shall lose the post if I say a word more. You thoroughly and in every nook and corner of your heart

forgive me for my letters? Indeed, indeed, Poole! I
know no one whom I esteem more—no one friend whom
I love so much. But bear with my Infirmities! God
bless you, and your grateful and affectionate

'S. T. COLERIDGE.

'*Sunday Morning*' [*? December* 18, 1796].

' He commenced his residence in Nether Stowey,
according to this letter,' is the entry opposite No.
17 in Mr. Thomas Poole's catalogue. It was in
all probability in the Christmas week of 1796.

CHAPTER XII

'. . . Beside one friend,
Beneath the impervious covert of one oak,
I've raised a lowly shed, and know the names
Of husband and of father ; not unhearing
Of that divine and nightly-whispering voice
Which, from my childhood to maturer years,
Spake to me of predestinated wreaths
Bright with no fading colours ! '

COLERIDGE (*May* 26, 1797).

IN after years, when the Coleridge family had
removed to the north of England, and Coleridge
himself had drifted gradually into an almost complete cessation of intercourse with his oldest friends,
it began to be a custom that Mrs. Coleridge should,
as often at least as once a year, take pen in hand
and write a long letter to Mr. Tom Poole, entering
into the minutest details concerning her children
and surroundings, and always giving the latest intelligence in her possession of her husband's state
of health and spirits.   These letters were evidently
a pleasure to her to write, and they were undoubt-
edly much valued by Mr. Poole, yet when the long

and closely-written sheet was finished, she often seems to have been half inclined to question whether such very domestic records were really worth posting, and she frequently ends with a kind of apology for sending them, somewhat after the fashion of the following extract from a letter written in April 1819, which is inserted here because of the allusion to the home at Stowey into which S. T. Coleridge had installed himself and his family, with such a passion of high-wrought expectation and eager enthusiasm in the last days of 1796 :—

'Dear Mr. Poole,' she writes, at the close of a long letter, overflowing with joy at Hartley's election to the Oriel Fellowship, and full of details about Derwent and Sara, 'I scarcely could have ventured this long and egotistical epistle, if I could ever forget that he whom I address is the same person who, in days long past, made so many and so friendly exertions to render a miserable cottage an abode of comparative comfort.'

Let us hope that that zealous assistance, together with the sweet-tempered acquiescence of Charles. Lloyd in the 'inconveniences of cottage accommodation,' and 'his gentleness to little Hartley,'[1] may have sufficiently comforted the young mistress of the house to prevent her from disappointing her husband by too complete a want of sympathy. Certainly it would seem so, from the joyful little note

---

[1] See *Biographical Supplement*.

to Cottle (*Early Recollections*, 1837, i. 188), undated, as Coleridge's letters usually are,[1] but which
must have been written in January 1797.   To
another friend [2] he writes :—

'We are *very* happy, and my little David Hartley
grows a sweet boy. . . . I raise potatoes and all
manner of vegetables; have an orchard; and shall raise
corn (with the spade) enough for my family. We have
two pigs, and ducks and geese. A cow would not
answer to keep; for we have whatever milk we want
from T. Poole.'

Nevertheless, Mrs. Coleridge was not altogether
wrong when she remembered the house as a
'miserable cottage,' and, indeed, the day was not
far distant when Coleridge himself would write of
it as 'the old hovel.'   It is now transformed into
a small public-house, and, even thus, it is a better
and larger house than it was when Coleridge
inhabited it, for its size has been increased by the
addition of a miscellaneous block of building at
the back.   In Coleridge's time it would seem to
have consisted of two small and rather dark little
parlours, one on each side of the front-door, look-

---

[1] Fortunately Mr. Poole was in the habit of endorsing all those
which he received with the date of the month and the year in which
he received them.   Later on he had such letters, or parts of letters,
as were of general interest copied into a book by Thomas Ward.
This book was, I believe, given by him to the Coleridge family after
S. T. C.'s death.

[2] Thelwall, February 6, 1797.

ing straight into the street, and a small kitchen behind, wholly destitute of modern conveniences, and where the fire was made on the hearth in the most primitive manner conceivable. There cannot have been more than three, or, at most, four bedrooms above. The back-door gave access to a long strip of kitchen garden, along the bottom of which was the lane through which the communication into Tom Poole's garden, which ran down from another part of the town into the same lane, was effected. That a man of a strongly meditative turn, and whose chief occupations were study and composition, should adventure himself with a wife, a young baby, and a boarder, into a house which offered no practicable means of securing to himself any private retreat, where he could enjoy freedom from interruption, and whose close neighbourhood to the street must have brought with it a good deal of quite unavoidable noise and disturbance, reads like the height of rashness ; and we have, besides, to remember that, small as the cottage might be, and slender as were the resources of the family, they were rarely without visitors, who followed one another in a constant succession of distinguished names.

But then there was always Tom Poole's house close at hand, with the quiet 'Book-room' upstairs, where Coleridge could always take refuge ; or, if

the weather permitted working out of doors, there
was the 'Jasmine *H*arbour,' in Tom Poole's garden,
celebrated by Cottle as the scene of that idyllic
feast on 'bread and cheese and true Taunton ale,'
when there seemed to be 'downright witchery in
the provisions,' every one was so happy; and pretty
young Mrs. Coleridge, coming out to join them
with her boy in her arms, appeared like a poetic
embodiment of the idea of Woman, bringing with
her the 'smile of home' to complete the charm
of that delicious day. I do not think that rustic
arbour was, in itself, a particularly romantic spot,
but Coleridge so delighted in it that he called it
his 'Elysium.' In the copy of the first edition of
his *Poems*, which he gave Tom Poole on April 11,
1796, the following allusion is to be found in a
few lines written by him in the first page, where,
after saying that he sends his poems to Tom Poole
with a better heart than he should to most others,
because he knows *that he will read them with
affection*, he adds—

'I love to shut my eyes, and bring up before my
imagination that Arbour, in which I have repeated
so many of these compositions to you. Dear Arbour!
An Elysium to which I have often passed by your Cerberus, and Tartarean tan-pits!'

So the experiment of living at Stowey was by
no means a failure, though it worked out, as many

experiments do, quite differently from the anticipations and intentions of the projector.   But then
it must be allowed that Coleridge's scheme of life
and labour had been a perfectly impracticable
one, and Tom Poole was not the only person who
had misgivings.   'You seem to have set your
heart upon this same cottage plan ; and God
prosper you in the experiment !' wrote Charles
Lamb to his old schoolfellow on October 28,
1796.[1]   And when the removal from Bristol is
an accomplished fact, he sends his congratulations,
wishes success to all Coleridge's projects, and 'bids
fair peace' be to that house ; but still—

'Do, in your next letter,' he adds a little later,
'and that right soon, give me some satisfaction respecting
your present situation in Stowey.   Is it a farm you have
got ?   And what does your worship know about farming ?'

What indeed ?   But, in truth, what became of
the farming and gardening part of Coleridge's
plan may be easily judged from the well-known
anecdote in his *Table Talk* (July 27, 1830).

'Thelwall thought it very unfair to influence a child's
mind by inculcating any opinions before it should come
to years of discretion, and be able to choose for itself.   I
showed him my garden, and told him it was my botanical
garden.   "How so?" said he ; "it is covered with weeds."
"Oh," I replied, "*that* is only because it has not yet

---

[1] Talfourd's *Letters of C. Lamb.*

come to its age of discretion and choice. The weeds, you see, have taken the liberty to grow, and I thought it unfair in me to prejudice the soil towards roses and strawberries." '

How Thelwall must have laughed to himself if he remembered a certain letter [1] in which Coleridge had described himself as getting up before breakfast to work in his garden *from seven to half-past eight*—that is to say, before sunrise in the chilly month of February ! But that, if it were anything more than an over-confident forecast of unaccomplished intentions, certainly betokened a zeal too extravagant for continuance.

It was not till almost the end of the time of roses, and long after the time of strawberries, that Thelwall first made his appearance in Stowey, thereby exciting no little commotion in the minds of many, and reviving all the prejudices against Tom Poole's literary friends as Jacobins and Atheists, which had become fixed in the general mind by that unlucky and oft-repeated anecdote of the remarks of *isti duo ignoti*, now certainly no longer *ignoti*, upon the death of Robespierre. Thelwall was, of course, drawn thither by the presence of Coleridge, with whom he had been for some time in correspondence, though they had never met. The fact that Thelwall had suffered

---

[1] Coleridge to Thelwall, February 6, 1797. Mr. Cosens' Collection.

imprisonment for his political utterances, and that
he was even then—to use his own word,[1] which is
not at all too vehement for the occasion—being
'hunted from society' by a social persecution of
a very unrelenting kind, had strongly excited
Coleridge's sympathies, and his letters abound
with the most cordial overtures of friendship,
though without any attempt to disguise that on
the great question of religion their convictions
are wide as the poles asunder.   When a complete edition of Coleridge's best letters comes
to be published, perhaps few will be read with
deeper admiration than one written from Bristol in
December 1796, in which Coleridge remonstrates
with Thelwall for having *spoken contemptuously* of
the Christian religion, and charges him with anti-
religious bigotry.   And yet—

'I write freely, Thelwall!' he says, 'for though *personally* unknown, I really love you, and I can count but
few human beings whose hand I would welcome with a
more hearty grasp of friendship. . . .'

And though he does show how unworthy of
any man who can think and feel is the attitude of
contempt towards the convictions of others, he is
not so much eager to prove an opponent in the
wrong as he is to set forth, with all the glow and
fervour of a believing heart, the glory and beauty

[1] Prefatory Memoir to the 'Fairy of the Lake,' by John Thelwall.

of the Christian hope, the loftiness and purity of the Christian standard of morals.

Thelwall had given up politics, and was anxiously in search of some peaceful retreat, where he might make, 'if not a comfortable, at least a quiet establishment for his encreasing family'; and it may not be irrelevant to remark that he was 'particularly happy' in his 'domestic' relations. His 'Stella' has been described as the 'good angel of his life,' and the friends at Stowey admired in him not only 'a man of extraordinary talent,' but a most 'affectionate husband and a good father.' Much more than in the neighbourhood of Bristol, whence Coleridge once wrote to him [1]—

'we have an hundred lovely scenes about Bristol which would make you exclaim, O admirable *Nature!* and me, O Gracious *God!*'

—did 'lovely scenes' abound in the vicinity of Stowey to make it very soon apparent that 'Citizen Thelwall,' though 'brought up in the city on a tailor's board,' was acutely sensible to that beauty of nature which was as the breath of life itself to Wordsworth and Coleridge, to Lloyd and to Thomas Poole; and he could talk brilliantly, and listen with appreciation, how was it possible but that he should be often in their society, even

[1] Coleridge to Thelwall, 1796. Mr. Cosens' Collection.

though he was opposed to many of their most cherished opinions, and in such bad odour, both theologically and politically, that they cultivated his acquaintance at the peril of the many inconveniences involved in becoming objects of popular suspicion ?

This, however, was later in the year. Coleridge's first visitor, and a very frequent one, seems to have been poor George Burnett—the wreck of Pantisocracy, listless, disappointed, broken in spirit, and utterly unable to turn his energies into some more practical channel. He was the clever son of a Somersetshire farmer, probably the very ' Mr. Burnett' who in March 1793 carried with him up to Oxford a letter of introduction from Tom Poole to his Cousin John :—

' He comes to Oxford,' wrote Tom Poole, ' entirely alone, and he will consider himself much obliged to you if you will assist him on his entrance into the University, and give him your advice respecting the arrangements it will be necessary for him to make. . . . He is a young man, I believe, of good dispositions and good sense, and enters into his present line of life with a full conviction that he has nothing to expect but from his own merits. This I esteem a good groundwork on which valuable acquisitions generally arise. . . . One circumstance may be mentioned : he has some acquaintance with Mr. White, Vicar of Huntspill, who, from Burnett's account, will be very ready to lend him any

assistance in his power, as I believe his father was one
of the few who did not molest Mr. White in his parish.
As Burnett designs entering at Baliol, Mr. W. may be
of some use to him. . . .'

Now the village of Huntspill lies between
Stowey and the Mendip Hills, and almost opposite
the ford at Combwich (Cummage, Coleridge
spells it), and the road to Bristol, whether from
Stowey, Bridgwater, or Huntspill, being across
the Mendips, nothing could be more easily within
probability than such an encounter as happened
to Coleridge once, when, 'during a pedestrian
excursion in Somersetshire,' he was asked by a
countrywoman whether he knew 'one Coleridge,
of Bristol,' and on answering that he had heard
of him, became the involuntary auditor of a violent
denunciation of *himself* as the 'vile Jacobin
villain' whose pernicious eloquence had drawn
away 'a young man of our parish, one Burnett.'

Coleridge, appreciating the humour of the
situation, listened very particularly, said 'dear
me!' several times, and in fine, so 'won the
woman's heart by his civilities that he had not
the courage to undeceive her.' And yet, perhaps,
when it became more and more evident how little
Burnett possessed the necessary strength to recover from a lost illusion, though neither Coleridge
nor Southey are to be blamed for his want of

moral stamina, a time may have arrived when the recollection of that country-wife's words cannot have been without pain.

Presently Coleridge, absent in Bristol attending to the publication of the joint volume in which his own poems were to appear together with those of Lamb and Lloyd, was recalled to Stowey by the news that Burnett was 'very ill with jaundice,' and returned to find him 'ill enough, Heaven knows'—as he writes to Cottle (p. 141).

'I wish,' he adds in a quaint postscript, 'my pockets were as yellow as George's phiz.'

A smaller trouble, incidentally mentioned in the same letter, is that the cottage is overrun with mice, which, says Coleridge—

'Play the very devil with us. It irks me to set a trap. By all the whiskers of all the pussies that have mewed . . . since the days of Whittington, it is not fair. 'Tis telling a lie. 'Tis as if you said, "Here is a bit of toasted cheese: come, little mice! I invite you!" when (O, foul breach of the rites of hospitality!) I mean to assassinate my too credulous guests. No! I cannot set a trap, but I should vastly like to make a Pitt-fall (smoke the pun?). But, concerning the mice, advise thou, lest there be famine in the land. Such a year of scarcity! Inconsiderate mice! Well, well, so the world wags. . . .'

Sure proof that the stress of life has relaxed, and that the whole man is, for the moment, at ease and happy, when the spirit of fun awakes, and he breaks forth into drolleries. This is a special characteristic of Coleridge at Stowey. A very small matter will set him off into some grotesque joke, a gambol rather than a play of wit, sometimes without much point, sometimes extremely humorous, sometimes disfigured by a mischievous and, as it were, *elvish* delight, in shocking ears polite with coarse expressions. It is curious to remember that in the character of Hamlet, between whom and Coleridge it is no new thing to trace the remarkable resemblance, there is the same combination of a deep refinement of nature, and a spirit that is most at home on the rarest intellectual heights, with a fantastic inclination to the grotesque, giving us strange shocks of astonishment at seemingly incongruous outbreaks of irrelevant and superficial coarseness. Coleridge not unfrequently jars upon the sensitiveness of a severely exclusive taste in precisely the same way, by some deliberately clumsy joke, unsavoury metaphor, outrageous pun, or over-homely simile. The cause is perhaps to be sought in an involuntary relaxation of nature, seeking relief from tension by an antic or a caper. In after years the impulse passes away, and men take their relaxation in silence, but almost all vigorous natures have it in boyhood.

Here, for instance, is a grotesque gambol in

rhyme, scribbled on the back of a prospectus of his own lectures, and addressed to T. Poole, one day in January 1797.[1]

> 'Plucking flowers from the Galáxy [2]
> On the pinions of Abstraction,
> I did quite forget to ax 'e,
> Whether you have an objaction,
> With us to swill 'e and to swell 'e
> And make a pigstie of your belly.
> A lovely limb most dainty
> Of a *ci-devant* Mud-raker,
> I makes bold to acquaint 'e
> We've trusted to the Baker ;[3]
> And underneath it satis
> Of that subtérrene apple
> By the Erudite 'clep'd *taties*—
> With which, if you'd wish to grapple,
> As sure as I'm a sloven,
> The Clock will not strike twice one,
> When the Dish will be out of the Oven,
> And the dinner will be a nice one.'

And who but Coleridge—or Hamlet—would ever have used the following comparison in speaking of some poems sent by him to Cottle ?—

---

[1] 'S. T. Coleridge proposes to give in six lectures a Comparative View of the English Rebellion under Charles the First, and the French Revolution.'

[2] Evidently a caricature of Poole's own line—

> 'He's gone—for us to cull celestial sweets
> Amid the flow'rets of the milky way."

[3] The 'miserable cottage' did not possess an oven.

' . . . If you do not like these verses, or if you do not think them worthy of an edition in which I profess to give *nothing but my choicest fish, picked, gutted, and clean'd,* get somebody to write them out, and send them, with my compliments, to the editor of the new Monthly Magazine. . . .'

During the early months of 1797, Coleridge seems to have been often to and fro between Bristol and Stowey ; and, at last, in May the joint volume appeared, with, among other novelties, the sonnets on the birth of Hartley, the lines on leaving Clevedon, and the 'Dedication' to his brother George. Lamb's poems were dedicated to his sister ; and the letter in which he asks Coleridge's opinion upon this is so touching and characteristic that I think most of my readers will not be sorry to see it quoted here, though those who are already acquainted with Lamb's letters will remember it quite well :—

' . . . I have another sort of dedication,' Lamb writes, 'for my few things, which I want to know if you approve of, and can insert. I mean to inscribe them to my sister. It will be unexpected, and it will give her plea-sure ; or do you think it will look whimsical at all ? As I have not spoke to her about it I can easily reject the idea. But there is a monotony in the affections which people living together, or, as we do now, very frequently seeing each other, are apt to give in to ; a sort of indif-ference in the expression of kindness for each other,

which demands that we should sometimes call to our aid
the trickery of surprise. . . .

' I am wedded, Coleridge, to the fortunes of my sister,
and of my poor old father. O, my friend! I think
sometimes could I recall the days that are past, which
among them should I choose? Not those "merrier
days," not the "pleasant days of hope," not those
"wanderings with a fair-haired maid," which I have so
often and so feelingly regretted, but the days, Coleridge,
of a *mother's* fondness for her *schoolboy*. What would I
give to call her back to earth for *one* day!—on my knees
to ask her pardon for all those little asperities of temper
which, from time to time, have given her gentle spirit
pain!—and the day, my friend, I trust will come.
There will be "time enough" for kind offices of love,
if " Heaven's eternal year" be ours. . . . O my friend,
cultivate the filial feelings! and let no one think himself
released from the kind "charities" of relationship; these
shall give him peace at the last; these are the best
foundation for every species of benevolence. I rejoice to
hear . . . that you, my friend, are reconciled with all your
relations. 'Tis the most kindly and natural species of
love, and we have all the associated train of early feelings
to secure its strength and perpetuity. . . .'

Shy and sensitive, living always under the
shadow of a heavy family affliction, and almost
entirely isolated from any congenial companionship except that of his sister, the friendship of
Coleridge was the chief treasure and embellish-
ment of Lamb's life, a life of much restraint

and of many limitations, patiently accepted and bravely endured.

> '. . . Believe thou, O my soul,
> Life is a vision shadowy of truth ;
> And vice, and anguish, and the wormy grave,
> Shapes of a dream . . .'

were his favourite lines in the *Religious Musings*. In after years he had many friends, and was, if we may use the expression, free of the whole brotherhood of literature ; but, in early manhood, the appreciation and sympathy which were needed to draw out those special gifts of fine taste and delicate humour which were his by nature, came to him from Coleridge alone ; and the relations between them were peculiarly intimate and affectionate.

'. . . You are the only correspondent, and, I might add, the only friend I have in the world,' Lamb wrote ; 'I go nowhere, and have no acquaintance. Slow of speech, and reserved of manners, no one seeks or cares for my society, and I am left alone. . . . I can only converse with you by letters, and with the dead in their books. My sister, indeed, is all I can wish in a companion ; but our spirits are alike poorly ; our reading and knowledge from the self-same sources ; our communication with the scenes of the world alike narrow. Never having kept separate company, or any company *together*—never having read separate books, and few books *together*—what knowledge have we to convey to each other ? . . .

'I know I am too dissatisfied with the beings around me, but I cannot help occasionally exclaiming, "Woe is me that I am constrained to dwell with Meshech, and to have my habitation among the tents of Kedar." . . . I gain nothing by being with such as myself. We encourage one another in mediocrity. I am always longing to be with men more excellent than myself.'

So wrote Lamb in 1796-97 ; but before the end of the latter year almost all Coleridge's closest friends were his friends also. He had become one of the Stowey set, as it may not incorrectly be called, since Stowey was the centre of meeting, his name to be henceforward inseparable from theirs, and to be caricatured and celebrated, admired and abused, as one of that much honoured, and much vituperated company. The first extension of his acquaintance in that direction was a visit from Charles Lloyd, who, being in London in the winter of 1797, called upon Lamb as a friend of Coleridge's. Lloyd was deficient in humour, but he had great refinement of literary taste and feeling; his uncertain health and spirits were an appeal to pity and sympathy, and his gentle, quiet manner was very congenial to Lamb, who expressed his pleasure at the unexpected visit in the verses—

'Alone, obscure, without a friend,
A cheerless, solitary thing,
Why seeks my Lloyd the stranger out,

What offering can the stranger bring
Of social scenes, homebred delights,
That him in aught compensate may,
For Stowey's pleasant winter nights,
For loves and friendships far away?'

Of course Coleridge, least consecutive and most parenthetical of mortals, did sometimes vex Lamb's gentle, self-distrustful spirit, by unaccountable intervals of silence; but, as a rule, the letters seem to have been just what Lamb's heart and mind craved for. In 1797 they always contained a pressing invitation to come with his sister and visit Stowey; but Lamb was but a clerk in the India House, with a slender salary, and one short annual holiday, of which he could not himself fix the time.

'I will come as soon as I can,' he wrote, 'but I dread naming a probable time. It depends on fifty things, besides the expense, which is not nothing. . . . As to——, caprice may grant what caprice only refused, and it is no more hardship, rightly considered, to be dependent on him for pleasure, than to lie at the mercy of the rain and sunshine for the enjoyment of a holiday. In either case we are not to look for a suspension of the laws of nature—"Grill will be Grill." *Vide* Spenser.[1] . . .'

Unless we are to consider the matter decided by the date 'June 1797' prefixed to Coleridge's

---

[1] *Faery Queen*, Book II. Canto xii.

lines, 'This Lime-tree bower my prison,' it is a little difficult to be sure at what particular period the 'laws of nature' relented, and Lamb got his holiday; for he, like Coleridge, was not in the habit of dating his letters, and the one which speaks of his visit to Stowey has been assigned to the year 1800, a manifestly impossible date. From internal evidence it would seem to have been written just *before* Thelwall's first appearance on the scene, which we know to have been in July 1797.[1]

'I am scarcely yet so reconciled to the loss of you,' Lamb writes, on his return to town, 'or so subsided into my wonted uniformity of feeling, as to sit calmly down to think of you and write to you. But I reason myself into the belief that those few and pleasant holidays shall not have been spent in vain. I feel improvement in the recollection of many a casual conversation. The names of Tom Poole, of Wordsworth and his good sister, with thine and Sara's, are become "familiar in my mouth as household words." You would make me very happy, if you think W. has no objection, by transcribing for me that inscription of his.[2] I have some scattered sentences ever floating on my memory, teasing me that I cannot remember more of it. You may believe I will make no improper use of it.

[1] Since the above was written Canon Ainger's edition of Lamb's Letters has appeared, in which this question is definitely settled. The visit took place in July.

[2] This must have been the 'Lines left upon a Seat by a Yew-tree,' Wordsworth's *Poems* (Edition 1858), vol. i. p. 38.

Believe me I can think now of many subjects on which I had planned gaining information from you ; but I forgot my "treasure's worth" while I possessed it.   Your leg[1] is now become to me a matter of much more importance, and many a little thing which, when I was present with you, seemed scarce to *indent* my notice, now presses painfully on my remembrance.

'Is the Patriot come yet?   Are Wordsworth and his sister gone yet?   I was looking out for John Thelwall all the way from Bridgwater, and had I met him I think it would have moved me almost to tears.   You will oblige me, too, by sending me my greatcoat, which I left behind in the oblivious state the mind is thrown into at parting.   Is it not ridiculous that I sometimes envy that greatcoat lingering so cunningly behind?   At present I have none, so send it to me by a Stowey waggon, if there be such a thing, directing for C. L., No. 45 Chapel Street, Pentonville, near London.   But above all, *that Inscription!* It will recall to me the tones of all your voices, and with them many a remembered kindness to one who could and can repay you all only by the silence of a grateful heart.   I could not talk much while I was with you, but my silence was not sullenness, nor, I hope, from any bad motive ; but, in truth, disuse has made me awkward at it.   I know I behaved myself, particularly at Tom Poole's and at Cruikshanks',[2] most like a sulky child ;

---

[1] See 'This Lime-tree bower my prison,' Coleridge's *Poems*.

[2] A son of Lord Egmont's agent, and known to Poole from boyhood.   He and his wife lived at Stowey, and were pleasant, good-natured young people, though with a taste for show and expense which led to trouble later.   Their garden had a gate into the same lane into which the gardens both of Coleridge and of Poole opened, and this led to frequent meetings and some intimacy.

but company and converse are strange to me. It was kind in you all to endure me as you did.

'Are you and your dear Sara—to me also very dear, because very kind—agreed yet about the management of little Hartley? And how go on the little rogue's teeth? . . .

'My love and thanks to you and all of you.

'C. L.'

It may be well to remind ourselves that this year 1797 was a very critical moment in the history of Europe, by transcribing the following letter, written on May 10, to Poole's old friend Purkis. It is rather a shock to realise that the 'joy' of which it is the expression must have been for Napoleon's second victorious campaign in Italy, and the Preliminaries of Leoben ; but then Napoleon was not yet revealed as the Autocrat of Europe, and we have to remember that, at this stage, Tom Poole and his friends viewed the war as an assault by Government upon the liberties of the French people, and would rejoice at the humiliation of Austria as a popular triumph. It may be mentioned that the Battle of St. Vincent had been fought in February ; Camperdown was yet to come, in October. The mutiny at Spithead had been suppressed in April, that of the Nore was just breaking out. The country was struggling with grave financial difficulties, and Ireland

was on the brink of a rebellion.   Still it was
natural enough that those who had detested the
formation of the First Coalition should rejoice at
its overthrow.

'MY DEAR FRIEND—At the moment of the arrival of
your last letter, I was returned from Bridgwater Market,
and sitting in a meditative state of languor by one side
of the parlour fire, while my mother, Mr. and Mrs. King,
and a neighbour, were playing a rubber of whist at the
other.   My mind had been in an anxious suspense for
the preceding week or ten days respecting the situation
of Buonaparte, which I deemed extremely critical.   On
glancing over your letter an involuntary exclamation
arrested the attention of the card-table.   I read aloud
as well as I could.   It was indeed a letter such as no
man can hope to write, or to receive, more than once in
his life, and I do most cordially congratulate you on the
events there mentioned.   They are in truth the seal of
the liberties of Europe.   I sent for the Bard,[1] and two or
three benevolent souls besides, and we read and re-read
till the heart overwhelmed was sad with joy. . . .

'And now let us see the situation in which we are :
1st, our own internal state ; 2d, our relation to France.
In England the earnest longings of one party for reformation complete and full, and the anticipations of the other,
which, in their own minds, amount almost to certainty,
lead, I think, inevitably to the consummation of the
event ; and these notions are not confined to the
speculative few, but pervade all ranks.   Strange if it
were not so, since such active and opposite means are

[1] S. T. Coleridge.

abroad to induce men to think; events which fill the
heart; incessant conversation; books; but, above all,
the weight of government, which our ministry has cause
to touch and yark every individual where he never felt
it before. The soldiers, as I understand we shall hear
soon, and sailors are awakened; they will no longer be
blind instruments. They must be convinced that they
have due recompense for their exertions, and that those
exertions are for the general good, and not for the support of the privileged. If this be the true state of
society in England, can the present order of things
continue to exist? It would be a moral miracle if it did.
The aristocrats are mad not to give reformation in the
present plan of government, to save themselves and to
prevent revolution. The picture of Ireland is too
horrible to be contemplated. The system carried on
there might have done 500 years ago; but are the men
FOOLS? I really expect the French will get Ireland in
less than six months, if an instant change of measures
does not take place there.

'As to our relations with France: will the French
make peace with us on *any* honourable terms?
If they will, it will be an instance of their modera-
tion. If the war continue, they have nothing to
fear: they will grow rich by it; they will, if they please,
retake their foreign possessions; they will prey on our
commerce; they will keep us in a continual state of
fever by their numerous armies. The only chance we
have is that at present they are satiated with vulgar glory,
and that, if we would change our ministry, and place
men at the head of affairs in whom they could confide,
they would make peace in the spirit of peace, in a spirit

to prevent wars between the two nations in future, and in the world in general, and recall to Frenchmen those ideas of Englishmen which warmed their hearts at the opening of the French Revolution. Such a connection, I do believe, is yet possible ; but it must be by the annihilation, even in thought of those principles by which our Government has been actuated during the present war.

'I have room for no more. I will only add that I have this minute heard of the fresh and dreadful disturbances at Portsmouth. Why has not Parliament sanctioned. what was granted to the sailors? What I alluded to above respecting the military was that I understand various discontents exist among the subalterns respecting pay, etc. . . .

'The Bard is very well—but he must be the only subject of a letter when I write of him particularly. . . .'

As an instance of the clash and conflict of public opinion, this chapter shall conclude with an extract from Charlotte Poole's journal :—

'*June* 4, 1797.—The newspapers are filled with melancholy news from the Fleet, which is still in a state of mutiny, occasioned by the black contrivances of the Democrats, who have got into the Fleet and poisoned the minds of the sailors.'

CHAPTER XIII

M. Guizot avait essayé de caractériser le XVIIIième Siècle en l'appelant, ' Un siècle de sympathie et de confiance, jeune et présomptueuse, mais sincère et humaine, dont les sentiments valaient mieux que les principes et les mœurs, qui a beaucoup failli parcequ'il a trop cru en lui-même, doutant d'ailleurs de tout, mais pour qui il est permis d'espèrer qu'un jour, quand ses fautes paraîtront suffisamment expiées, il lui sera beaucoup pardonné parcequ'il a beaucoup aimé.'—*Histoire des idées morales et politiques en France au XVIIIième Siècle.* Jules Barni.

THE month of June, 1797, was a very notable one in the life of S. T. Coleridge ; it was the month of his visit to Racedown, and first beginnings of intimate friendship with Wordsworth and his sister. Years afterwards, Wordsworth said ' Coleridge is the only *wonderful* man that I ever knew,' and the same epithet ' wonderful' is used to convey the impression made by him at their first meeting. ' He is a *wonderful* man,' wrote Dorothy Wordsworth ; ' his conversation teems with soul, mind, and spirit.' At first she thought him very plain—' that is, for about three minutes ; ' but let him once begin to speak and every other feeling was soon forgotten in astonishment and admiration. The one thing that everybody remembered about his countenance was that they had never seen such eyes in any human face before—light gray eyes they were, 'large and full,' with fine, dark eyebrows, and an overhanging forehead. 'I have the brow of an angel, and the mouth of a beast,'[1] he used to say, in mockery of his own personal appearance. He was quite as much impressed by Wordsworth as Wordsworth was by him, and dwelt with special pleasure upon the rare satisfaction of recognising in his new acquaintance an intellectual giant. 'I speak with heartfelt sincerity,' he wrote to Cottle, 'when I tell you that I feel myself a little man by his side, and yet I do not think myself a less man than I formerly thought myself.' That 'Wordsworth and his exquisite sister' should at once return his visit by coming to see him at Stowey was, of course, his immediate proposal, and as Lloyd was just then at Birmingham, there was a present possibility of accommodating two guests in the cottage at Stowey.

During their fortnight's visit the brother and sister were much delighted with the beautiful neighbourhood, but especially with Coleridge's society. 'There is everything here,' wrote Miss

---

[1] A Stowey tradition told me by Mrs. J. Anstice.

Wordsworth, 'sea, woods as wild as fancy ever painted, brooks clear and pebbly as in Cumberland, villages so romantic. . . .' She describes how she and Wordsworth, 'in a wander by ourselves,' found their way into a *coomb*, which she calls a *dell*, where was concealed a sequestered waterfall, and whose steep sides were covered with 'full-grown timber trees.' Following the course of the brook, and 'prying into its recesses,' they continued their ramble as far as Alfoxden, where they paused to admire the enchanting situation, and indulged in 'dreams of happiness in a little cottage, and passing wishes that such a place might be found out.' A few days later they learnt that Alfoxden itself was to be let, and that at a rent so merely nominal that the sole object seems to have been to keep the house inhabited during the minority of the owner. I hold in my hand the original agreement, written out in Tom Poole's handwriting, and signed by W. Wordsworth and John Bartholomew, who would appear to have been the tenant of the St. Albyn family for the home farm, with some power of subletting the house ; but his exact position is not very easy to determine.

'Mem. of Agreement made the 14th day of July, 1797, between John Bartholomew and William Wordsworth. That is to say, the said John Bartholomew agrees to let the said William Wordsworth Allfoxen House, Furniture,

Gardens, Stables, and Coach-house, and to put him in
immediate possession, to hold the same one year from
Midsummer last, at the rent of twenty-three pounds.
The said John Bartholomew to discharge every rate and
tax whatever, and to keep the premises in good tenant-
able repair.   And the said William Wordsworth agrees in
case he quits the house, &c., at the end of the year, to give
the said John Bartholomew three months' notice.   And
it is further agreed that in case the said William Wordsworth retains the house, &c., beyond the present year, he
shall be allowed by the said John Bartholomew, out of
the rent of £23, any diminution he might secure in the
present assessed taxes.   As witness our hands

' JOHN BARTHOLOMEW.
' WILLIAM WORDSWORTH.

'*Witness*—THOMAS POOLE.'

The whole matter was very quickly arranged,
for within the next two or three days Wordsworth
and his sister, with the child Basil Montagu, of
whom they were just then taking charge, were
established in their new and sufficiently splendid
quarters, of which the following is Dorothy Wordsworth's description :—

'The house is a large mansion, with furniture enough
for a dozen families like ours. . . . The garden is at the
end of the house, and our favourite parlour . . . looks that
way. . . . The front of the house is to the south, but it
is screened from the sun by a high hill which rises immediately from it.   This hill is beautiful, scattered irregularly . . . with trees, and topped with fern. . . . Where-

ever we turn we have woods, smooth downs, and valleys with small brooks running down them ; . . . the hills that cradle these valleys are either covered with fern and bilberries,[1] or oak woods, which are cut for charcoal. . . . Walks extend for miles over the hilltops, the great beauty of which is their wild simplicity : they are perfectly smooth, without rocks. . . .'

Amid these appropriate surroundings Words-worth settled down for the year which was to be both to himself and to Coleridge so 'pleasant' and so 'productive' a time. It is quite a re-lief to miss, in almost all the various mentions of Coleridge which refer to this period, the con-stant notices of pain and suffering that seem to predominate at every other period of his life. He was better in health, and happier in mind, than he had almost ever been before, or ever was to be again. There were moments when he was even radiantly happy. And yet, even here, the harass-ing uncertainty about ways and means could not but follow him. It may have been at the very time when Wordsworth and his sister were staying at the cottage, for the letter makes mention of Wordsworth's conversation, that, on his return from a resultless visit to Bristol, he wrote to Cottle of what he terms—

---

[1] They are called whorts or whortle-berries in the south, bil-berries in the north of England, where also the stems from which the berries are gathered are known as 'bilberry wires.'

'A depression too dreadful to be described—

> "So much I felt my genial spirits droop,
> My hopes all flat ; Nature within me seemed
> In all her functions, weary of herself."

Wordsworth's conversation aroused me somewhat, but, even now, I am not the man I have been, and I think I never shall. A sort of calm hopelessness diffuses itself over my heart. Indeed every mode of life which has promised me bread and cheese has been, one after another, torn away from me ; but God remains. . . .'

He adds that he is in no immediate pecuniary distress, having just received £10 from Lloyd ; but there was, then as always, a total absence of any certain and sufficient expectation of making an income, which weighed like lead upon his spirits. Tom Poole, however, was unceasingly watchful over his friend's worldly affairs, and he lost no time in putting into his hands his own and his brother's subscriptions to the little fund that had been planned a year before, while he wrote to Mr. Estlin and one or two other friends, to remind them of their resolve to repeat the offering that had then been made, if Mr. Coleridge's circumstances should seem to require it. There is a mingled tenderness and dignity in Mr. Poole's letters on this delicate subject, which I think very touching :—

                                        '*June* 5, 1797.

'DEAR LLOYD—When we parted it was, I believe, pretty well understood that some occasional communications should take place between us.   In writing to you it is natural that the main subject should be our dear friend Col., and, indeed, his concerns are the immediate occasion of my letter.   You know, I believe, that last year some of his friends subscribed five guineas apiece, which they presented to him, and pledged themselves to continue the same subscription, if wanted, for seven successive years.   Their object was to relieve his mind from painful anxieties respecting pecuniary concerns, so that it may be left at ease to exert its own great natural energies—not doubting but that those energies would, long before the expiration of that period, procure him more than he wants.   In conformity with this plan, they are now again making the same offering, and I am certain that if I permitted a thing of this kind to pass over without informing you of it, you would justly complain of my unkindness. You will, I know, become one of us.

'The money is remitted to Estlin, who is treasurer-general in this little concern, and by him sent to Col. If you know any who are worthy to become members of this little society, apply to them, and get the money remitted accordingly.   I say worthy, for, in truth, I know not what purity of heart it requires to present, with due associations, such assistance to such a man.   All this you are more capable of feeling than any one I know, and to your discretion I refer it. . . .

'I observed in one of your letters to Col. you reminded me of transmitting to you the letters I received from him containing an account of his life.[1]   The truth is I have as yet received but two.   I excuse him; for his mind has been, and is, deeply engaged in the pro-

[1] These letters are printed in the *Supplement* to the *Biog. Lit.*

duction of his tragedy.   Three acts are completed.   The
remaining two will, he says, be finished in a week.   What
is written is deeply interesting and admired by all. . . .
He has reproduced all his former with many new
excellences, and I have little hesitation in saying he will
be more admired in dramatick than in any other species
of writing.   At Stowey we are much as you left us.   My
dear mother still suffers daily.   She desires to be kindly
remembered to you. . . . From your sincere friend,

'THOS. POOLE.'

The letter to Mr. Estlin was written the same
day.

'MY DEAR SIR—Some time ago Mr. Garnett[1] of Bristol
was here at Stowey, and he being a sincere wellwisher
of our dear friend Coleridge, we had some confidential
conversation respecting him.   Mr. Garnett was no
stranger to the plan we last year proposed, and in part
executed.   I stated to him that, according to our agreement, it was necessary we should again come forward, and
desired him to call on you, and make the necessary
arrangements.   He promised he would, and give me
a line in a few days.   However, I have heard nothing
from him.

'This, I am sure, knowing him as I do, arises from no
unfriendly disposition to the cause, but to that incomprehensible habit of procrastination, to which he, and such
men as he, are subject.   You will now, my dear Sir, see
him, Dr. Beddoes, and Coleridge's other friends, and
state to them what we are doing.   You must be treasurer,

---

[1] This must have been Poole's American friend, the inventor of
the 'anti-friction rollers' and the 'new bark mill.'

and through you the money must reach our Bard. Do not apply but to those who love him, for it requires affection and purity of heart to offer, with due associations, assistance of this nature to such a man. I have paid him my subscription and will receive my brother's for him, and I have written to Lloyd who will, I doubt not, write to you. We are going on pretty much as when you were at Stowey. Coleridge is industrious, considering the exertion of mind necessary when he works. The race-horse cannot always be on the turf. He has committed three acts of the tragedy to paper; the other two have being, but as yet in the chambers of his brain. He promises to produce them in a week. All who have seen what he has written admire it. I refer you to Mr. Garnett for our opinion. . . . Believe me, my dear Sir, your very sincere friend,   THOS. POOLE.

'*P.S.*—Coleridge preached an excellent sermon at Bridgwater last Sunday, on the necessity of religious zeal in these times. Most of the better people in the town were present, and I believe all admired him.'

The rough draft of the first act of Coleridge's tragedy of *Osorio*, as it was then called, was left in Thomas Poole's hands, and I have it by me as I write. It is scribbled on a quire of common paper, stitched into the form of a rude copy-book, and has, it would seem, been a good deal carried about in the pocket between Stowey and Alfoxden. Wordsworth, too, was busy with a tragedy, the heaviest and most unreadable thing he ever wrote,

and in spite of Poole's admiration, it must be
admitted that Coleridge's tragedy too (*Remorse*)
is very far from being a success, though it can be
read with pleasure, and is full of noble and elevated
feeling.   Both poets were giving sedulous toil and
pains [1] to produce a kind of work that was alien to
their special gifts, and it is a curious instance of
the paralysis of the critical faculty, which scarcely
any one can escape in judging his own work, that
neither of these great poets realised at the time that
that which had been so laboriously accomplished
was below the level of his own reputation.   Only,
side by side with the *Magnum Opus*, Wordsworth
wrote, for pure pleasure, some of his most delicious
lyrics, and Coleridge composed the first part of
Christabel, and *The Ancient Mariner*.

John Thelwall was expected in Stowey, as it
would seem, on the very day of the Lambs'
departure.   A letter from him to his wife, dated
Alfoxden, July 18, 1797, describes his actual
arrival (Mr. Cosens' Collection) :—

'Everything but my Stella and my babes,' he writes,
'are now banished from my mind by the enchanting
retreat (the Academus of Stowey) from which I write
this, and by the delightful society of Coleridge and of

[1] 'My tragedy employed *and strained* all my thoughts and
faculties for six or seven months ; Wordsworth consumed far more
time, and far more thought, and far more genius.'—Coleridge to
Cottle, *Reminiscences*, p. 176.

Wordsworth, the present occupier of Allfox Den. We have been having a delightful ramble to-day among the plantations, and along a wild, romantic dell in these grounds, through which a foaming, rushing, murmuring torrent of water winds its long artless course. There have we . . . a literary and political triumvirate, passed sentence on the productions and characters of the age, burst forth in poetical flights of enthusiasm, and philosophised our minds into a state of tranquillity, which the leaders of nations might envy, and the residents of cities can never know.'

[Every one will remember Wordsworth's reminiscence, probably of the same occasion. Coleridge exclaimed, 'This is a place to reconcile one to all the jarrings and conflicts of the wide world.' 'Nay,' said Thelwall, 'to make one forget them altogether.']

'Samuel was not at home (he was here) when I arrived last night, nor would Sara have been, but that she had quitted this friendly retreat to superintend the wash-tub. I have spoiled the soapsuds, however. . . . I slept at Coleridge's cot, and this morning we rose by times, and came here time enough to call Samuel and his friend Wordsworth up to breakfast. Faith, we are a most philosophical party . . . the enthusiastic group consisting of C. and his Sara, W. and his sister, and myself, without any servant, male or female. An old woman, who lives in an adjoining cottage, does what is requisite for our simple wants. "Delightful spot, O were my Stella here!" . . .'

[He is thinking of Coleridge's Brockley Coomb
line—

'Delightful spot, O were my Sara here!']

Upon personal acquaintance, Coleridge considered Thelwall

'a very warm-hearted honest man; and disagreeing,
as we do,' he wrote to Cottle, 'on almost every point of
religion, of morals, of politics, and philosophy, we like each
other uncommonly well. He is a great favourite with
Sara. Energetic activity of mind and of heart is his master
feature. He is prompt to conceive, and still prompter
to execute; but I think he is deficient in that patience
of mind which can look intensely and frequently at
the same subject. He believes and disbelieves with
impassioned confidence. I wish to see him doubting.
He is intrepid, eloquent, and honest—perhaps the only
acting democrat that is honest; for the patriots are ragged
cattle, a most execrable herd, arrogant because they are
ignorant, and boastful of the strength of reason because
they have never tried it enough to know its weakness.'

By Coleridge, by Wordsworth, and by Thomas
Poole, Thelwall found himself received with that
perfect kind of tolerance which is, as it were, a
spontaneous effect of nature, therefore happily unconscious of its own merits; and he thus enjoyed
the singular advantage of being able to speak with
absolute freedom on such great subjects as 'religion,
morals, politics, and philosophy,' with men whose
intellectual power he could not but recognise, who

habitually thought much and deeply on those very
subjects, who could listen with patient comprehension, and answer without missing the point of what
had been said, and yet whose conclusions were
entirely opposite to his own.   No wonder that he
made up his mind to use the most earnest endeavours
to find in the same neighbourhood the retired home
that he himself was seeking at that very time.

But the Stowey world shuddered at his very
name, and the feeling with which his appearance
in their neighbourhood was regarded, may be
judged by the following extract from Charlotte
Poole's journal :—

'*July* 23, 1797.—We are shocked to hear that Mr.
Thelwall has spent some time at Stowey this week with
Mr. Coleridge, and consequently with Tom Poole.
Alfoxton house is taken by one of the fraternity, and
Woodlands by another.   To what are we coming?'

Woodlands had been taken by a Mr. Willmott,
the son of a silk manufacturer in Sherborne.   Why
he should be reckoned as 'one of the fraternity' I
cannot tell.   He was a man of singular upright-
ness and activity, and was recommended by Mr.
Poole to the Wedgwoods when they needed a
confidential steward to manage their estates in
Dorsetshire.[1]   But it was a time of great political

---

[1] 'Willmott is extremely useful to me.'—J. Wedgwood to T.
Poole, April 1811.

excitement, and a little thing alarmed the public mind. All sorts of reports began to be circulated as to the presumably dangerous character of men who made Thelwall their chosen associate ; nor, indeed, can it be denied that Thelwall had been guilty of the use of very violent language, and was apt to think it almost a merit to insult the convictions, and outrage the prejudices of those to whom he felt himself opposed.

'Such passages are offensive,' Coleridge once wrote to him, 'they are mere *assertions*, and can, of course, convince no person who thinks differently, and they give pain and irritate.'

His very appearance upon the scene was enough to make the position of all the others well-nigh untenable, and the mischief that had been already done was past undoing, when Coleridge wrote the following letter, representing to Thelwall the reasons that existed why Tom Poole, at any rate, should not be asked to find a house for him in Stowey. The letter is undated, but must certainly have been written from Nether Stowey or Bridgwater, some time in the autumn of 1797 :—

'DEAR THELWALL—This is the first hour that I could write to you anything decisive. I have received an answer from Chubb, intimating that he would undertake the office of procuring you a cottage, provided it was thought right that you should settle *here*. But this (*i.e.* the whole

difficulty) he left for T. Poole and me to settle. . . .
Consequently, the whole returns to its former situation,
and the hope which I had entertained that you could have
settled here, without any, the remotest interference of
Poole, *has vanished.* To such interference on his part
there are insuperable difficulties. The whole malignity
of the Aristocrats will converge to him, as to one point.
His tranquillity will be perpetually interrupted; his
business and his credit hampered and distressed by
vexatious calumnies; the ties of relationship weakened,
perhaps broken; and lastly, his poor old mother made
miserable—the pain of the stone aggravated by domestic
calamity, and quarrels betwixt her son and those neighbours with whom and herself there have been peace and
love for these fifty years.

'Very great odium Tom Poole incurred by bringing
me here; my peaceable manners, and known attachment
to Christianity, had almost worn it away, when Wordsworth came, and he, likewise by T. Poole's agency,
settled here. You cannot conceive the tumult, calumnies,
and apparatus of threatened persecutions which the
event has occasioned round about us. If *you*, too,
should come, I am afraid that even riots, and dangerous
riots, might be the consequence. Either of us separately
would perhaps be tolerated; but *all three* together—
what can it be less than plot and damned conspiracy?—
a school for the propagation of Demagogy and Atheism?

'And it deserves examination whether or no, as
moralists, we should be justified in hazarding the certain
evil of calling forth malignant passions, for the contingent
good that might result from our living in the same
neighbourhood. Add to which; that in point of *public*

interest, we must put into the balance the Stowey Benefit
Club. Of the present utility of this T. Poole thinks
highly—of its possible utility, very, very highly indeed ;
but the interests, nay, perhaps, the existence of this
Club is interwoven with his character as a peaceable and
undesigning man. . . .'

[In Mr. Cosens' Collection.]

So Thelwall must not come to Stowey, or, at
any rate, *not yet.* It is evidently very painful to
Coleridge to have to say so, and yet he cannot
but affirm that this is his ' sad but clear conviction.'

How correct were his anticipations may be
clearly seen in the reception Thelwall met with,
when, after a four months' pedestrian excursion
' in unavailing search for an eligible retreat,' he
took his family to a little farm at Llys-Wen, an
' obscure and romantic ' village in Brecknockshire,
where he hoped, but hoped in vain, to be beyond
the reach of his own notoriety, and to live in
forgotten and undisturbed tranquillity.[1]

Meanwhile, the uneasiness created by his visit
to Stowey was so great that a spy had actually
been employed to watch Wordsworth's movements.
It is curious that it should have been so particularly
upon Wordsworth that popular suspicion fastened,
while Coleridge was left comparatively undisturbed,
but I think the explanation is to be sought for in
the far more strongly marked incomprehensibility

[1] Prefatory Memoir to ' The Fairy of the Lake,' by John Thelwall.

of Wordsworth's character and position. Coleridge was, at any rate, living in the very middle of Stowey. People saw him daily and knew, or thought they knew, all about him. Besides, he had a wife, a comfortable young woman with a baby, just like any one else, who enjoyed talking about the little commonplace concerns of life, and was even indiscreet enough to betray to sympathising friends, how trying it was when Samuel *would*[1] walk up and down composing poetry, instead of coming to bed at proper hours. I have sometimes thought Ophelia might have been like Mrs. Coleridge if she and Hamlet had lived to be married. In her girlish grace and softness she belonged to the very type of woman that a Hamlet, in early youth, most easily falls in love with, for she personifies womanhood to him. In after years the likeness to Polonius would come out more and more ; she would be a loving mother and a careful housewife ; but Hamlet might wake up to perceive that she was a very unsympathetic companion for a man of high intellectual rank, especially if he detected in her a quiet sense of superiority to himself in all practical matters, and a bad habit of frequently wishing that he were a little bit more like other people.

Mrs. Coleridge was, as we have said, exactly

[1] Told me by Miss Ward.

like other people, and her innocent chit-chat may
have been really a kind of protection to her
husband, making every one clearly understand that
he was only a harmless genius, and quite incapable
of conspiring to bring the French over, or anything
else of the sort.   It was otherwise with Wordsworth.   His sister was as great a mystery to the
rustic imagination as he was himself.   The pro-
found seclusion in which they lived, the incomprehensible nature of their occupations, their strange
habit of frequenting out-of-the-way and untrodden
spots, the very presence of an unexplained child
that was no relation to either of them, all combined
to produce an impression of awe and mistrust.
Mrs. St. Albyn became alarmed, and found fault
with Mr. Bartholomew for having let Alfoxden
House to a person concerning whom such unsatisfactory rumours were abroad, and finally Wordsworth received notice to quit in June 1798 ; that
is to say, the moment his first year's tenancy
should expire.

The following letter from Tom Poole apparently
produced no effect ; but it is interesting, and
almost amusing that any one could ever have
needed to be assured of William Wordsworth's
' respectability ' !—

'MADAM—I have heard that Mr. Bartholomew of
Putsham has incurred your displeasure by letting Allfoxen

House to Mr. Wordsworth. As it was through me that Mr. Wordsworth was introduced to Mr. Bartholomew as a tenant, I take the liberty of addressing to you this letter, simply to state the circumstances attending the business, and to say a few words of Mr. Wordsworth and his connections. Mr. Wordsworth happened to be on a visit at Stowey. In the course of a walk he saw Allfoxen, and was delighted with its situation. It was just at that time known . . . that it was to be let. Mr. Wordsworth desired me to apply to Mr. Bartholomew, which I did, and strongly recommended Mr. Wordsworth as a tenant, in consequence of which, after two or three meetings, Mr. Wordsworth took the house of Mr. Bartholomew for a twelvemonth. Mr. Bartholomew knew nothing of Mr. Wordsworth but through me, and therefore can deserve no blame; and I can truly say when he was letting the house he seemed more anxious to have a tenant who would take care of it and not abuse the premises around than to promote his own advantage. These circumstances considered, I am sure your goodness and justice will acquit him of any the least intentional misconduct in this transaction.

'As for Mr. Wordsworth, I believe him to be in every respect a gentleman. I have not known him personally long, but I had heard of his family before I knew him. Dr. Fisher, our late Vicar, and one of the Canons of Windsor, had often mentioned to me as his particular and respected friend, Mr. Cookson, Mr. Wordsworth's uncle, and also one of the Canons of Windsor. This circumstance was sufficient to convince me of the respectability of Mr. Wordsworth's family. You may, upon my honour, rest assured that no tenant could have been found for Alfoxen whom, if you knew him, you would prefer to Mr. Wordsworth. His family is small, consisting of his sister, who has principally lived with her uncle, Mr. Cookson, a child of five years old, the son of a friend of his, and one excellent female servant. Such a family can neither wear nor tear the house or furniture, and I will venture to say they were never both in better order. How different would be the case with a large family—full of careless servants, a run of idle company, hunting, breaking down fences, etc.

'But I am informed you have heard that Mr. Wordsworth does keep company, and on this head I fear the most infamous falsehoods have reached your ears. Mr. Wordsworth is a man fond of retirement—fond of reading and writing—and has never had above two gentlemen at a time with him. By accident Mr. Thelwall, as he was travelling through the neighbourhood, called at Stowey. The person he called on at Stowey took him to Allfoxen. No person at Stowey nor Mr. Wordsworth knew of his coming. Mr. Wordsworth had never spoken to him before, nor, indeed, had any one of Stowey. Surely the common duties of hospitality were not to be refused to any man; and who would not be interested in seeing such a man as Thelwall, however they may disapprove of his sentiments or conduct?

'God knows we are all liable to err, and should bear with patience the difference in one another's opinions. Be assured, and I speak it from my own knowledge, that Mr. Wordsworth, of all men alive, is the last who will give any one cause 'to complain of his opinions, his conduct, or his disturbing the peace of any one. Let me beg you, madam, to hearken to no calumnies, no party spirit, nor to join with any in disturbing one who only wishes to live in tranquillity. I will pledge myself in every respect that you will have no cause to complain of Mr. Wordsworth. You have known me from my youth, and know my family—I should not risk my credit with you in saying what I could not answer for. Believe me, with sincere respect, your very obedient and obliged, THOMAS POOLE.

'*September* 16, 1797.'

It was, perhaps, the rumours of Thelwall's visit to Stowey, and of his intention of settling there, that grouped his name with that of Coleridge in the Anti-Jacobin. There is a kind of irony in the curious circumstance that the 'friends of order and religion' should have selected so irreverent a medium as a jingling parody of Milton's magnificent *Morning Hymn*, when they wanted to make atheists and revolutionaries look absurd—a thing that no one possibly could have done who had ever realised that Hymn as a Psalm of Praise to the Creator of Heaven and Earth! But the literature of attack can seldom pause to be scrupulous, and least of all when ridicule is the weapon employed. Lepaux was a French charlatan, whose name would have been entirely forgotten but for the celebrity of the lines—

'Thelwall, and ye that lecture as ye go,
  And for your pains get pelted,
        Praise Lepaux!

And ye five other wandering bards that move
In sweet accord of harmony and love,
C——dge and S——th–y, L——d and L——b, and Co.,
Tune all your mystic harps to praise Lepaux !'

On October 9, Charlotte Poole records in her
journal that, being at Tom Poole's, she 'saw Mr.
Wordsworth and Mr. Coldridge.'   It is typical of
the attitude of the cousinly mind at Marshmill
that she has not, even yet, mastered the ortho-
graphy of Coleridge's name.   His letters, which
almost always contain not only some word of loving
remembrance of Tom's mother—'*Our* Mother,'
he calls her in one letter—but also many little
messages to Stowey friends and acquaintances,
have never a word for the cousins at Marshmill.

Once Tom Poole, being there with his friends,
begged Penelope to sing 'Come, ever smiling
Liberty !' (*Judas Maccabæus*) for Coleridge and
Wordsworth.   Many years afterwards she related
the circumstance to her daughter, and told how
she persistently selected another song.

'I *could* not sing it,' she said ; 'I knew what
they meant with *their* liberty.'

CHAPTER XIV

'Life's best warmth still radiates from the heart.'
S. T. COLERIDGE, *Remorse*, Act V.

IT must not be supposed that the new sympathies and friendships which were giving such hitherto untasted interest and freshness to Tom Poole's existence, had at all the effect of making him indifferent to the humbler opportunities of local usefulness in which he had been so long accustomed to spend a large portion of his energies. Coleridge was even inclined to complain that local and family attachments had too strong a hold upon him, a fault which, if it be a fault, is certainly one of those failings which lean to virtue's side. Wordsworth, to whom strong local and family attachments, and a deeply-rooted loyalty to old associations, were as the very groundwork of all healthy national character, thoroughly esteemed and appreciated Tom Poole as a type—surely rather an uncommon type—of the very best sort of rural Englishman. 'During my residence at

Alfoxden,' he wrote, 'I used to see much of him, and had frequent occasion to admire the course of his daily life, and especially his conduct to his labourers and poor neighbours. Their wishes he carefully encouraged, and weighed their faults in the scales of charity.'[1]   So much, indeed, was Wordsworth delighted with *this* side of Thomas Poole's character, that he perhaps hardly gave sufficient weight to the strength of his *literary* tastes and sympathies ; but then, there was always a certain austerity in Wordsworth that kept most people at a distance, and great as was the regard he and Poole sincerely entertained for one another, they never became intimate, however often they might meet.

One of Poole's minor interests at this period was the improvement of the Nether Stowey Church Choir.   Perhaps, however, modern minds may cavil at the word *improvement*, when it becomes clear that his ideal of Church music must have been Nebuchadnezzar's band.   We find him writing to Dr. Langford,[2] in December 1797, to report that 'our singers are more than commonly active'; those who had been dissatisfied with certain arrangements made by their new vicar had come round, and had at length joined the choir that

---

[1] Wordsworth's *Memoirs*.
[2] Successor to Dr. Fisher as Vicar of Stowey.

he had established, and if he would now send 'the
Bassoon and the Music' that he had promised,
'I think, sir,' says Tom Poole, 'that we shall
make good use of them.'

Those who are fond of noticing the little
coincidences of literary circumstance, will be
amused to recognise in that bassoon an instrument
of music destined to a celebrity little dreamed of
by the Stowey singers ; for who can feel much
doubt that this and no other was the very original
and prototype of 'the loud Bassoon' whose sound
moved the wedding-guest to beat his breast, whilst
none the less he continued to sit spell-bound
listening to the Ancient Mariner?

That wonderful poem in which Coleridge once
for all touched that supreme height in poetry, which
is neither to be found by seeking nor attained by
striving, originated, as we all know, in a walking
expedition from Alfoxden to Porlock, Linton, and
Lynmouth.   Porlock is, perhaps, the most beautiful spot in all the beautiful West Country—where
the brown tint of the Severn Sea merges, at last,
into Atlantic blue ; where the coombs run down
to the very water's edge ; and where the sea is
bordered by rich red sandstone cliffs, crowned with
the overhanging woods that are the latest haunt
of the wild red deer.   The walk from Porlock
to Lynmouth, keeping 'close to the shore about

four miles . . . . through woods rising almost
perpendicularly from the sea, with views of the
opposite mountains of Wales,'[1] is almost the most
charming bit of English scenery that I know.   I
have walked it more than once, and each time with
fresh delight and admiration,—for my husband was
a true nephew of Thomas Poole, and loved the
Quantocks as if he had been born amongst them,
—but certainly we never selected November for
such an excursion.   It seems to me that a walking
tour, begun at 'half-past four,' on a 'dark and
cloudy' November afternoon, is a fairly good
illustration of the fantastic waywardness in their
proceedings, which excited such unreasonable
suspicions in the breasts of the West Country
folk concerning the tenants of Alfoxden.

What possible *good* motive could any three
people have—one a lady—for stealing out of the
comfortable shelter of their own roof at such a
time, and not coming back for days?   It is true
they might have done all this and more in the
north, and no one would have made a remark, or
hazarded a conjecture ; but in the north Wordsworth was a privileged person, as no doubt he
would soon have become in Somersetshire if he
had stayed there long enough.   But in 1797
there was a disposition to question everything he

---

[1] Wordsworth's *Memoirs*.   Letter of Dorothy Wordsworth.

did, and we can easily imagine the stories Mrs. St. Albyn may have heard from her maid, illustrating only too well the weightier misgivings of those local magnates who would, perhaps, think it their duty to call, to ask her if she were aware of the kind of person to whom Alfoxden had been let.

The tour was to be paid for out of the proceeds of a poem, to be sent to the newly-started Monthly Magazine; and as the trio plodded along in the oncoming darkness for 'the first eight miles,' they eagerly struck out the general plan. Coleridge began by speaking of a remarkable dream of John Cruikshanks', which he had thought of making the subject of a poem ; and then, as they walked, the outline gradually suggested itself. The old Navigator, 'as Coleridge afterwards delighted to call him,' should by some crime bring upon himself a spectral persecution. Wordsworth had been reading Shelvocke's Voyages, and had been struck by his description of that 'grand and graceful creature,' the albatross ; let the Ancient Mariner kill one of these birds, he suggests, and let the tutelary spirits of the region avenge that act of cruelty. The pedestrians must have spent that first night at Watchett, a little seaside village where Severn mud still encumbers the shore. It is rather a primitive place even now, and in those days must have been quite primeval in its simplicity.

Probably the friends scarcely noticed the rudeness of the accommodation, so eager were they to begin to put their thoughts on paper. But the joint composition originally planned was found to be impracticable, their 'respective manners proved so widely different.' Besides, the *idea* was Coleridge's, he alone knew what he meant—indeed, the vivid succession of perfect and clearly-defined images carries with it the impression of actual vision, and though Wordsworth contributed a few lines and some suggestions, the point was soon reached when the 'making mind' must be left to proceed alone. The next day the chillness of the November sun seems to have formed no bar to enjoyment, and the travellers fulfilled their intention of exploring the coast line as far as Linton, returning by an inland route through Dulverton—the poem moving and stirring in Coleridge's imagination, and doubtless, even then, finding voice from time to time in an occasional verse or stanza as he journeyed on with his two congenial companions. It reminds one of Walt Whitman's saying that he believes all *most* beautiful poems to have been composed in the open air. But the Monthly Magazine was left far behind, and, on their return to Stowey, 'the *Ancient Mariner* grew and grew,' until finally it stood forth complete, a perfect poem, and, as he himself said, 'not imitable.'

A little later in the same year, December 19, 1797, there was a General Thanksgiving 'for the three signal victories obtained over the Fleets of the French, the Spaniards, and the Dutch, and Miss Charlotte Poole 'observed with satisfaction' the largeness of the congregation that met in Over Stowey church, 'since,' she wrote in her journal, 'it proves that disaffection has not reached us.'

There seems to have been a kind of freemasonry in Thomas Poole's circle of friendships, within which something like the ideal brotherhood of Coleridge's imagination was actually realised. Some of the fraternity, like Tom Poole himself, and the Wedgwoods, were simply *tradesmen* (a name applied in those days to any one engaged in trade [1]), members of that same middle class which has so often been reproached for its lack of sweetness and light, and in which, nevertheless, every new movement of the human mind, whether moral or intellectual, has been apt to find the very earliest response of faith and sympathy. Wordsworth and Coleridge were men of the highest genius in the kingdoms of thought and poetry; Lloyd and Lamb, and perhaps we might add, Southey, though he never came quite within the innermost line of intimacy at Stowey, all possessed literary gifts of high individuality and value; Davy was the

---

[1] Not merely, as now, to shopkeepers, carpenters, etc.

most remarkable scientific man of his day; Rickman was an able economist, deeply versed in the knowledge of facts and statistics; Clarkson's whole soul was given to the leadership of the greatest philanthropic effort of the century, the heroic work of his whole life;—the bond which brought them all into fellowship with one another was a common enthusiasm for truth and goodness, a common passion for excellence, a common sense of duty, governing the entire direction of their minds, and a common persuasion that life was worthless and gifts abused, unless both were spent in the service of God and man. Service to their generation was the master-thought in the two leading minds of the group; and though poor Coleridge's life trailed on a broken wing, the spirit truly was willing if the flesh were weak, and he did not die without having accomplished much, and handing on an unextinguished torch to others. To be useful was the first ambition of Tom Poole's youth, and, long before he knew Coleridge, to fit himself for usefulness had, as we have seen, been the object of all his patient self-culture; and the Wedgwoods, weighted—overweighted some would think—with that burden of a great fortune which is so apt to smother in material comforts all the nobler aspirations and faculties of the higher nature, have, nevertheless, made good their title to a place amongst the unforgotten names of their epoch, chiefly by the enlightened liberality of their conviction that money was a trust, which it was their duty to employ carefully for the use and benefit of their fellowmen.

Cottle tells us that Mr. Poole introduced Coleridge to the Wedgwoods ; it seems probable that his first acquaintance with them began when Tom Wedgwood came into Somersetshire in 1797, to be near Dr. Beddoes, who had first settled in Clifton in 1793, with his mind full of the idea of starting an institution in which the question 'how far pneumatic chemistry could aid in the cure of disease' should be regularly tried and tested.[1] His earliest experiments in the virtues of 'medicated airs' had been made in Shropshire, at the house of that Mr. Reynolds with whom William Anstice, the William Anstice who married Penelope Poole, afterwards entered into partnership.

Beddoes was 'sanguine to a fault, hasty in judgment, and prone to theories which, in many respects, proved little more than day-dreams;'[2] but nothing attracts converts like a sincere enthusiasm, especially in a man of tried and trustworthy attainment, and though there was much difficulty in finding a home for the Pneu-

---

[1] He had been Chemical Lecturer at Oxford from 1788 to 1791.

[2] Meteyard's *Group of Englishmen*.

matic Institution, on account of a popular impression
that 'medicated airs' were explosive, and that the
complaints, which were to be cured by inhaling
them, might be infectious, which caused a general
unwillingness to be next-door neighbour to so
suspicious a novelty, he had none in obtaining the
necessary funds to accomplish his design ; and
when at last a Cornish undergraduate,[1] who had
attended his lectures at Oxford with much interest
and pleasure, introduced 'young Davy, the carver's
son,' of Tredrea, who was so fond of making chemical
experiments, and had burst into absurd 'tumultuous delight' at the first sight of a well-appointed
laboratory, to the doctor's notice, and Beddoes
discovered in him the very person he was seeking
as superintendent of his new institution, and a
house was at last found in Dowry Square, Hot
Wells, Thomas Wedgwood actually subscribed
£1000 to complete the sum required to make
it possible to begin immediately.   It would
be worth that sum, he declared, even to be sure
'that the elastic fluids would *not* be serviceable in
medicine.'

This was in 1798, when Thomas Wedgwood
had already been for some time a patient of Dr.
Beddoes, and had already more than once visited
Poole at Nether Stowey, where he must have met

---

[1] Mr. Davies Giddy, afterwards Sir Davies Gilbert, P.R.S.

both Coleridge and Wordsworth, and have learnt to appreciate them as men of unusual and transcendent gifts. [[He was himself a man of parts considerably above the average ; he was an excellent chemist—indeed it is generally admitted that the 'silver pictures' or 'heliotypes' which were printed off by him at Etruria in 1791 and 1793, when he was little over twenty years of age, establish his rights to be considered as the earliest discoverer of photography ; [and in metaphysics he had a reach of thought that even Coleridge spoke of with respect. His brothers were men of excellent sense and considerable culture, but he was something more, and the pride with which his abilities were regarded by his own family, rendered the disappointment all the more bitter, when it gradually became certain that, young as he was, he was stricken with incurable disease, and would never be well enough to do anything but drag out an invalid's existence, moving listlessly from place to place in the vain search after health.

Still, until he became a prey to that saddest of all maladies, an utter weariness of life, he must have been a very delightful companion, and to Tom Poole he was ever the object of a tender, considerate affection, quite different from the solid mutual regard which existed between him and his brother Josiah, and of which the expression remains

in a large collection of sensible and straightforward
letters,[1] full of practical details concerning purchases
of land, farm and dairy management, family plans
and projects, and other matters of everyday concern.   With the third brother, John, who was the
eldest of the three, and whose main intention in
settling at Cote House, near Bristol, seems to have
been to supply the comforts of a home to poor
Tom Wedgwood, whenever he wished to be within
reach of Dr. Beddoes, Tom Poole was never
intimate ; but it was at his house that Coleridge
went to meet Tom Wedgwood on his return from
Shrewsbury, to make his personal acknowledgments of the offer of the annuity which he had
just made up his mind to accept.

He had, as we know, refused, though with
some hesitation, their first gift of £100.   The
letter in which he did so is copied out, in Ward's
boyish hand, into the pages of Mr. Poole's copying-
book, where it is immediately followed by a copy,
in the same writing, of the letter in which Mr.
Josiah Wedgwood replies by the offer of the
annuity of £150 a year, from his brother Thomas
and himself, an amount corresponding to the
income that would have been his, if he had undertaken the charge of the Unitarian pulpit at
Shrewsbury.   Coleridge had already started for

[1] These letters begin in 1797.

Shropshire when this important letter reached
Stowey, and was opened by Mr. Tom Poole, who
seems to have been left in charge of Coleridge's
correspondence, and who took immediate measures
for communicating the contents to him. One
copy, with a letter from himself on the same
sheet, earnestly recommending him to accept, was
addressed to Coleridge in the first instance at Mr.
Estlin's, and thence forwarded to the Rev. John
Rowe's, at Shrewsbury.

'PENZANCE, *January 10th, 1798.*

'DEAR SIR—*In the absence of my brother, who has
an engagement this morning, I take up the pen to reply to
your letter received yesterday. I cannot help regretting
very sincerely that, at this critical moment, we are separated
by so great a length of the worst road in the kingdom. It
is not that we have found much difficulty in deciding how
to act in the present juncture of your affairs, but we are
apprehensive that, deprived of the benefit of conversation,
we may fail somewhat in explaining our views and intentions with that clearness and persuasion which should
induce you to accede to our proposal without scruple or
hesitation—nay, with that glow of pleasure which the
accession of merited good fortune, and the observation of
virtuous conduct in others, ought powerfully to excite in the
breast of healthful sensibility. Writing is painful to me.
I must endeavor to be concise, yet to avoid abruptness.
My brother and myself are possessed of a considerable
superfluity of fortune; squandering and hoarding are
equally distant from our inclinations. But we are*

VOL. I   S

earnestly desirous to convert this superfluity into a fund of beneficence, and we have now been accustomed for some time, to regard ourselves rather as Trustees than Proprietors. We have canvassed your past life, your present situation and prospects, your character and abilities. As far as certainty is compatible with the delicacy of the estimate, we have no hesitation in declaring that your claim upon the fund appears to come under more of the conditions we have prescribed for its disposal, and to be every way more unobjectionable, than we could possibly have expected. This result is so congenial with our heartfelt wishes, that it will be a real mortification to us if any misconception or distrust of our intentions, or any unworthy diffidence of yourself, should interfere to prevent its full operation in your favour.

'*After what my brother Thomas has written I have only to state the proposal we wish to make to you. It is that you shall accept an annuity for life of £150, to be regularly paid by us, no condition whatsoever being annexed to it. Thus your liberty will remain entire, you will be under the influence of no professional bias, and will be in possession of* a "permanent income not inconsistent with your religious and political creeds,"[1] *so necessary to your health and activity.*

'*I do not now enter into the particulars of the mode of securing the annuity, etc.—that will be done when we receive your consent to the proposal we are making; and we shall only say that we mean the annuity to be independent of everything but the wreck of our fortune, an event which we hope is not very likely to happen, though it must in these times be regarded as more than a bare possibility.*

[1] Quotation from S. T. C.'s last letter.

'Give me leave now to thank you for the openness with which you have written to me, and the kindness you express for me, to neither of which can I be indifferent, and I shall be happy to derive the advantages from them that a friendly intercourse with you cannot fail to afford me.—I am very sincerely yours,

'JOSIAH WEDGWOOD.'

'STOWEY, *Saturday*, 12 *o'clock.*

'MY DEARLY BELOVED—Such is the answer which is sent to your letter. I received it this morning by nine o'clock, and immediately informed Mrs. Coleridge of it, scrawled two notes to you, one directed *the Rev. Mr. Rowe's, Shrewsbury*, the other enclosed in a short letter I wrote to Estlin, desiring him immediately to send or give it to you, and sent off little Tommy to the post-office, where I trust he arrived before the mail went off. In my letter to Estlin I informed him of the contents of the above; told him that when I considered the ministry, and your peculiar character, that I thought you ought not to hesitate to accept the annuity proposed, and that I trusted he would be of the same opinion, as I was satisfied that his approbation of every part of your conduct formed no small ingredient of your happiness.

'I now repeat that my opinion is that you ought not to hesitate to accept the annuity. When I consider the MANNER in which the proposal is made, the persons from whom it comes, the property they possess, and the uses to which they have destined that property, I really think it would be palsying that benevolence, which, God be praised, does exist in the human breast, to think of refusing it. This benevolence, in the present case, is

deduced from reason; the utility of it is clearly seen
before the feelings are permitted to colour the deed with
all that can give joy to the heart of man.   The existence
of such benevolence is the pledge, and the only pledge,
of our perfectibility; it is, alas! so overgrown by the
various wickedness which has been so systematically
excited in the world, that it is rarely seen.   You have
called it forth in this instance ; don't drive it back to the
honourable breast where it seems peculiarly to keep its
court.   Excuse my warmth of expression.   You can
have but two reasons to hesitate : first, that it is more
honourable to gain one's own living than to be dependent
upon another ; second, that you possibly may be of more
use in promoting Christianity as a minister than as a
private man.   The first can only be answered by considering the *true use* which the possessors of wealth ought
to make of it, and by your own immutable resolves of
falling in with that use—in which case you are not dependent, but you labour as effectually for that which
you receive, as if you took a spade, and worked for me
a day, and received a shilling.   You and your friends
are only moving in the small sphere which approaches
to perfection, which is, by beginnings like these, I trust,
to conquer and to involve the whole.   Would you prefer
sticking to the great circle of vice which heavily, very
heavily, now drags itself on?   The second objection is
so frivolous that it need not have been mentioned.   The
nicest notion of honour can only preclude your being an
hired minister, while you receive this annuity.   You
don't think Christianity more pure by coming from the
mouth or pen of an hired man?   You are not shackled.
Your independence of mind is *part of the bond.*   You

are to give to mankind that which you think they most want. Religion, if you please, may be, as it will be, the basis of your moral writings—it may shine in your lighter productions, inspire and purify your poetry. You may, if you please, occasionally preach, and these occasional addresses are heard with the attention which novelty, as the world is, always excites, and, being gratuitous, possess the aid of disinterestedness on your part, and gratitude on the part of the hearers, to impress on the mind the doctrines you teach. All are well here. Heaven bless and direct you,   Thos. Poole.'

Copies of a letter from Stuart asking for contributions, and of a note from Tom Wedgwood begging Coleridge to meet him at Cote House, are forwarded a few days later. Meanwhile Poole has heard of his friend's decision, and adds on the same sheet[1] a few words of exuberant joy and sympathy :—

'The receipt of your last letter,' he says, 'made me so happy that I went to a party here in town, and was never so chearful; never *sung* so well, never so witty, never so agreeable,—so I was told ten times over ! They little knew the cause which made joy beam from every feature and action.

'Make as much haste home as you can, provided it be *good speed*. You will, of course, stay the necessary time at Cote House. God bless you for ever. . . . Yours affectionately,   Thos. Poole.'

---

[1] Undated ; but Stuart's letter is dated January 20, 1798.

In so primitive a place as Nether Stowey, and
with a housekeeper so careful as Mrs. Coleridge,
and a standard of living so plain as that to which
the little family were accustomed, £150 a year
was sufficiency, even though Lloyd had withdrawn
himself and returned to Birmingham, and £20
had to be subtracted, which Coleridge regularly
allowed, year by year, to his wife's mother.   For
the moment the gnawing pressure of straightened
means was removed, Coleridge's nature rose elastic
to enjoy the new sense of freedom, and both to
him and to Wordsworth, the next six months
became one of the very happiest periods in their
lives.   Wordsworth was under notice to leave
Alfoxden in June, and the certainty that the time
is limited, during which a particular kind of enjoyment will be within reach, does certainly add
intensity to the pleasure we take in it while it lasts.
Nature, too, was kind, and the spring and early
summer of 1798 were radiantly soft and beautiful.
The coombs looked their loveliest, and the two
poets fairly lived out of doors together.   It is
almost painful to trace the allusions to '*that*
summer*' in the closing book of Wordsworth's
'Prelude.'   He remembers 'the buoyant spirits,
that were their daily portion, when they first
together wantoned in wild poesy'—the 'kindred
influence' which found its way to his 'heart of

hearts' from 'that capacious soul, placed on this
earth to love and understand,' and in whose
society

> ' . . . Thoughts and things
> In the self-haunting spirit learned to take
> More rational proportions; mystery,
> The incumbent mystery of sense and soul,
> Of life and death, time and eternity,
> Admitted more habitually a mild
> Interposition—a serene delight
> In closelier gathering cares, such as become
> A human creature howsoe'er endowed,
> Poet, or destined for a humbler name.
> And so the deep, enthusiastic joy,
> The rapture of the hallelujah sent
> From all that breathes and is, was chastened, stemmed
> And balanced by pathetic truth, by trust
> In hopeful reason, leaning on the stay
> Of Providence; and in reverence for duty,
> Here, if need be, struggling with storms, and there
> Strewing in peace life's humblest ground with herbs,
> At every season green, sweet at all hours.'

Recalling the 'memory of that happiness,' he
knows well enough that Coleridge too, in looking
back, must see, '*in clearer view than any liveliest
sight of yesterday, that summer, under whose indulgent skies, upon smooth Quantock's airy ridge
they roved unchecked, or loitered 'mid her sylvan
coombs.*' The Lyrical Ballads were almost ready
for publication, and Coleridge, in the simple glad-

ness of his heart, sure of a sympathetic listener, went chaunting '*in bewitching words*,' the '*vision of that Ancient Man, the bright-eyed Mariner*'; or recited that lovely fragment of the Lady Christabel, which, amid such surroundings, certainly ought to have been finished, but for that fatal spell of incompleteness which Coleridge never but once seems to have been able to elude ; or listening to Wordsworth '*murmuring of him who, joyous hap, was found, after the perils of his moonlight ride, near the loud waterfall ; or her who sate in misery near the miserable Thorn. . . .*'

The entire poem of the 'Idiot Boy' was suggested by some words actually used by a hapless half-wit who was well known in the Stowey neighbourhood : 'The cocks did crow, and the moon did shine so cold.' The poem is full of the most tiresome faults and the most exquisite beauties, such as, for instance, the following description of morning twilight :—

> ' By this the stars were almost gone,
>   The moon was setting on the hill,
>   So pale you scarcely looked at her :
>   The little birds began to stir,
>   Though yet their tongues were still. . . .'

—a stanza which almost makes me forgive Wordsworth for having written a poem which, if he had

had any sense of humour, he would certainly never have published. It was composed, 'almost extempore,' in the groves of Alfoxden, and was evidently a favourite with the poet himself, perhaps, as his own words would suggest, '*in gratitude to those happy moments of which it was the offspring.*'

It was at Holford, a village near Alfoxden, that the incident occurred, commemorated by Wordsworth in the 'Last of the Flock,' which to me has always seemed one of the most pathetic poems ever written. Simon Lee, too, had been 'huntsman to the Squires of Alfoxden,' and his 'moss-grown hut of clay' stood on the common, a little way from the entrance of the park, and 'near the waterfall.' Wordsworth knew him well, and had often noted the flicker of former joys in the old man's face whenever 'the chiming hounds were out.' Word for word from his own lips did he take the expression, 'I dearly love their voice, . . .' and that simple, but vividly natural picture of the mingled feebleness and courage of old age among 'the poorest of the poor' was sketched from life. The hearty outpouring of thanks is specially characteristic of the native-born peasant of the Quantock hills, where, together with the old Celtic names and tricks of pronunciation, there lingers a certain Celtic grace of inbred courtesy of manner—

a simple, rustic dignity, rendering to all their due—
which I have often observed with admiration,
especially in the older people whom I remember
in my youth.   I trust it is not beginning to die
out with the dialect.

CHAPTER XV

' I cannot doubt that they whom you deplore
Are glorified ; or, if they sleep, shall wake
From sleep, and dwell with God in endless love.
Hope, below this, consists not with belief
In mercy, carried infinite degrees
Beyond the tenderness of human hearts :
Hope, below this, consists not with belief
In perfect wisdom, guiding mightiest power,
That finds no limits but her own pure will.'

WORDSWORTH, *The Excursion*, Book IV.

IN that same year, 1798, which was, upon the whole, such a happy one to his friends, a sudden cloud of sorrow, heavy and dark, descended upon Tom Poole. On May 9, the news arrived from Sherborne that his brother Richard had been taken alarmingly ill, and Tom, hurrying off to see him, found him stricken with a malignant fever, whilst his young wife, forced from his side by the pains and perils of childbirth, had, on the very day of Tom Poole's arrival, brought into the world a little daughter. The mother was a widow and the child fatherless before the babe was a week old.

From the manner in which the letter is addressed
we gather that Richard Poole was not actually
dead, but evidently beyond any hope of recovery,
when Coleridge penned the following letter on
May 14 :—

'MY DEAREST FRIEND—I have been sitting many
minutes with my pen in my hand, full of prayers and
wishes for you, and the house of affliction in which
you have so trying a part to sustain—but I know not
what to *write*. May God support you! May He re-
store your brother—but, above all, I pray that He will
make us able to cry out with a fervent sincerity, Thy
Will be done! I have had lately some sorrows that
have cut more deeply into my heart than they ought to
have done, and I have found religion, and *commonplace
religion* too, my restorer and my comfort, giving me
gentleness, and calmness, and dignity. Again and again,
may God be with you, my best, dear friend! O believe
me, believe me, my Poole! dearer, to my understanding
and affections unitedly, than all else in this world!

'It is almost painful and a thing of fear to tell you
that I have another boy; it will bring upon your mind
the too affecting circumstance of Mrs. Richard Poole.
The prayers which I have offered for her have been a
relief to my own mind; I would that they could have
been a consolation to her. Scripture seems to teach us
that our fervent prayers are not without efficacy even for
others; and though my reason is perplexed, yet my
internal feelings impel me to a humble faith, that it is
possible and consistent with the divine attributes. . . .'

A few days later Thomas Poole returned home in such grief that even Coleridge shrank from approaching him, till assured that his presence would be acceptable. Here is a note, written on 'Sunday morning,' and endorsed 'from Coleridge. May 20, '98':—

'MY DEAREST POOLE—I was all day yesterday in a distressing perplexity whether or no it would be wise or consolatory for me to call at your house—or whether I should write to your mother, as a Christian friend—or whether it would not be better to wait for the exhaustion of that grief which must have its way. . . .

'. . . Do you wish to see me to-day? Shall I call on you? Shall I stay with you? Or had I better leave you uninterrupted?

'In all your sorrows as in your joys, I am, indeed, my dearest Poole, a true and faithful sharer. May God bless and comfort you all!   S. T. COLERIDGE.'

Poor Tom Poole took his trouble very hard; there had been a more than ordinary closeness of sympathy between himself and his brother, and his departure left a wound which was, perhaps, only healed by the gradual comfort that came to him through his intense devotion to his brother's fatherless child. 'You can scarcely conceive,' writes one who remembers them both, 'the extraordinary vehemence of Mr. Tom Poole's affection for his niece.' But this was years later, when the babe had grown into a girl ; in her baby days she was indeed a treasure, but one whose very sight recalled painful memories.

'I shall be more likely to see you at Salisbury than at Sherborne,' he writes to the eldest of the Miss Warwicks,[1] who had informed him of an intended removal of their school to Salisbury. ' My associations concerning Salisbury are at any rate neuter, nay, rather pleasant. But when I think of Sherborne, Miss Warwick, there is such a load at my heart, such a tumult of agony in my mind, as are altogether intolerable. I little thought how dependent a being I was. It was right that I should be taught. Be it so. I cannot bow in resignation. You will remember me, I pray, first, to Henrietta and all your family ; next, to all that loved my brother and knew his value. Mrs. Poole is tolerably well. The precious little infant is her comfort. She has just passed through the smallpox very favourably [2]—and is a most interesting baby.'

But in moving on to October, I have too much anticipated the course of events, and must go back to the days when the date fixed for Wordsworth's departure from Alfoxden was drawing nearer and nearer ; and in the consideration of future plans, the idea of going to Germany to study the language and literature had been suggested, perhaps by Thomas Wedgwood, in one of his visits at Tom Poole's, and was being enter-

---

[1] In October 1798.   [2] *i.e.* inoculation.

tained with some eagerness, by Coleridge even
more than by Wordsworth, whilst the generous
Wedgwoods, acting on their principle that wealth
is a trust to be wisely and thoughtfully expended
by those to whom it is confided, for the general
good, were ready and willing to provide the
necessary funds. It seems to have been principally for conference on this subject that Coleridge
visited Mr. Josiah Wedgwood at Stoke, in June,
stopping on the way first at Bristol and then at
Brentford, at which latter place he was the guest
of Poole's old friend, Mr. Purkis, of whom he thus
gives his impressions :—

'MY DEAR POOLE—I arrived in Bristol on Monday
evening, spent the next day at Estlin's, who opposed my
German expedition *furore per-religioso, amicissimo furore.*
At Brentford I arrived Wednesday evening, and was
driven by Mr. Purkis great part of the way to Stoke on
Thursday evening; and here I am, well, etc. etc. . . . Purkis
is a *gentleman*, with the free and cordial and interesting
manners of the man of literature. His colloquial diection
is uncommonly pleasing, his *information* various, his *own*
mind elegant and acute. These are but *general* expressions ; but this I can say, that if he liked me as well as
I liked him, I have left very agreeable thoughts and
feelings in the mind of an excellent man. And I like
Mrs. Purkis.

' The Wedgwoods received me with joy and affection.
I have been metaphysicizing so long and so closely with
T. Wedgwood, that I am a *caput mortuum*, mere lees

and residuum. . . . This place is a noble, large house in a rich, pleasant country; but the little Toe of Quantock is better than the head and shoulders of Surrey and Middlesex. These dull places, however, have the effect of liveliness from their being a variety to me. May you say the same by this letter, for it is scarcely worth the postage. . . .—Yours ever,   S. T. COLERIDGE.'

In that same month of June Wordsworth and his sister quitted Alfoxden, and after a short stay at Coleridge's house at Stowey, and a week at Cottle's, started together on a walking tour along the banks of the Wye, of which the poetical fruits were the lines on Tintern Abbey. Then they took lodgings in Bristol, so that Wordsworth might be near the printer, whilst the *Lyrical Ballads* were issuing from the press. Here Coleridge visited them, and the German plan began to take definite shape. On August 3, 1798 he writes to lay the matter before Poole, telling him he thinks 'the realisation of the scheme of great importance to his intellectual activity, and, of course, to his moral happiness.' Whether to take Mrs. Coleridge and the children is another question, both on account of the expense and of the unsettled state of the continent. It will be more prudent to go alone in the first instance, for three or four months, after which he can either fetch over his family, or return 'with his German for his pains.' Poole must consider the whole scheme, and be ready to advise him, for in another week he will be in Stowey. He intends to 'dart into Wales,' and return by Swansea 'usque ad Bridgwater sive Cummage. . . .'

When the printing of the *Lyrical Ballads* was completed, the Wordsworths removed to London. About a fortnight afterwards, on September 16, they sailed from Yarmouth, together with Coleridge, and arrived at Hamburgh two days later, after a voyage of which Coleridge wrote an amusing description in a long letter to Mr. Poole. His very last act, before the packet started, had been to pen a few lines of affectionate farewell :[1]—

'MY VERY DEAR POOLE—We have arrived at Yarmouth just in time to be hurried into the packet—and four or five letters of recommendation have been taken away from me, owing to their being wafered. Wedgwood's luckily were not.

'I am on the point of leaving my native country for the first time, a country which, God Almighty knows, is dear to me above all things for the love I bear to you. Of many friends whom I love and esteem, my head and heart have ever chosen you as the friend—as the one being in whom is involved the full and whole meaning of that sacred title. God love you, my dear Poole, and your faithful and most affectionate S. T. Coleridge.

'We may be only two days, we may be a fortnight going.

---

[1] Postmark, September 17, 1798.

The same of the packet that returns.   So do not let my
poor Sara be alarmed if she do not hear from me.   I
will write alternately to you and to her, twice every week
during my absence.   May God preserve us, and make
us continue to be joy, and comfort, and wisdom, and
virtue to each other, my dear, dear Poole !'

In the following month, July 1798, Charlotte
Poole went to live in Bridgwater, to keep house
for her brother Ruscombe.[1]   Here is an extract
from her journal of October 3 in the same year :—

'The mail came in covered with laurels, and brought
the account of the complete defeat of the French fleet,
at the mouth of the Nile, by Admiral Nelson.   The
cannons were instantly set firing, and an almost general
illumination took place.   One obstinate democrat who
refused to put up lights had his windows entirely
destroyed.'

In those far-off days telegrams and railways as
yet were not ; the earliest intimation of great news
from the seat of war always arrived at Bridgwater
in the form of some tumultuous rumour, flying
from mouth to mouth, of laurels on the London
Coach, which would bring everybody into the
streets to learn the truth, and to see Mr. Anstice

[1] The writer's grandfather.   He, too, had a passion for usefulness.
When his children desired to raise some monument to his memory,
the thing that occurred to them as most appropriate, was a school for
the education of the children of the poor, in what was then a neglected
part of the town.

come hurrying out to get his newspaper—for that Mr. Anstice took in a London newspaper was an important and well-known fact. Then, almost before he had it well into his hand, lo! there was a barrel reared up on end near the Market Cross, which he was then and there expected to mount, and to read the news aloud to his fellow townsmen, which, indeed, he always did, upon such occasions, in the most patriotic manner, and amid the eager acclamations of the crowd.

The arrival of a telegram is not half so dramatic, though no doubt a far swifter and surer mode of obtaining intelligence ; just as the present Cornhill, as the open space in the centre of the town is still called, with circular-fronted market-house adorned with pillars, is as much more convenient as it is less picturesque than the old one, with its fine old Market Cross, bearing the excellent motto, ' Let every one mind his own business,' which was destroyed over half a century ago by a set of wild young men, who had formed themselves into a Committee of Grievances, and having voted the Market Cross to be obstructive, decided that it was their business to pull it down.

The news of the battle of the Nile has a special connection with what I think may be considered as the *second* greatest friendship of Tom Poole's life ; for it was in the very same week of October,

1798, that Humphrey Davy, then a lad of nineteen, left Penzance for Bristol, where, as we have seen, he was to undertake the superintendence of Dr. Beddoes' Pneumatic Institution.   The news of the great naval victory reached Devon one day later than it reached Somerset, therefore it was not till October 4 that the happy-hearted youth, strong in the modest consciousness of his own powers, and fairly overflowing with exultation at having obtained his first opportunity of showing what he could do, met at Okehampton the laurel-crowned coach, streaming with ribbons, that was bearing the tidings westward, and was lifted to a still higher pitch of exhilaration by the glorious intelligence.

A scheme to which Tom Wedgwood had given £1000 could not fail to be a subject of interest to Tom Poole, and some time in 1799 he was introduced to Davy at the Pneumatic Institution, where he 'inhaled his nitrous oxide with the usual extraordinary and transitory sensations.'[1]   But 'the interesting conversation, manners, and appearance of the youthful operator' made no transitory impression; and it is easy to understand how delightful to a nature like his the discovery of such a being as Davy must have been, and what a consolation it must have afforded in the flatness which

---

[1] Poole's letter to Dr. Paris.   Published in *Fragmentary Remains of Sir H. Davy*, by his brother.

the departure of Coleridge had left, to find himself
enjoying once again that rare pleasure of intercourse
with *genius*, which to him was the crowning charm of
life.   Acquaintance quickly ripened into friendship,
and the foundations were soon laid of a lasting
lifelong regard.

Meanwhile Coleridge had not, of course, written
as often as he had planned to do ; was it to be
expected that he should ?   But he had written,
and did write, pretty fully and continually, and
many of his letters are already known to the public,
having been published in the *Biographia Literaria*
under the name of Satyrane's Letters.[1]   In these,
however, all that is intimate and personal has
been omitted ; nor perhaps was it necessary to re-
produce the exceeding homeliness of the details
which occasionally passed between the two friends.
Some readers, however, may be interested in the
following selections from Thomas Poole's side of
the correspondence, illustrated by quotations
from those passages in Coleridge's letters to
which they refer.

I

'Stowey, *October* 8, 1798.

' MY VERY DEAR COL.—We have received all your four

---

[1] Spenser's Satyrane—

> ' Plain, faithful, true, and enemy of shame,
> Who far abroad for strange adventures sought.'

Faery Queen, Canto VI.

letters [1] . . . and have been made most happy to hear
from each stage that you were well. May God preserve
your health till you return, and always. This homespun
wish is at last the very best we can feel for our friends.
We are going on at Stowey just as when you left us.
Mrs. C. and the children are perfectly well. Mrs. C.
keeps up her spirits, and I believe every one is anxious to
make her happy. My poor mother suffers—still she
suffers. What a mysterious affliction for so good a woman!

'If we have no domestic news, we have had brilliant
publick news: the resplendent victory gained by Nelson
has, I imagine, lit up the world from the north to the
southern pole. We illuminated at Stowey, all except
that mulish fellow W.

'We long for your journal. Be sure to be particular,
and don't mind a little trouble in writing—and write
with good pens upon large paper; let the hand be very
small, and the lines very close together. . . .

'We were amused by your account of the sea and your
companions during your passage.[2] The sparkling waves,
I imagine, charmed away your share of sickness. You
have seen Klopstock! Be particular in describing the
physiognomy and stature of all such men, as well as
noting their habits and sayings. The Wordsworths have
left you—so there is an end of our fears about amalga-
mation, etc. I think you both did perfectly right. It
was right for them to find a cheaper situation; and it
was right for you to avoid the expense of travelling,
provided you are where *pure German* is spoken. You
will, of course, frequently hear from Wordsworth. When

[1] Two to Mrs. Coleridge, two to himself.
[2] Satyrane's Letters.

you write remember me to him and to his sister, and
thank him for his tragedy, which I am to receive from
the Wedgwoods. Thank him in proportion as I value
the present, which is indeed very highly. . . .

'You are now, dear Col., fixed in Germany, and what
you have to do is to attend *wholly* to those things which
are better attained in Germany than elsewhere. Let
nothing divert you from them. And, on this consideration, I should spend no time to send anything to Stewart
but what was involved in the progress of those pursuits.
If any matter to *narrate* occurred, which, *for certain*,
could be despatched without exertion of mind, or any
great *consumption* of time, send it to him. But *begin*
no poetry—no original composition—unless translation
from German may be so called. One thing which you
must determine to acquire while you are in Germany is
as perfect a knowledge of the language as possible.
You will thus have to show one distinct and almost
tangible addition to your stock of knowledge, for the
trouble and expence to yourself, for the anxieties and
fears of your family and friends, incurred by this journey.
. . . Beware of being too much with Chester. I could
wish you had not both been in one house. Speak nothing
but German. Live with Germans. Read in German.
Think in German. Don't mind a few pounds while you
are out for any assistance in learning German; nor,
while you are out, must you regard a few weeks or
months of time. You must *stay long enough to do the
business you are gone to do;* but do it as quick as you
can do it well. . . .

'Make a strict arrangement of your time and chain yourself down to it. This may not be advisable for the gener-

ality, but I am persuaded it would counteract a *disease*
of your mind—which is an active subtilty of imagination
ever suggesting reasons to push off whatever excites a
moment of languor or *ennui.* This many of your friends
falsely call irresolution. No one has more resolution and
decision than you ; no one sooner sees the side of a
question on which the balance of argument turns. But
then that same habit of giving free scope to the activity
of your imagination, makes it death to you to chain
the mind long to any particular object. This habit to
acquire a language must be conquered, and I am sure is
conquerable. To acquire a language—nay, to acquire
excellence in any point. . . . You desired me to send
you some agricultural queries. . . . I can find no
general ones in the reports of the Board of Agriculture
which would suit your purpose ; I should think it would
be a good object for Chester to take a very accurate account of the agriculture, horticulture, implements relating to those objects, and, in short, of every species of
rural and domestic management which he has the
opportunity of observing, or collecting information on.

'I know not that I can say anything more. I thank
you for the books I am to receive, which I will read—
Horne Tooke's work, if I can, with particular attention.
I feel how little I know of English, and I would wish to
know it well. Mrs. C. will write you a long letter
next. . . . My mother desires her dear love to you.
She weeps with a mother's affection at hearing your
letters read. Sir John Sinclair, in his plan for reward-
ing useful discoveries by an agreement among the
European powers and America, states that it is said a
German physician has found out a very effectual pallia-

tive, if not a cure, for the stone. Do inquire about it. And though you shall not fly home, yet let a letter fly with all speed if such a thing is to be found. God bless you, my dear Col. I shall just take and read this letter to Mrs. C. and send it off by the boy who is waiting. From your sincere friend, THOS. POOLE.

'*P.S.*—I see there were very general queries given by the Board of Agriculture to the Surveyors of the Counties of England, and as they will answer pretty well for all countries, Ward shall copy them and I will send them in my next. Ward's kind love.'

II

'*November* 22, 1798.

' MY VERY DEAR COL.—We have received your letters, and I need not say how delighted and happy we are when we receive them. You have by this time, I hope, re-ceived Mrs. Coleridge's long letter. . . . Mrs. Col. and the little ones are perfectly well. Berkeley was, as you have heard, well peppered with the smallpox, but never in any danger. . . . He is a delightful boy, and we begin to think him very like you. Hartley speaks everything, and knows two or three letters. . . . He knows the names of all the books in the house which have pictures in them. . . . My dear mother is much better. She gets up now by ten, and sits up frequently after me. I went to bed and left her and Mrs. Coleridge chatting two nights ago. Lime water was the last thing she took, and to the last thing, you know, we always attribute the most efficacy. . . . Your progress in the German language amazes us. Proceed, proceed. Make your-self, I charge you, compleatly master of it. I shall post-

pone *looking* at it before you come home, and then, before
I look, we must *talk* about it. The wish that I should
know what you know is very natural—'twas what I always
felt when I used to urge you to learn French. I do not
say I *won't* apply to it ; but a language—and the German
language—is an arduous task. . . . You say you wish
to come home ; I need not say we wish to see you—but
I trust you and we can submit to absence till every object of your journey be attained. Be unremittingly
diligent in attaining those objects, but stay till they are
attained. Have you heard from the Wordsworths ? Let
us hear how they go on. Stuart has written a very
kind letter to Mrs. Coleridge. He is afraid that he
offended you, as you did not call before you left London.
He says he hopes you consider his engagement as existing with you. He has been anxiously expecting the communication you promised him respecting German literature. . . . Why have you not sent it? Though I repeat that
I advise you not to suffer your thoughts to stray from the
main objects, to send communications to Stewart, if in
pursuing those objects suitable matter occur, transmit
it. By way of a little remuneration for the advantages
I gain by Stewart, I have taken it into my head to
write an essay concerning the encroachments of men on
the employments of women—which Mrs. C. this day
sent him. She has told him if it suit his purpose it is at
his service ; if not, to throw it aside without ceremony.
To finish on the plan I have begun with will take half
a dozen essays about the length of a *Spectator.* The
subject is important, and though old, is interesting, and
one on which I think a man may honestly write with
the hope of doing good. . . .

'Mrs. Coleridge desires me to ask you if you have any objection to your letters being read when she goes to Bristol to your friends there? Ward copies them all into a book. I read extracts from the letters, according to the dispositions and capacities of the hearers.'

The promised list of agricultural questions follows, copied in Ward's handwriting.

'You'll have enough to do, even with the assistance of the Muses, to answer all these questions ; and if those ladies, (though once so complaisant to Virgil) should turn up their noses if enlisted by you into the service, I would recommend you to consign those inquiries to Chester, or, at any rate, to make him your pioneer in the business. . . . Well, my dear, dear Col., I don't know that I have anything more to say. May God Almighty bless you and ever make you happy. May you live long to undeceive the miserable reptiles who have been so busy to disturb your tranquillity ; and while you are respected and beloved by the best of your own country, and by the most respectable strangers whom you meet, let those tapers which blink in the noontide sun burn out and die away by their own nature.—Once more believe me, with entire affection, yours ever,   THOS. POOLE.

'*P.S.* . . . Have you the opportunity of any good libraries where you are? Is your host a man of literature? You will, of course, buy some German books. . . . Write *particularly, long,* and *frequently.* Write all about your own pursuits above all. This is writing about ourselves, for you are a part of ourselves. Once more Adieu. My mother desires her dear love to you. And kind remembrances I am desired to give by dozens.'

III

'STOWEY, *ye* 2*4th January* 1799.

'MY VERY DEAR COL.—We were rejoiced last night by
the receipt of your two letters, one for Mrs. Coleridge, the
other for me. When letters from Hamburg were announced
Ward jumped up and twirled round like a whirlygig,
in spite of the barricade of chairs and tables that were near
him, to the great derangement of the bread and cheese,
and two or three full glasses of beer which were splashed
over. I sat *grinning* and broke the seal. Why will you
make yourself unhappy at not hearing from us? It is
true I cannot account any more than you for the irregularity of the packets, but I consider it utterly impossible,
situated as we are, with the feelings we reciprocally
possess, that we can neglect writing sufficiently frequently
to satisfy those feelings; therefore, if I had not known
that the ice prevented the arrival of the Hamburg mails,
I should have attributed our not hearing from you to an
irregularity in the conveyance of which I knew nothing.
Be assured, unless we are all taken off in a whirlwind,
that, if you do not hear from us, it will always arise from
the miscarriage or delay of a letter.

'Mrs. Coleridge went to Bristol the last day of the old
year. . . . She arrived safely at Bristol with the little ones,
and is very well. Hartley is very well; nothing ails
him. He is a most amusing rogue. Berkeley had a
cough which prevailed amongst the children here. I
find from my sister that the change of air has been of
great service to him; but the particulars of the children
Mrs. C. will inform you of. Let, my dear Col., nothing
trouble you. When Berkeley had the small-pox, and gave

his mother trouble, I assure you she and all of us rejoiced you were not at home. I forwarded this morning the letter for Mrs. C. I did not open it, as she told me I must not if it was a *small* letter; however, I desired her, after she had had the first view of it, and if it was *not too foolish*, to send it to me. I am delighted to hear of your progress in German; delighted to hear of your progress in mastering the untired and unbidden excursions of your mind. Perfect yourself, oh perfect yourself, I pray you, in this latter discipline, for who knows how to do well like you, if you could acquire *power* to do it. . . .

'I am highly pleased with your intended removal to Göttingen. Being a university it must possess advantages which your present situation does not—to say nothing of the economy of the plan. . . . But once more, my dearly beloved, let me entreat you not to over-interest yourself about your family and friends here; not to incapacitate yourself by idle apprehensions and tender reveries of imagination concerning us. Those things are wrong. They can do no good, and you are not fit to see many people, and many nations, if you indulge in them. Mrs. Coleridge has sent me from Bristol the letter you wrote her. Was it well to indulge in, much less to express, such feelings concerning *any* circumstance which could relate to two infants? I do not mean to check tenderness, for in the *folly* of tenderness I can sympathise— but be *rational*, I implore you—in your present situation, your happiness depends upon it. I was grieved to hear of your eyes. Take care of your health, remember that. Water and vegetable food will not do for you. . . .

'We received from Johnson six copies of the poems

the *Account of Paraguay*, and the *Essay on Population*, but *not* the *Diversions of Purley*. Every one admires the poems, and I am told they are much admired in London. As to the house—I have long felt that in Lime Street is unsuitable for you. The old house at Woodlands, Wilmott intends living in himself; the new house is too large. What think you of the house in which Hancock lived at Stowey? . . . There is a communication with the fields behind, a good garden, and a noble room adjoining the garden, retired from the house. The rent . . . may be £16 or £18 a year; perhaps I am beyond the mark. However, you *may be certain* I shall keep an eye on every house to be had here and in the neighbourhood. *I will not part from you, if you will not part from me;* be assured of that. I can truly say that your society is a principal ingredient of my happiness, a principal source of my improvement. The time will, I trust, come, when it will contribute still more than it has done both to the one and to the other. God send you in due time safely home is my present prayer. I have lately been very idle. I began learning Greek, and am now oscillating whether I shall attend to it or go on with what I had in my mind[1] before you left Stowey. The only advantages I see in Greek are, reading the New Testament in the original language, knowing something which forms a part of a good education, and being made happy by *the magick of sound*—for the sense at any rate which *I* should find in the Greek writers I presume we have translated. Perhaps it is my *duty* to proceed with the other; it may be working the works of Him that sent me ere the night cometh. The night

---

[1] Political Economy, I fancy.

descended, as you know, on one half of our family *suddenly*, and so it may on me. Think of that, Col., when, if you hear an infant, an unconscious infant, is recovered from an illness, you indulge in tumultuous feelings. Remember me affectionately to the Wordsworths. Should they settle near Stowey they may depend on all my good offices to make them comfortable. But has Wordsworth any idea of returning soon from Germany?'

Messages and greetings and details of his mother's improved health follow, and the letter concludes :—

'Once more I implore you to permit no circumstance, of whatever nature, to make you unhappy. *All that depends on you*, you do; therefore you have no cause to be unhappy. Whatever is external—independent of you—*what have you to do with it?*—For ever your affectionate THOS. POOLE.'

This letter was re-addressed at Ratzburg to Göttingen.

CHAPTER XVI

'Life! Power! Being! Organisation may be and probably *is* their
effect; their *cause* it cannot be! . . .'
'Oh! this strange, strange, strange Scene-shifter, Death! . . .'
S. T. C. to T. P. on the death of his infant.

WHEN Thomas Poole wrote the last sentences
it is probable that he foresaw an approaching trial
which his friend would be certain to feel more
deeply than he was at that time able to com-
prehend, tender and true as his sympathies
usually were. Thomas Poole was not a father,
and the quaint simplicity with which he sets forth
the unreasonableness of any vehement going forth
of the affection to an unconscious infant, discovers
a most masculine absence of sentiment in relation
to babies. Perhaps it is only fathers and mothers,
but especially mothers, who instinctively recognise
the individual soul with its infinite possibilities in
the little undeveloped human creature; certainly
Tom Poole writes as if, in his mind, a baby
scarcely ranked as a human being. Still, in

sympathy, it is personality that conveys comfort, not the actual words that are said ; and Poole suited Coleridge.   The letter, such as it was, in which he informed him of the infant's death, drew forth just such an outpouring in response as more than anything else relieves a burdened heart, and which it is a victory of sympathy to win from sorrow.

Inoculation was a process always attended with much discomfort and inconvenience, and the fact that this or that infant has 'got safely over the smallpox' is often recorded with expressions of thankfulness in the family letters of this period. Little Berkeley Coleridge was supposed to have passed happily through the ordeal, yet there had been some anxiety on his account, and perhaps he did not really recover as he should have done. Presently, as we have seen, he contracted a cough, which had resisted all the usual remedies, but which his mother hoped might yield to change of air.   In February, 1799, an undated letter, written in the first tumult of her grief, comes to say that all is over.

'*Monday, Noon.*

'Oh, my dear Mr. Poole, I have lost my dear, dear child !   At one o'clock on Sunday morning a convulsive fit put an end to his painful existence.   Myself and two of his aunts were watching by his cradle.   I wish I had not seen it, for I am sure it will never leave my memory.

Sweet babe ! what will thy father feel when he shall hear
of thy sufferings and death? I am perfectly aware of
everything you have said on the subject in your letter.
I shall not yet write to Coleridge, and when I do, I will
pass over all disagreeable subjects with the greatest care,
for well I know their violent effect upon him—but I
account myself most unfortunate in being at a distance
from him at this time, wanting his consolation as I do,
and feeling my griefs almost too much to support with
fortitude. . . . I suppose you will have received from
Coleridge the promised letter for me. I long for it, for
I am very miserable. . . .'

Southey, with his usual kindness, was seeing to
the little funeral, and would take the bereaved
mother, and her remaining child, back with him to
his home at Westbury immediately afterwards; but
still she begs Tom Poole to come to her, and con-
fides to him the little details of her situation as to an
almost father. Her money is nearly spent. Can he
supply her till Samuel makes some provision? She
does not choose to be obliged to any one at Bristol.
Perhaps her husband thinks she has enough to last
till his return, not knowing her situation. To
Tom Poole, also, was entrusted the task of breaking
the news to Coleridge, which he does as follows:—

IV

'*March* 15, 1799.[1]

'MY EVER DEAR COL.—The Hamburg mail at length
arrived, but it brought no great weight of pleasure for

[1] Bristol postmark, March 18.

me. One letter came for Mrs. Coleridge, which, as she
desired, I opened. . . . I sent it to Mrs. C. at Bristol,
and desired her not to write to you till I had written,
and that I would forward her my letter to read. I have
this morning heard from her. . . . She is very well, and I
shall send her this letter that she may read it and forward it to you. Perhaps even by reading so far, you *feel
the reason* for my wishing to write to you before Mrs.
Coleridge. I suspect you feel it by the anticipations in
your last letter. You say there that you have serious misgivings concerning Berkeley—well—you now, my dear
Col., know the worst. I thus give you to understand the
catastrophe of the drama, without heightening it by first
narrating the circumstances which led to it ; but, as you
will hear by and by, those circumstances were purely
natural, and such as probably no human conduct or fore-
sight could have averted. The child was got perfectly well
out of the smallpox, and enjoyed a clear interval of health
before he was seized with a cough. . . . As he did not get
better, the medical men, and indeed all of us, advised
Mrs. C. to go to Bristol and try change of air, or
rather to carry into execution the visit she intended. For
some time the child appeared better, but the cough again
returned, and he lost flesh and grew weaker daily—in
short, from the accounts Mrs. Coleridge wrote me, I was
quite prepared for the event. . . . On examination it
was found that he died of a consumption. Mrs. Coleridge was much fatigued during the child's illness, but
her health was very good, and she very wisely kept up
her spirits. . . .

'I have thus, my dear Col., informed you of the
whole truth. It was long contrary to my opinion

to let you know of the child's death before your arrival
in England. And I thought, and still think myself
justified in that notion, by the OVER-anxiety you expressed in your former letters concerning the children.
Doubtless the affection found to exist between parents
and *infant* children is a wise law of nature, a mere instinct
to preserve Man in his infant state. . . . But the moment
you make this affection the creature of reason, you
degrade reason. When the infant becomes a reasonable
being, then let the affection be a thing of reason, not
before. Brutes can only have an instinctive affection.
Hence, when that ceases to be necessary, all affection
ceases. This seems to me to be a great line of demar-
cation between Men and Beasts, between Reason and
Instinct. If then the love of infants be a mere instinct, it
is extraordinary that sensible men should be much disturbed at the counteraction of it, particularly when the
end of that action, if I may so speak, becomes a nullity.
Certainly, if I had an only child, and no hopes of
another, who alone was to be the solace of my age,
who was to take my property, to bear my name, to represent myself; in short, to be another self—certainly, if
this child were to die, I should feel my *earthly* being as
it were suddenly stopped, and something like a feeling
of annihilation would occur, which of all others is the
most disconsolate. But this is not your case. Hartley is
brave and well, and like to give you grandchildren and
great-grandchildren, *ad libitum ;* and, I need not add,
very likely to have a plenty of brothers and sisters.
The truth is, my dear Col., it is idle to reason about a
thing of this nature. Therefore I talk quaintly—your
mind must suggest everything I can suggest and more.

Only let your *mind* act, and not your *feelings*. Don't
conjure up any scenes of distress which never happened.
Mrs. Coleridge felt as a mother . . . and, in an exemplary
manner, did all a mother could do. *But she never forgot herself.* She is now perfectly well, and does not
make herself miserable by recalling the engaging, though,
remember, mere instinctive attractions of an infant a few
months old.[1] Heaven and Earth! I have myself within
the last month experienced disappointments more weighty
than the death of ten infants. There are two particular
friends of yours and mine,[2] who offered, ten days ago,
£22,000 for a delightful estate within seven miles of
Stowey. But for a most untoward circumstance which I
have not now room to explain, they would have had it. . . .
I was much interested, and for a fortnight busily employed about this business. They came down and saw
the estate, and were determined, I believe, to purchase
it almost at any price. Now as to the pecuniary disappointment, as far as it relates to them, or as to the
personal one, as far as it relates to you and me, it may
not be very weighty, though whatever it be, it is
rational; but the loss to the neighbourhood is incalcul-
able. A humane and wise expenditure of a large income
would have been an example so novel and extraordinary

[1] Poor Mrs. Coleridge! It may be questioned whether Tom
Poole knew what he was talking about. Neither he nor Coleridge,
after this exchange of letters, ever mention the lost child, but
years afterwards *she* alludes to him again and again as a loved and
living memory in her letters to Tom Poole. She remembers his
birthday, realises what his age would have been, and once almost
breaks down with emotion when a Stowey acquaintance visits her, of
whom she recollects that, when last they met, she sat long by
Berkeley's cradle.

[2] The Wedgwoods.

to our country gentlemen, that I could not help antici-
pating much good from it, to say nothing of the happiness
they would have conferred on individuals immediately
within the sphere of their action.   The failure of a plan
of this nature I take to be a justifiable cause for regret.

'Another circumstance has occurred to me within a
month, which mixes so much feeling with so much
rational cause for regret, that it has altogether made me
very unhappy.   I have been used ill by some of my
servants whom I treated best, whom I most confided in
—in a word, whom I most loved.   Now this is a proof
of such melancholy insensibility on their part, not to say
depravity, and so damps every benevolent feeling of my
own mind, as far as relates to their class of society,
that it is difficult to say how injurious to me, and to
them, the consequences of it may be.   Say nothing
about this to anybody.   I hope I have made them
sensible of their errors, and that in future they will be
better, that I may be prevented from being worse.   Thus,
my dear Col., we must look to ourselves, and I am afraid
to ourselves alone, for happiness.   Woe be to him who
cannot in these days turn with satisfaction from the
contemplation of the species to the contemplation of
himself—who cannot keep the little court of his own
breast swept clean of the degrading passions and low
vices, which alone brave the sun, and triumph in the
face of day.   Let us hear from you circumstantially,
let us hear that you are happy. . . . We long to see
you.   But still I say, don't come till you have done
your business.   My mother is better, ten times better
than she has been these two years.   Heaven bless you,

'THOS. POOLE.'

Coleridge did not weep, he tells Poole, when he received the news of his infant's death. ' I walked out into the open fields, oppressed—not by my feelings—but by the riddles which the thought so easily proposes—and solves, never!' And when he returned he sat down to cover the first half of a large sheet of paper with a series of reflective 'fancies' upon the phenomena of Life, Consciousness, and Personal Identity. If Poole's letter was designed to raise a barrier against violent agitation, by exciting a train of metaphysical speculations, it succeeded.

' I am perplexed,' wrote Coleridge, ' I am sad ; and a little thing, a very trifle, would make me weep ; but for the death of my baby I have *not* wept.'

Nevertheless, he could write of nothing else that day ; it is not till two days later that he takes up his pen again to finish the sheet, and to answer the concluding portion of his friend's letter—

' *April* 8, 1799.—I feel disappointed beyond doubt,' he says, ' at the circumstance of which you have *half* informed me . . . but still, we can *hope*. If you live at Stowey, and my moral and intellectual being grows and purifies, as I would fain believe that it will, there will always be a motive, a strong one, to their coming.

' As to your servants and the people of Stowey in general, Poole, my beloved! you have been often unwisely fretful with me when I have pressed upon you their

depravity.   Without religious joys and religious terrors,
nothing can be expected from the *inferior* classes in
society.   Whether or no any *class* is strong enough to
stand firm without them, is to me doubtful.   There are
favoured *individuals* but not *classes*. . . .'

Expressions of almost filial joy at the improved
health of Poole's mother come next, and then
some account of his own studies ; lastly—

'With regard to the house in Stowey,' he says, 'I
must not disguise from you that to live *in* Stowey, and
in that house which you mention, is to me an exceedingly
unpleasant thought.   Rather than go anywhere else I
assuredly would do it, and be glad, but the thought is
unpleasant to me.   I do not like to live *in* a town, still
less in Stowey, where, excepting yourself and mother,
there is no human being attached to us, and few who do
not dislike us.   Besides, it is a sad tyranny that all who
live in towns are subject to, that of inoculating all at
once, etc.   And then the impossibility of keeping one's
children free from vice and profaneness, etc.

'If I do not send off this letter now, I must wait
another week.   What must I do?   How you will look
when you see the blank page !   My next shall make up
for it.   Heaven bless you

'and S. T. COLERIDGE.'

It is amusing to find an apology for brevity at
the close of a letter which entirely covers two
sides of an immense sheet of paper, with minute
and closely compressed handwriting ; but it was
not at all uncommon at this period of their lives

for Coleridge to write to Tom Poole upon paper
of this description, and to fill the entire sheet,
only leaving the vacant space required for the
address, in the centre of the last page. The
child's death, for which he had not wept, must
nevertheless have preyed a good deal upon his
mind, if we may judge from the tone of passionate
home-sickness which pervades the next letter, dated
'May 6, 1799, Monday morning'; and, indeed, it
must have taken the entire morning to write it,
for it occupies the whole of just such another
sheet of paper as the last. That part of it which
refers to the relations between Poole and Coleridge, and to the question of returning to live at
Stowey, may be transcribed here :—

'MY DEAR POOLE! MY DEAR POOLE! I am home-sick.
Society is a burthen to me; and I find relief only in
labour. So I read and transcribe from morning to
night, and never in my life have I worked so hard as
this last month, for indeed I must sail over an ocean of
matter with almost spiritual speed, to do what I have to
do in the time in which I *will* do it, or else leave it
undone! O my God! how I long to be at home! My
whole being so yearns after you, that when I think of the
moment of our meeting, I catch the fashion of German
joy, rush into your arms, and embrace you. Methinks
my *hand* would swell, if the whole force of my feeling
were crowded there. Now the Spring comes, the vital
sap of my affections rises as in a tree. And what a

gloomy Spring! But a few days ago, all the new buds
were covered with snow; and everything yet looks so
brown and wintry, that yesterday the roses (which the
ladies carried on the Ramparts, their Promenade), beautiful as they were, so little harmonized with the general
face of nature they looked to me like silk and paper roses.
But these leafless Spring woods! O how I long to hear
your *whistle* to the Rippers![1] There are a multitude of
nightingales here (poor things! they sang in the snow).
I thought of my own verses on the nightingale, only
because I thought of Hartley, my *only* child. Dear
lamb! I hope *he* won't be dead before I get home.
There are moments in which I have such a power of life
within me, such a *conceit* of it, I mean, that I lay the
blame of my child's death to my absence. Not *intellect-
ually;* but I have a strange sort of sensation, as if while
I was present none could die whom I intensely loved.
And doubtless it was no absurd idea of yours that there
may be unions and connections out of the visible world.

'Wordsworth and his sister passed through here, as
I have informed you. I walked on with them five English
miles, and spent a day with them. They were melancholy and hypp'd. W. was affected to tears at the
thought of not living near me—wished me, of course, to
live in the north of England near them and Sir Frederic
Vane's great library. I told him that, independent of
the expense of removing, and the impropriety of taking
Mrs. Coleridge to a place where she would have no
acquaintance, two insurmountable objections, the library
was no inducement, for I wanted old books chiefly, such
as could be procured anywhere better than in a gentle-

[1] Blackbirds.

man's new fashionable collection. Finally, I told him plainly that *you* had been the man in whom *first* and in whom alone I had felt an *anchor!* With all my other connections I felt a dim sense of insecurity and uncertainty, terribly uncomfortable. W. was affected to tears, very much affected. But he deemed the vicinity of a library absolutely necessary to his health, nay, to his existence. It is painful to me, too, to think of not living near him : for he is a *good* and *kind* man, and the only one whom in *all* things I feel my superior; and you will believe me when I say, that I have few feelings more pleasurable than to find myself, in intellectual faculties, an inferior.

But my resolve is fixed, *not to leave you till you leave me.* I still think Wordsworth will be disappointed in his expectations of relief from reading, without society ; and I think it highly probable that where I live there he will live, unless he should find in the North any person, or persons, who can feel with and understand him, can reciprocate and react on him. My many weaknesses are of some advantage to me ; they unite me more with the great mass of my fellow-beings—but dear Wordsworth appears to me to have hurtfully segregated and isolated his being. Doubtless, his delights are more deep and sublime, but he has likewise more hours that prey on his flesh and blood. With regard to Hancock's house, if I can get no place within a mile or two of Stowey, I *must* try to get that; but I confess I like it not. . . .'

Written across the paper, in the folded oblong piece below the cover, comes a tiny note to Mrs. Coleridge :—

'My dear Sara—On Saturday next I go to the famous Harz Mountains, about twenty English miles from Göttingen, to see the mines and other curiosities. On my return I will write you all that is writable. God bless you, my dear, dear, dear Love! and your affectionate and ever faithful husband, S. T. Coleridge.

'With regard to money, my Love! Poole can write to Mr. Wedgwood, if it is not convenient for him to let you have it.'

Such were the almost more than brotherly terms that existed between the two young men; but Sara, perhaps, would have preferred greater ceremony, and the wholesome, commonplace routine of regular remittances. It seems likely that the above note may have been an answer to some kind of representation on her part that she had been again obliged to apply to Mr. Poole, for a letter of hers exists, dated April 2, 1799, in which, after a variety of domestic details, and some comments on the letters from Germany, mingled with longings for her husband's return, she goes on :—

'My principal reason for troubling you now is, to beg you will send me ten guineas, for I expected Coleridge would have thought of it, but he has not, probably thinking I can do without till he arrives. . . . I shall want the cash as soon as you can provide me with it conveniently, for I have many little bills to pay, and must purchase a few things to bring with me to Stowey.'

Then follows a petulant postscript :—

'The Lyrical Ballads are not liked at all by any.'

And then, yet another afterthought :—

'It is very unpleasant to me to be often asked if Coleridge has changed his political sentiments, for I know not properly how to reply. Pray furnish me.'

In later years this perplexed, and sometimes much provoked young wife, with her warm affections and her untrained mind, had grown to her surroundings, and we smile to find her writing to Mr. Poole in 1815 of Wordsworth's *Excursion* and the *White Doe*, that 'there are still two very opposite opinions concerning his poetry, *you know ours*, and Sir George and Lady Beaumont think him the first of living poets.'

In 1799 there was no Sir George or Lady Beaumont to be quoted against the unappreciative multitude ; the general voice was still her standard, and she had not that happy, blind belief in her husband that might have led her to take his side against the clamour of the crowd, with dogged, uncritical conviction of the excellence of anything that 'he' had done. Popularity would have instantly opened her eyes to their merits, but if they were *not* popular, how, she seems to ask, could the *Lyrical Ballads* be anything else but a failure?

And yet the collection included the *Ancient Mariner*, Coleridge's one absolutely perfect achieve-

ment.   Be sure he knew its excellence himself,
and was aware that he had done what he could
never surpass, and had produced something that his
countrymen should not willingly let die—and measure, if you can, his sense of disappointment, almost
of despair, when this, like everything else, met with
no recognition, and was actually received with a
howl of derision.

'The *Lyrical Ballads*,' writes Sara, in another of her
postscripts, ' are laughed at and disliked by all with very
few exceptions. . . . '

Even Southey and C. Lloyd were not among
the ' few exceptions.'

' If you wrote that review . . . ,' says Charles Lamb to
Southey in November 1798, ' I am sorry you are so spar-
ing of praise to the *Ancient Marinere*. . . . You have
selected a passage fertile in unmeaning miracles, but have
passed by fifty passages as miraculous as the miracles they
celebrate.   I never so deeply felt the pathetic as in that
part—

> ' "A spring of love gushed from my heart,
> And I blessed them unaware."

It stung me into high pleasure through sufferings.
Lloyd does not like it.   His head is too metaphysical,
and your taste too correct ; at least I must allege something against you both to excuse my own dotage.

> ' " So lonely 'twas that God himself
> Scarce seemed there to be ! " etc. etc.

But you allow some elaborate beauties.   You should
have extracted 'em. . . . '

Let us hope that the few who felt with Charles Lamb may have consoled Coleridge for the many who stood cold and unresponsive to his highest effort.

'I pine, languish, and waste away to be at home,' he wrote to Thomas Poole in May 1799, 'for though in England only I have those that hate me, yet there only I have those whom I love ;' and some time in the summer of that year saw him at Stowey again, but only for a short time. Early in September he was with the Wordsworths in the North, and one or two notes written from 'Southey's lodgings in Exeter' later in the same month, tell us that he had then been, with Mrs. Coleridge and little Hartley, visiting his kindred, and taking a few days' tour in Devonshire, a county which he vehemently declared to be very inferior to Somersetshire in everything except perhaps 'clouted cream, bless the inventor thereof,' and 'the views of Totness and Dartmouth.'

'I shall be back in Stowey in three weeks,' he writes, and there, as of old, the spirit of drollery reawakens, and we find him sending a bundle of quill pens over to Ward to be mended, and acknowledging their return in what I should think must be the only monosyllabic note that he ever wrote in his life :—

'*October* 7, 1799.

' Thank you !

'S. T. COLERIDGE.'

This is speedily followed by a quaintly folded epistle, addressed as follows :—

'To Mr. WARD.

' This *pen*tagonal letter comes *pen*cil'd as well as *pen*n'd.'

And on the reverse :—

'Your messenger neither came nor returned *pen*niless.'

'MOST EXQUISITE PENNEFACTOR—I will speak dirt and daggers of the wretch who shall deny thee to be the most heaven-inspired, munificent Penmaker that these latter times, these superficial, weak, and evirtuate ages have produced to redeem themselves from ignominy! And may he, great Calamist, who shall vili*pend* or derogate from thy *pen*making merits, do *pen*ance, and suffer *pen*itential *pen*alty, *pen*n'd up in some *pen*urious *pen*insula of *pen*al and *pen*etrant fire, *pen*sive and *pen*dulous, *pen*ding a huge slice of Eternity. 'Were I to write till *Pen*tecost, filling whole *Pen*tateuchs, my expressions would still remain a mere *pen*umbra of my debt of gratitude. Thine,

'S. T. COLERIDGE.'

But unluckily Ward never handled those pens at all ! Coleridge's message arrived in his absence, and they were mended by Govatt, the clerk, as a matter of course ; though, later in the day, and perhaps not knowing what Govatt had done, Ward on his return mended and despatched a second batch of pens himself, but only to meet with the following uncomplimentary reception :—

'Ward! I recant, I recant! solemnly recant and disannul all praise, puff, and panegyric on your damned pens. I have this moment read the note wrapped round your last present, and last night therefore wrote my Elogy on the assured belief that the first batch were yours, and before I had tried the second. The second! I'm sick on't. Such execrable Blurrers of innocent white paper. Villains with uneven legs, Hexameter and Pentameter Pens. Elogy. No, no, no. Elegies written with Elegiac pens—Elegies on my poor Thoughts doing penance in white sheets, filthily illegible.

'My rage prevents me from writing sense. But O Govatt, dear Govatt! kick that spectacle-mongering son of a Pen-hatchet out of creation, and remain alone, from the date hereof, invested with the rank and office of Penmaker to my immortal Bardship, with all the dignities and emoluments thereunto annexed.

> 'Given from Apollo's temple in the odoriferous Lime Grove Street, in what Olympiad our Inspiration knows not, but of the usurping Christian Æra 1799, Oct. 8.
> 'S. T. COLERIDGE.'

Govatt is expected to express his gratitude by an immediate present of half a dozen pens,

amended—if indeed the reprobates be not in-
corrigible.

Probably the 'Devil's Walk' was written with
one of these very pens ; for this, too, belongs to the
same month of October.   The poem in Southey's
version concludes with the lines—

'Therewith in second-sight he saw
   The place, and the manner, and time,
   In which this mortal story
   Would be put in immortal rhyme.

'That it would happen when two poets
   Should on a time be met,
   In the town of Nether Stowey,
   In the shire of Somerset.

'There, while the one was shaving,
   Would he the song begin,
   And the other when he heard it at breakfast,
   In ready accord join in.

'So each would help the other,
   Two heads being better than one,
   And the phrase and conceit
   Would in unison meet,
   And so with glee the verse flow free,
   In ding-dong chime of sing-song rhyme,
   Till the whole were merrily done.

'And because it is set to the razor,
   Not to the lute or harp,
   Therefore it was that the fancy
   Should be bright and the wit be sharp. . . .'

In its original shape the 'Devil's Walk' went up to the *Morning Post*, and created a great sensation. It is grotesque, and rather in the manner of Southey than in Coleridge's own manner; but there is a searching quality in the irony of which Southey possessed not the secret, and a fantastic extravagance in the wit, which has a good deal more of Coleridge's fling than of Southey's fancy in it. By November Coleridge had accepted an engagement to write regularly for the *Morning Post*, and was settled with his wife and child in what he describes in a letter to Tom Poole—whom he invites to come and stay with him—as 'quiet and healthful' lodgings in London, where his first occupation was to prepare and to publish his fine translation of *Wallenstein*, that work which cost him so much labour, and which brought him in so little profit and so little fame. The newspaper work paid; but the unbought copies of *Wallenstein* were actually sold for waste-paper! It was from these lodgings that he penned that loving greeting to Tom Poole, on New Year's Eve, 1799, which stands on the first page of these Memoirs.